THE GUARDIANS OF ZOONE

THE BOOKS OF

The Secret of Zoone
The Guardians of Zoone

THE GUARDIANS OF ZOONE

LEE EDWARD FÖDI

HARPER

An Imprint of HarperCollinsPublishers

Library of Congress Control Number: 2019944598
ISBN 978-0-06-284528-3

Typography by Michelle Taormina
20 21 22 23 24   PC/LSCH   10 9 8 7 6 5 4 3 2 1

First Edition

To Hiro—everybody needs a crew,
and I'm so glad I'm a part of yours.

SNEAK ATTACK

The dragon exploded through the doorway in a burst of iridescent green, nostrils flaring, eyes bulging, smoke leaking from the corners of its mouth. It paused for the briefest of moments, as if to take in its surroundings—and then it charged straight toward Ozzie.

He quickly puffed out his chest, windmilling his arms and trying to look as big as possible. He had heard that sort of thing intimidated some wild animals. Unfortunately, the technique didn't appear to work on dragons—because, even though this one wasn't very big, it didn't stop. Instead, it flew straight into Ozzie, sending him sprawling. Then it scrambled onto his chest and proceeded to lick him with a bright green and slightly warm tongue.

Just another day on the job, Ozzie thought.

Working as a porter was never predictable—especially at a place like Zoone, the nexus of the multiverse, where a thousand doors led to a thousand worlds. Missing suitcases, flustered travelers, and runaway pets were all just hazards of working the platforms, helping people get from one side of the 'verse to the other. The dragon currently lapping at Ozzie's cheek was about the size of a bulldog and was wearing a bejeweled collar with a long leash trailing behind it—which definitely put it in the runaway-pet category.

"Puffy!" a demanding voice called. "Where are you?! Help! Someone's snatched my girl!"

Ozzie craned his neck to see a short, round man waddle out of the door from Garalond. He was wearing a ridiculous top hat, a broad waistcoat, and even a monocle. His skin was as green as the dragon's, and he had a mustache that made his nose look like it was wearing a bow tie.

Could this guy be more pompous? Ozzie wondered.

Then the man caught sight of Ozzie. "How dare you steal my precious Puffy?!" he roared. "Do you have the faintest idea of who I am?"

Puffy sure seemed to know. As soon as Sir Pomposity

began galumphing toward her, she leaped off Ozzie's chest and made her escape across the platform.

Ozzie should have sprung to his feet and chased the pet dragon—that's what any good Zoone porter would do. But he didn't have to make that decision, because Puffy's leash made it for him; the end had looped around his ankle, and so Ozzie found himself being yanked unceremoniously across the north platform. He yelped in pain as he bounced on the cobblestones.

"THIEF!" Sir Pomposity thundered. "Come back here! Don't you know who I . . ."

Ozzie was whisked out of earshot. Legs, luggage, and doors whipped past in a blur.

"What the—?!" a magenta-skinned traveler yelped as they slipped between her ankles.

"Hey! Watch the jamb!" a door knocker snarled as they swept over its doorstep.

"OOF!" Keeva, a fellow porter, gasped as Ozzie careened into her stack of suitcases.

Puffy kept going—and Ozzie with her. He fumbled for the whistle in the breast pocket of his uniform so he could call for help. The whistle was meant only for emergencies—but as far as he was concerned, this definitely qualified! Unfortunately for Ozzie, as soon as he got hold of the whistle, it slipped out of his grip and rattled away across the cobblestones.

Puffy made an abrupt turn into the forest that surrounded Zoone Station. It was called the Infinite Wood, which, Ozzie realized, didn't bode well for coming to a stop anytime soon.

But when a giant man stepped out from behind one of the trees, Puffy slammed into him, bringing them to an instant halt.

Ozzie woozily sat up and rubbed his head. "Cho?"

The captain of Zoone security was a large man. With the long scar on his left cheek and the intricate tattoo on his right, he probably should have looked menacing. But his eyes were so friendly that they chased away all other impressions.

"Just another day at Zoone, isn't it?" Cho said, a smile spreading across his brown face. He lifted the dragon by her collar and she dangled in the air, squirming. "We'd better get this little lass back to her owner."

They had just begun their trek through the woods when another tiny creature came bolting toward them. There was nothing dragonish about this one—if anything, it looked more like a mouse. It was Ferbis Fusselbone, Zoone's chief conductor.

"This is preposasterous, absolutely preposasterous!" Fusselbone squealed at Ozzie. "That's the prized pet of Lord Snogget of Garalond! It's a pug-nosed Sellandrian dragon, my boy! Extremely rare!" He began hopping from foot to foot. "Did it burn you, my boy? Bite you? *Breathe* on you?"

That was Fusselbone for you, Ozzie thought; he was a whole lot of emergency with nowhere to go.

"I'm fine," Ozzie said. "But—"

Fusselbone jabbed him in the knee with one finger. "You've got to watch your heels, my boy!"

Cho chuckled at Fusselbone's outburst and continued toward the north platform, with Ozzie and Fusselbone—still yammering—following. The platform soon came into view, along with the magnificent station house. With its towering turquoise spires, whimsical archways, and rosette windows, the station had always reminded Ozzie of a castle—but the stunning view was shattered by the commotion on the platform. Sir Pomposity—Lord Snogget, rather—was standing on a suitcase and wailing so loudly that his cheeks had turned bright green. Well, a brighter green than they had been. As soon as he saw Ozzie, the lord pointed a blunt finger at him and yelled, "There he is! PETNAPPER! I demand restitution! I demand—"

"No harm was done," Cho told him. He held out a still-wriggling Puffy as evidence.

Lord Snogget snatched the dragon away and squeezed

her against his chest. "This boy must be punished!" he bellowed. "Don't you—"

"Bugs and blight!" came a crackling voice. "What a lot of mayhem!"

The voice belonged to Lady Zoone, steward of the nexus. Ozzie turned and looked up at her—way up, because Lady Zoone was the kind of tall that meant she knew it was raining a half minute before anyone else. Her height was emphasized by her impossibly long neck and towering nest of greenish hair. Creatures lived in that nest: squirrels, mice, and birds, all rustling and fluttering in and out of her curls. She was what you would get, Ozzie liked to think, if a tree could walk and talk. She had a comforting aura about her—though Ozzie wondered if even she would be able to soothe Lord Snogget.

Lady Zoone planted one of her spindly hands on the man's shoulder, guided him down from the suitcase, and gave him the sort of smile that made you want to curl up and take a nap in her shade. "How about a complimentary refreshment at our tavern?" she offered. "The Squeaky Hinge serves the best whistlefizz in the multiverse. Or perhaps you'd prefer a bottle of Orakian ale?"

"Well, I'm not sure," Lord Snogget huffed. "I have a connection to catch!"

"Ah, do not fret," Lady Zoone interjected. "We'll make

alternate arrangements for you." She cast a meaningful look at Fusselbone.

"Yes, my lady—at once! AT ONCE!" The little mouse-man scampered up to Lord Snogget and began to escort him toward the station.

Cho took his leave as well, and the crowd that had gathered to gawk at the scene slowly dissipated, leaving behind only Ozzie and Lady Zoone.

The tall woman tilted toward Ozzie and held out a small silver object. "I believe you dropped this?"

"My whistle!"

"Can you hear it?" Lady Zoone asked. "The alarm is sounding."

"Huh?" Ozzie stared at her in confusion.

"It means trouble is approaching," she continued gravely.

Ozzie could hear the sound clearly, though it wasn't the kind that normally came from his whistle. It sounded more like an old-fashioned telephone. Like something from Earth. Or, as they liked to call Ozzie's home world here at Zoone, Eridea.

Then, looking past Lady Zoone, he spotted his two best friends approaching from the station house: Tug, the winged blue cat known as a skyger, and Fidget, the princess with inappropriately purple hair.

"Guys!" Ozzie called. "You'll never guess what happened!"

He began to rush toward them, only to feel a hand grab him by the shoulder and pull him back. "Ozzie!" a voice urged, but it didn't belong to Lady Zoone.

"Let me stay!" Ozzie cried, trying to wriggle free. He wanted to see Tug and Fidget. He *needed* to see them.

"OZZIE!"

He was being shaken now. Heavy with resignation, he turned, blinked, and found himself staring into the perplexed face of Aunt Temperance.

"Huh?" Ozzie mumbled groggily.

Aunt Temperance sighed. "You drifted off. *Again.*"

Ozzie's eyes darted around him. Just like that, Zoone was gone, instantly melting away into the reality of Apartment 2B, where he lived (sort of) with Aunt Temperance. Ozzie glanced down at the table in front of him. He had been using his math textbook as a pillow. Which meant it had all been a dream. An incredibly vivid dream. Not real.

Except it had been once.

Ozzie *had* been to Zoone. The nexus was real. Even the situation with Lord Snogget had happened—in fact, getting entangled with a pesky pet dragon had been tame compared to the rest of his adventures there. He had faced glibbers, fought a dark wizard, and played a part in saving the entire nexus. Most important, he had met his friends there. True friends. Like Tug and Fidget . . .

Aunt Temperance shook him again. "Ozzie, stay with me."

It was only now that he realized she was clutching the receiver to Apartment 2B's ancient phone in her free hand, and there was someone squawking through it.

"Oh," Ozzie said. It had been the ringing phone that had cut into his dream.

"It's your mom," Aunt Temperance mouthed.

Ozzie's stomach lurched. His mom, Renowned Journalist Extraordinaire, was on assignment—and *adventure*—in Kenya. She usually only called Ozzie when she had important news. Correction: important *bad* news.

Aunt Temperance passed him the phone, and as Ozzie stared at it in trepidation, she thrust a pamphlet toward him, too.

He was suddenly struck with the suspicion that this whole moment had been planned. He narrowed his eyes at Aunt Temperance. "What is that?"

She waved the pamphlet at him, not seeming to have the courage to look him in the eye. Instead, she turned her head and stared purposely into the corner of the kitchen.

"Talk to your mom," she whispered.

This is a sneak attack, Ozzie thought as he lifted the receiver to his ear.

And he was right.

Because it wasn't just important news his mom was delivering. It wasn't even just important *bad* news.

It was the worst news that Ozzie had ever heard.

THE BUG IN THE KEYHOLE

Ozzie slammed down the phone, glared at his aunt, and released a growl. It wasn't the sort of sound normally heard in Aunt Temperance's living room on a Monday evening.

Aunt Temperance's eyes went wide behind her thick-rimmed glasses, a strand of long silver hair trembling at her cheek. Her mouth slowly dropped open, but no words came out.

"You," Ozzie accused, crumpling the pamphlet in his fist. "You could have told me."

Then, even though he didn't have his shoes on, he tore out of the apartment, into the hallway, and down the stairs that led into the crypt-like cellars of their old apartment building. Downward he spiraled, into what Aunt Temperance referred to as "The Depths." He didn't even stop to catch his breath at the bottom, just kept running until he arrived at the door to Zoone. Then he wound up and kicked it with all his might. Without a shoe on, it hurt. A lot.

Ozzie stood back, fuming, and tried to ignore his throbbing toes. He had no way of seeing or even communicating with Zoone because the portal had been damaged when he had first crossed through it. He had been able to get back home after his adventures—but just. Then the door had closed up again. All he had now were his dreams of his time in the nexus, all those weeks ago. It was beyond frustrating—especially after the news Ozzie's mom had just delivered over the phone.

"Just work again, already," Ozzie pleaded with the door.

It just stood there, silent and obstinate. Ozzie contemplated it for what felt like the zillionth time. Its wooden planks were weathered and gray, barely showing a trace of the vibrant turquoise color it had once been painted. Its long, whimsically shaped hinges were streaked with rust, as was the decorative letter "Z" that dangled halfway up its face. The door looked as if it had been getting pummeled by wind and rain for a hundred years—except there was no wind or rain down here in The Depths. Ozzie knew the door didn't look so miserable because of weather.

It looked this way because its magic was dying.

Ozzie plopped to the cold cement floor, uncurled his fist, and flattened out the crumpled pamphlet. The header read: *Dreerdum's Boarding School for Boys.* The photo on the cover featured a horde of boys wearing identical navy blue uniforms. Their faces were plastered with the sort of smiles that always seemed to dupe teachers: They looked innocent enough on the surface, but any kid trained in Bully Survival 101 knew they harbored an undercurrent of malice and the threat of insult and injury. Dreerdum's looked like the worst place in the multiverse.

And Ozzie's parents were sending him there. Just because of one bad report card. Okay, admittedly, it wasn't *one* bad report card, just the worst so far. But it wasn't his fault! How was he supposed to worry about mundane things like fractions and percentages when there was an entire multiverse out there? He knew tons of stuff—like how to handle a pug-nosed Sellandrian dragon, for example. Unfortunately, those sorts of skills didn't matter in Eridea.

He heard Aunt Temperance's footsteps approaching from a long way off. She came to a halt alongside him, but Ozzie kept his eyes trained on the door, willing himself to melt into the shadows, like a ninja.

Which, of course, didn't work.

"Ozzie?" Aunt Temperance said, setting down a tray. "I've brought comestibles."

She could have just said "snacks." But Aunt Temperance relished her heavy words. Ozzie glanced at the tray she had set beside him. It held a blender full of some slightly green concoction and a glass.

"Vitamin shake?" he hazarded.

"Mint chocolate chip milkshake," Aunt Temperance corrected him. "I guarantee there is nothing healthy about this drink. It's completely devoid of nutrition."

She knelt and poured Ozzie a glass. He took a begrudging sip and discovered she was telling the truth: It tasted like ice cream, which Aunt Temperance never allowed except sometimes on weekends. But Ozzie didn't feel like giving her the satisfaction of a compliment. Instead, he returned his attention to the door.

Aunt Temperance sighed. "That conversation with your mom didn't go very well."

"No kidding."

He couldn't go to Dreerdum's. It would mean moving a plane-flight away from Apartment 2B, Aunt Temperance, and . . . the door to Zoone. It would mean being alone. Even *more* alone than he was now.

"Ozzie, don't drift off. Tell me what you're thinking."

Ozzie turned his red-hot glare on her. "Why didn't you warn me? You had this pamphlet the whole time, then she calls, and you just shove it in my hands and walk away."

"I don't want you to go," Aunt Temperance said. "But your parents . . ."

Ozzie buried his head in his hands.

His parents were always gone, more interested in their careers than anything else—including him. His mom was reporting in Africa and his dad was—well, as far as Ozzie understood, he spent his time gallivanting across the globe looking for precious minerals for his company to mine. Ozzie couldn't even remember where he was right now, just that it was multiple time zones away.

"Your mom," Aunt Temperance began, "is just trying to—"

"She told me to grow up," Ozzie growled. "She said I get worked up too easily. That I'm 'too sensitive.'"

Aunt Temperance sat down beside him, even though the floor was filthy and frigid. "I don't think you're too sensitive," she told him. "As far as I'm concerned, being sensitive just means you've got good instincts. Awareness. You're a thinker and a . . ." She trailed off.

"But?" Ozzie prompted—because he knew one was coming. Like it was standing at the front door working up the nerve to knock.

"*But*," Aunt Temperance continued delicately, "I don't

think sitting down here in the cold will solve anything. You can't just live in the hope that this door will magically open, Ozzie. Sometimes things don't turn out the way you want."

"What I want is to try the door again," Ozzie said, leaping to his feet. "Right now."

Aunt Temperance tucked the loose strand of silver hair behind her ear. "We tried yesterday, Ozzie. We try every day."

"There's no harm in trying again."

Aunt Temperance frowned. Ozzie knew what she was thinking: *You'll just be disappointed.*

"I keep telling you how great it is at Zoone!" he insisted. "There're a thousand doors, a thousand worlds! And some of the doors will even *talk* to you. The mail is delivered by quirls, and there's all my friends—you've met Lady Zoone, and there's Tug and Fidget and—"

"I know, Ozzie, I know," Aunt Temperance cut him off. "But . . ."

Ozzie stared her down.

"All right," she relented. "We'll try. But then we go back upstairs. You can finish your shake and read your manga."

She plucked at the cord around her neck, revealing a large, tarnished key with a "Z" for its bow. She passed it to Ozzie and he clenched it hopefully. Every other time he had tried the key, the door had opened—but only revealed a wall of dusty bricks. That wasn't supposed to happen, not with Aunt Temperance's key. What he should see was a pathway leading through a swirl of stars. At least when the door was working.

Ozzie stood up, took a deep breath, and inserted the key.

He was greeted by a clunk.

Ozzie grimaced and tried again. Another clunk. He tried wriggling and turning the key, but something was blocking it.

"Here, let me," Aunt Temperance said, bending to peer at the peculiar key. She used both hands to try to twist it in the lock, but with no success.

"It's never done that before," Ozzie fretted. He took a step back and regarded the door. Was it getting worse? *More* closed? Was that even possible?

Aunt Temperance suddenly stood to her full height. "Did you hear that?"

"I don't hear any—"

"Shh!" Aunt Temperance hissed.

Ozzie fell silent, and that's when he detected a faint humming. It soon turned into a buzz, reminding Ozzie of an angry wasp.

"It's coming from the door!" Aunt Temperance cried. "Quick, get back!" She grabbed Ozzie by both shoulders and dove back against the far wall.

The droning sound intensified—and then, suddenly, the key shot out of the door like a bullet. Aunt Temperance gasped and Ozzie instinctively ducked, just in time. The key ricocheted off the bricks exactly where his head had been, then clattered to the floor, glowing hot and orange. There was a smell of scorched metal, like burning brakes on a car.

When Ozzie looked back to the door, he could see a wisp of smoke curling from the lock. Then a tiny metal antenna emerged, soon followed by another.

"What is *that*?" Aunt Temperance whispered.

A miniature metallic creature poked through the keyhole. It had a cluster of bulbous eyes, multiple legs, and a pair of pincers that twitched menacingly. It began scuttling across the surface of the door, quickly and erratically, metal feet clicking on the wood.

Ozzie groaned. Being a boy meant being tough (according to his dad, at least), but he wasn't—at least not when it came to creepy-crawlies. Especially creepy-crawlies that could *fly*. Because that's exactly what the miniature bug now did: It sprouted what looked like a tiny propeller and launched itself into the air to hum around the corridor, its round eyes probing every corner. Ozzie maneuvered himself slightly behind Aunt Temperance.

"Did that thing come from Zoone?" Aunt Temperance asked.

"It must have . . . but I've never seen anything like it," Ozzie said, staring nervously at the metallic bug. "They don't have robots in Zoone."

"Hmm," Aunt Temperance replied.

The bug pivoted toward Aunt Temperance and seemed to contemplate her, its antennae telescoping up and down. It made a few loops around her head, then landed on top of her hair.

"Tickles," Aunt Temperance murmured.

She obviously wasn't afraid of the bug, which was something of a surprise to Ozzie. It wasn't that Aunt Temperance was old or frail—she was, in fact, neither—but he was pretty sure the most terrifying thing she had dealt with in her life was finding a carton of expired milk at the back of the fridge.

Then the bug must have stung her, because suddenly, Aunt Temperance *did* scream. And it wasn't an "I found expired milk" scream. It was a shriek loud enough to rouse the dead—and possibly Mrs. Yang, who lived in Apartment 2A and had been known to sleep through fire alarms, sirens, and all the other commotion that comes from someone trying to make Mother's Day toast for his aunt when he's only four years old.

It was also a scream that snapped Ozzie into action. Aunt Temperance had dropped to her knees and was clutching her hair. Ozzie still had the pamphlet in his hand, so he rolled it into a makeshift club and swung at the bug. He missed—thankfully, he missed Aunt Temperance's head, too—but the gust from his swipe sent the bug back into the air with an angry buzz. Ozzie decided to keep swinging.

"Ozzie! Wait! Don't wreck it!" Aunt Temperance shouted.

Ozzie ignored her. No one had ever accused him of being athletic, but they had a saying at Zoone: Even a blind quirl sometimes delivers a message. What Ozzie finally delivered was a strike that sent the bug careening into the wall.

There was a mini explosion of sparks and the metal creature sputtered to the ground, where it lay on its back like a dying fly, its long feelers twitching. Ozzie inched over for a closer look. The bug's bulbous eyes flickered; then it released a quiet, mechanical groan before turning rigid.

Aunt Temperance stood alongside him, massaging her head with one hand.

"Are you okay?" Ozzie asked.

"It jabbed me," Aunt Temperance replied. "Didn't hurt that much, but it startled me." She prodded the bug with a finger. All its legs were curled up, just how a real bug looked after being clobbered.

"It's dead now, right?" Ozzie asked uneasily.

Aunt Temperance frowned. "Broken, anyway. I don't think robots can die, can they?"

Ozzie exhaled. "I guess not."

Aunt Temperance was still staring at the bug. "It *is* marvelous, though."

Sure, Ozzie thought, *if you consider a flying razor blade with eyes to be marvelous.* Which, incidentally, he did not.

"I think this specimen requires further inspection," Aunt Temperance announced. "Upstairs, in the proper light." She picked up the bug, cradled it in her cupped hands, then began wandering down the passageway.

Ozzie hurriedly scooped up the key from the floor. It still felt warm in his hands. Aunt Temperance had already disappeared around the corner, but he had to give the door another try—because the bug had gotten through, and that meant . . .

Has to work this time, he pondered. The key now slid easily into the slot, but when he opened the door, there was still only a wall of bricks.

Frowning, he leaned forward and examined the wall more closely. When he crouched down, he finally noticed it: a small key-shaped hole in the bricks. He peered through the gap—and could just make out a swirling starscape. The track to Zoone was there! The doorway was opening again, just enough to let the bug through.

"Maybe it's repairing itself!" Ozzie rejoiced. *But why did a robotic flying death bug come through? What's going on in Zoone?*

"Ozzie!" Aunt Temperance called from around the corner. "Hurry up!"

Ozzie closed the door, gathered up the blender and his glass, and reluctantly followed Aunt Temperance up the steps.

"Why are you in such a hurry?" he called. "You seem . . . I don't know, discombobulated."

It was a pretty impressive word, and he was proud of himself for coming up with it. But Aunt Temperance didn't even acknowledge it. She just kept moving steadily up the stairs, her gaze transfixed by the bug.

"This is the thing, Ozzie," she said eventually. "*You* may have never seen anything like this creature before. But I think I have."

3

NEWS FROM THE NEXUS

Ozzie chased after his aunt, his mind twisting like the set of steps they were climbing. Where would Aunt Temperance have seen a robotic flying death bug? She didn't lead a very exciting life. After all, what kind of person had a key to Zoone but never used it? Aunt Temperance had inherited the key from her grandfather and, as far as Ozzie understood, she had always known about the door—she had just never quite believed in its magic, never been tempted to go through it. Ozzie didn't understand it. As soon as *he* had discovered the existence of the key, he had, well, "borrowed" it and whisked himself off to find adventure.

But Aunt Temperance liked to play it safe, stay at home reading books or listening to the "classics" on the radio. Even her job was boring; she was a corporate librarian, which meant she spent her days preparing and organizing legal documents. Just the thought of it made Ozzie yawn.

They were soon back in Aunt Temperance's apartment—or, as Ozzie liked to think of it, *their* apartment. Technically, he lived with his parents, but because they were away so often, he spent most of his time in Apartment 2B. He even had his own room there.

Aunt Temperance set the bug down on the coffee table and continued to gaze at it with a quizzical expression. Then she disappeared into her bedroom, where she began to rummage around with an uncharacteristic loudness. When she returned, she was tugging a battered steamer trunk, covered with faded stickers that showed the names of distant cities and countries. Ozzie had never seen it before.

Aunt Temperance knelt down and hesitated a moment before clicking open the trunk. "Welcome to my old life."

Ozzie leaned over to see that the trunk was crammed with all sorts of curiosities. There were brightly colored playbills and posters, an assortment of trinkets and jewelry, and peculiar items of clothing, including a leotard that looked like it had drowned in glitter.

"This all belongs to you?" Ozzie asked in surprise.

"Yes," Aunt Temperance explained, "from my days in the circus."

"What?!" Ozzie gasped. He suddenly remembered Lady Zoone telling him that Aunt Temperance had once run away to join the circus, but he hadn't thought it was *true*. That was just an expression people used. Wasn't it? "I—I don't believe it," he finally stammered.

"Believe it," Aunt Temperance said, unrolling a poster and passing it to him.

In large gold letters, the poster said: *Culpepper & Merriweather's Circus of the Bizarre*. But it was the photo under the title that caught Ozzie's attention: It depicted a young woman in a dazzling sequined suit—the very suit sitting in the trunk!—swinging on a trapeze, long hair flowing out behind her. A starburst graphic boasted: *The One and Only Tempest of the Big Top!*

"Wait a minute," Ozzie said. "That's *you*?"

Aunt Temperance laughed. "Try acting a little less astonished."

"But . . . but . . ." What Ozzie really wanted to say was, "There's days when you can't even face making breakfast; how could you fly across a circus tent?" But he just continued to gape like a goldfish.

"Oh, here's one you should appreciate," Aunt Temperance said, passing over a second poster. It featured a woman with an impossibly long neck and similarly disproportionate arms, which were stretched out to serve as perches for dozens of birds. Underneath, it read: *Behold Madame Arborellia, freak of nature! She can stand hours on end without moving! Wild birds nest in her hair!*

"That's Lady Zoone!" Ozzie cried.

"Yes, she lived in our world for many years. We met in the circus." She paused. "In those days, we were friends. Good friends."

"They're calling the stationmaster for the nexus of the entire multiverse a . . . a *freak!*"

"Unfortunately, it sold tickets," Aunt Temperance said. "Though, why people would want to spend money just to watch her do absolutely nothing for hours on end is beyond m—oh! There it is."

A small box with a flowered pattern was nestled in one corner of the chest. Aunt Temperance plucked the box from its confinement and set it on her lap. She took a deep breath, then gingerly opened the box. Ozzie leaned in— only to leap back an instant later.

There was a bug in the box. A *metal* bug.

"It won't hurt you," Aunt Temperance assured him. "It's a cricket. A very cute cricket, I think." She gently placed the creature on the table.

Ozzie swallowed. The cricket looked like some kind of antique tin toy. It even had a clockwork key jutting from its back. It wouldn't have looked that out of place sitting among the other vintage knickknacks on the various shelves of Apartment 2B. He wondered why Aunt Temperance didn't have it out on display, too.

Curiosity won him over, and Ozzie found the courage to nudge the cricket with his finger. Then he picked it up, turning it over in his hands to see that its innards consisted of a complicated system of gears and wires. He set the cricket down again and twisted the clockwork key. Lights flickered in its bulb-like eyes, its wings juddered— but almost before it had started, it sputtered to a stop.

"Doesn't work properly," Aunt Temperance said. "Not anymore. Maybe . . . maybe it never did."

She picked herself up, sat in the nearest chair, and began staring into space, like she did whenever she was feeling overwhelmed. Ozzie had a feeling that she was talking about something bigger than the cricket.

"Why haven't you ever showed this stuff to me before?" he asked.

"Memories," she murmured. "Ones I've tried to forget. But things keep happening . . ."

She didn't finish her sentence, prompting Ozzie to feel a sudden spike of dread. Was this going to turn into one of her depressive episodes? Maybe it had been a good idea to keep this stuff locked up in a trunk. The last time she had fallen into a slump, she hadn't gotten out of bed for a week.

And now Ozzie felt guilty—because what had sparked her most recent downward spiral was him finding the door to the nexus, which had prompted Lady Zoone to come visit, and then . . . well, he wished he knew why it had upset her so much. Something must have happened in her past that he still didn't understand.

Ozzie's gaze wandered over to the robotic flying death bug, still lying upside down on the coffee table. Then he looked back at the cricket. "This is why you thought the death bug was familiar?"

Aunt Temperance slowly nodded.

She said nothing more, so Ozzie began stuffing the posters and playbills back in the steamer trunk—which was when he noticed a flyer with an illustration of a robotic cricket, just like the one on their table. Above the picture, in whimsical clockwork letters, it declared: *Visit the Menagerie of Mechanized Marvels! Only at Culpepper & Merriweather's Circus!*

"This doesn't make sense," Ozzie muttered. "I mean, the cricket came from the circus. From here, right? And the robotic flying death bug came through the door, which means it must have come from . . ."

"Zoone," Aunt Temperance added softly. "Which means . . ."

She trailed off again. Ozzie stepped right in front of

her. "Hello? Aunt T? Which means *what*?"

Aunt Temperance blinked and focused her eyes on Ozzie, as if only suddenly remembering that he was there. "Which means it's a clue to . . ."

"Will you stop doing that?!" Ozzie cried. "Finish a sentence! Are you okay?"

Aunt Temperance rose firmly to her feet, put her hand on Ozzie's shoulder, and looked him straight in the eye. "I'm more than okay, Ozzie. No more sitting around. As soon as that door opens, we're going to Zoone."

Aunt Temperance was a new woman. Ozzie had been worried about the trunk of memories upsetting her, and maybe it had, initially. But now it seemed to provoke a different result: rejuvenation. She hummed and danced— *danced*—around Apartment 2B. She even proudly hung one of the circus posters on the living room wall. Aunt Temperance wasn't hiding from her past now, Ozzie realized. She was embracing it.

On Wednesday, he came home from school to find her reorganizing the furniture. Which was odd. Aunt Temperance liked a certain consistency.

"Wait a minute," he said in a sudden moment of realization. "Why aren't you at work?" She usually arrived home after him.

"I quit," she declared proudly.

"What?!" Ozzie cried. "What are you going to do for money?"

"This apartment was left to me by my grandfather," Aunt Temperance replied. "Which means there's no rent to pay. I can live off my savings, at least for now. Nothing to worry about, Ozzie."

Sure, Ozzie grouched to himself. *Because you're not the one scheduled to be shipped off to Dreerdum's School of Torture. What if the door doesn't open? Ever? Or in time? Then I don't just lose Zoone . . .*

He stared at his aunt.

I lose you.

He did what he always did when he was upset: He borrowed the key, raced to The Depths, and checked the door. That was when he realized his aunt might be right; maybe there wasn't anything to worry about.

Because the track was definitely repairing itself.

The hole in the brick wall had expanded—just a little bit, but it was definitely bigger. With a sigh of relief, Ozzie turned and gazed up the long set of steps, toward Apartment 2B. Just between him and himself, he wondered if it was Aunt Temperance's doing. Maybe her new attitude—announcing her intention to go to Zoone, quitting her job—was speeding up the magical repair of the portal.

Every day was better than the last. On Thursday, Ozzie could put his fist through the hole. On Friday, he could fit his head. On Saturday, he and Aunt Temperance arrived home from the grocery store to find two visitors from Zoone sitting on their sofa: a humongous flying tiger and a princess with purple hair.

Aunt Temperance's jaw dropped. So did the grocery bag in her hands. It hit the floor with a crash.

"Don't worry," Ozzie assured her. "These are my—"

He didn't finish because at that moment the cat sprang from the sofa, bowled him over, and began lapping at his face with a long blue tongue. "I'm so happy to see you," Ozzie said, burying his hands and face in the skyger's luxurious blue fur.

"Me, too," Tug purred, tickling Ozzie's face with his whiskers.

Fidget tried to elbow the skyger aside, which, Ozzie knew, was like trying to move a cement truck. "Hey, I missed him, too!" When she finally managed to pull Ozzie free, she wrapped her arms around him. "Good to see you, Oz."

"You have no idea," he said as Tug thrust his giant head into their hug.

"Are you going to introduce us?" Aunt Temperance cut in eventually.

"Oh, right!" Ozzie said. He had spent countless hours

telling her about his friends—and finally, they were *here.* "This is Tug. He's a skyger, and—"

"Just to tell you, skygers come from the Skylands of Azuria," the enormous cat declared. "But I've lived at the nexus most of my life. Which means I'm a *Zoonian* skyger." His fur shimmered from blue to pumpkin orange, a sure sign of skyger—*Zoonian* skyger—exuberance.

"Ozzie said you were a cub," Aunt Temperance said faintly. "I thought you would be . . . *smaller.*"

Tug gave a twitch of his long bushy-tipped tail. During his time in Zoone, Ozzie had come to think of that tail as a calamity looking for a place to happen. In the tiny confines of Apartment 2B, it didn't have to look very long. A potted fern and a framed photograph from the sofa's side table toppled to the living room floor—though the cat himself was oblivious to the accident.

Aunt Temperance wasn't, but before she could say anything, Ozzie continued, "And this is Fidget. Well, her real name is Kaia, she's a princess of Quoxx, and—"

"Just call me Fidget," the purple-haired girl interjected. "Because, to be honest—"

"—her parents arranged for her to get married, even though she's only thirteen," Ozzie continued excitedly. "Remember, I told you? So she ran away. She lives at Zoone now."

"Your ears really are pointed," Aunt Temperance said,

studying Fidget. "And your hair! Ozzie did warn me, but I didn't realize it would be *that* purple. Even your *eyebrows* are purple."

"Really?" Fidget retorted, crossing her arms. "I hadn't noticed."

"Oh!" Aunt Temperance cried. "The door is still open." She promptly shut it, then, leveling a reprimanding glare at Ozzie, said, "*Someone* was supposed to lock it behind us when we left for the store."

"It's a good thing for us that you didn't," Fidget said. "I don't think you'd want us roaming around in your building."

"Um . . . no," Ozzie said, thinking of Mrs. Yang next door.

Aunt Temperance seemed to have the same thought. She whisked across the floor to the street-facing window and hastily drew the curtains shut. "The last thing we want is someone calling animal control."

"Ooh," Tug said with an excitable flutter of his wings. "Someone can control animals? They must be a wizard. Just to tell you, Fidget and Ozzie and me—we've met loads of wizards. But I'm not sure we've ever met one who could *control* animals. What's their name?"

Aunt Temperance gaped at the giant cat. "Whose name?"

Tug sat down on his haunches and flicked his long tail.

Ozzie quickly snatched it out of the air, saving the nearby lamp from obliteration. "The animal-controlling wizard you're worried about."

Aunt Temperance removed her glasses and began giving them a vigorous cleaning with the hem of her blouse. "I'm not sure things work in our world the same way they do in yours."

"No kidding," Ozzie agreed, before turning to Fidget to say, "You're *here*! That must mean the door to Zoone has reopened. What are we waiting for? Let's go!"

"Hold on, Oz," Fidget said, putting a hand gently to his chest. "You don't know what's going on there. There's a lot we have to tell you." She looked cryptically at Aunt Temperance. "Both of you, actually."

"Me?" Aunt Temperance wondered, slipping her glasses back on.

Fidget nodded. "Something's happened at the nexus. Something terrible. We're not visiting from Zoone, Ozzie. We're *escaping* it."

THE MESSAGE AND THE MEMORY MARBLE

Ozzie stared at the princess in bewilderment. Zoone wasn't a place you escaped *from*—it was a place you escaped *to*. Fidget knew that better than anyone. "We have to go," he insisted. "Like, *now*."

Fidget shook her head. "It's not safe."

Aunt Temperance's brow knitted in concern. She glanced briefly at Ozzie. "Not safe how?"

"Show them the marble," Tug suggested.

Fidget nodded, reached into a pocket, and fished out a round pebble. "Nespera Cruxx gave this to me after staying at the Zoone Inn during the Convention of Wizardry.

I guess it was supposed to be a tip for working so hard as a clerk."

"She gave you a rock?" Aunt Temperance asked skeptically.

"It's *not* a rock," Ozzie chimed in. "It's a memory marble. Remember, I told you about them?"

"I'm still getting used to all of this," Aunt Temperance admitted.

"Well, get used to it quicker," Fidget said. "I recorded something I need to show you. See, one day this strange— *really* strange—traveler shows up at the station. He's wearing armor and a helmet with all this . . . *stuff*. Like, hoses and switches and things. He dresses like a moto, I guess."

"What's a moto?" Ozzie asked.

"They're like people," Tug added. "Except not people-people. Metal people."

Ozzie gasped. "You mean robots? Where did they come from? I've never seen anything like a robot at Zoone."

Fidget shrugged. "Klaxon—this traveler—calls them *motos*. He shows up with a whole gang of them, then he and the motos have a private meeting with Lady Zoone. We're all wondering what's going on. Then, suddenly, one of Lady Zoone's birds flies through my window with a message from her, asking me to come to her study with my memory marble. But to pretend I'm delivering tea."

"Why would you have to pretend?" Ozzie asked.

"I think I should just show you," she said.

She threw the pebble to the floor, which made it crack open and beam a moving three-dimensional image into the room, a scene of Fidget standing at an open window. Ozzie felt as if he were standing right next to this memory version of Fidget. Peering through the window, he could see the platforms of Zoone, with its hundreds of doors of all different designs and shapes and, beyond, the lush turquoise trees of the Infinite Wood.

"Zoone!" he cried excitedly, inhaling the scene with every fiber of his being. "We're at Zoone!"

"This is a recording?" Aunt Temperance marveled. "It feels like we're right inside of it! I can hear the breeze through the trees—I can even smell the air."

"That's how a memory marble works," Fidget explained impatiently. "I'm showing you my memory of the last time I saw Lady Zoone. Just watch."

The Fidget inside the memory turned away from the window to reveal a new perspective: that of a cramped and cluttered chamber. Ozzie instantly recognized it as Lady Zoone's personal study. The room always looked like it was trying to do its best impression of a wizard's lair; there were books, maps, and arcane artifacts stuffed into every crook and corner.

Lady Zoone was now in the picture as well. She didn't

seem the same sturdy and sure figure that Ozzie had come to know during his time in the nexus. Her face, normally as rich and umber as tree bark, was pale with worry. Her willowy limbs were quivering.

"Did you bring your marble?" Lady Zoone asked.

"Yes, I brought it. I've already started recording," Memory Fidget told her. "What's going on? Why are motos guarding your door? And why did I have to pretend to be serving tea?"

"I thought it would be easier," Lady Zoone explained. "I wanted to make sure they let you in."

"Um, you're the steward of the nexus," Memory Fidget said indignantly. "You don't need anyone's permission."

Lady Zoone smiled—but it didn't seem to be a happy one. "I have a mission for you, Fidget. You and Tug."

"Okay," Memory Fidget said. "Anything—you can count on us."

"I need you to travel to Ozzie's world," Lady Zoone said, taking a key from around her neck. The birds and rodents in her hair chirped excitedly as she spoke.

"You're giving me *your* key?!" Memory Fidget exclaimed.

Ozzie was just as surprised. Lady Zoone's key was a fabulous device, clustered with gears and wheels—by turning them to different settings, you could open any door in Zoone. Ozzie watched with a hint of envy as

Lady Zoone pressed the key into Fidget's hands.

"As soon as the door is working, you must find Ozzie, and deliver this to his aunt." She produced a small cloth bag and passed it to Memory Fidget. "And my message."

"What message?"

"This one." She turned slightly, as if facing a camera, and called out, "Tempie?"

Aunt Temperance blinked in surprise. From her vantage point in the room, she was looking at Lady Zoone from the side. It was Ozzie who was looking at the steward directly; Aunt Temperance quickly shuffled him out of the way and gazed up at the image of Lady Zoone. "Zaria?"

Ozzie frowned. "It doesn't work that way. It's not interactive! It's just—"

"I need you, Tempie," Lady Zoone began, her green eyes wide and earnest. "Frost in summer—we all do. The entire multiverse."

Ozzie's expression turned to a scowl. Why was Lady Zoone begging for *her* help?

"I know what happened to him, Tempie," Lady Zoone called from the memory, anxiously clasping her hands. "He's in trouble—terrible trouble. I know you've resisted visiting Zoone, but if you're hearing this, that means the door to your world is open, and you *must* come to me."

Ozzie glanced at Aunt Temperance again. She had

turned stiff, as if Lady Zoone's words had caused her to petrify.

"We can save him, Tempie," Lady Zoone continued. "I can't do it without you—and we *must* do it. He's the key. Save Mercurio and we save Zoone. He's still—"

She came to an abrupt stop; there was the raucous sound of a door being thrown open. The image instantly disappeared. The memory was over.

"One of the motos interrupted us," Fidget explained into the sudden silence. "I managed to slip out of Lady Zoone's study with my marble and the stuff she gave me. But I haven't seen her since then. No one has. Not the real her."

"What's that supposed to mean?" Ozzie asked.

"No one's seen her up close," Fidget said. "Sometimes we glimpse her standing on one of the terraces. Otherwise, the only time you hear from her is if she issues some official proclamation. If you ask me, it's an imposter. Either that, or she's under an enchantment."

Aunt Temperance finally unstiffened. "Why do you think that?"

"I *know* Lady Zoone," Fidget replied. "When I first came to the nexus, she let me stay with her. She kind of looked after me. Now I'm stuck with Panya and Piper, those girls from the kitchen. You can't move for the gossip and drama in their room, and—"

"Where's Cho?" Ozzie interrupted. "He wouldn't let anything happen to Lady Zoone."

All the color drained from Fidget's cheeks. She glanced uncomfortably in Tug's direction. "I'm not sure how to say this, Ozzie. Cho's been fired."

Ozzie reeled. "Fired? *Fired?!* Lady Zoone would never fire him."

"Exactly," Fidget agreed. "Aren't you listening to a word I'm saying? She's not acting like herself."

"We don't know where Cho is," Tug added, his fur fading to a mournful gray. He flopped to the floor, which caused the picture frames on the wall to tilt sideways and a few of the books on the nearby shelf to thump over. "He just disappeared. He didn't even say good-bye."

"It's been a couple of weeks since he's vanished," Fidget explained, dropping down next to Tug—which caused absolutely nothing to happen to the apartment. "Klaxon is the captain of security now. And his motos are the new security force." She stared fixedly at Ozzie. "They're *machines*. Glorified tin cans. And now they're in control of Zoone."

"What are we doing standing around, then?!" Ozzie cried.

Fidget gritted her teeth. "Completing Lady Zoone's mission."

Ozzie turned to Aunt Temperance. He wondered how

she was digesting all this news. It was a lot to take in, even for him, and he'd had some experience with the strange situations that happened in the multiverse.

But Aunt Temperance didn't seem overwhelmed. She leaned intently forward, resting her chin on a fist. "Fidget, show me the pouch Zaria gave you."

"Zaria?" Ozzie asked, only to remember that was Lady Zoone's first name. It was strange to hear Aunt Temperance refer to one of the most important people in the multiverse in such a personal way.

Fidget reached into a pocket and passed over the pouch. Aunt Temperance fiddled with the drawstrings and shook the contents out onto her waiting palm.

"Oh!"

A long golden chain was spilling through her fingers. Attached to it was an old-fashioned locket and a peculiar ring. The band of the ring was plain and tarnished, but the gemstone was huge, round, and seemed to be *pulsing*. Ozzie reached out to touch it and immediately felt a zap. It didn't hurt him—but it was surprising. It hadn't felt like magic. It had felt like static electricity—or maybe *real* electricity, the kind you could use to power a car. Or, judging by how the gem was glowing, a small city.

"What is it?" Ozzie asked. "Why did Lady Zoone want *you* to have it?"

"Because . . . these things are mine. I didn't know she had them. I threw them away, but she must have . . ."

Aunt Temperance clicked open the locket and Ozzie leaned in over her shoulder to see a photo of a young man and woman. Even though the picture was tiny, the man's broad smile stood out, as did his wild, unruly hair. As for the woman—Ozzie suddenly recognized her as Aunt Temperance. She wasn't wearing her glasses, but it was definitely her. A long time ago.

Fidget crowded in and asked the question burning in Ozzie's mind. "Who's the guy?"

"Mercurio," Aunt Temperance answered, eyes still fixed on the photo.

The one Lady Zoone wants her to save, Ozzie realized.

"Yeah, but who *is* he?" Fidget pressed.

Aunt Temperance raised her gaze from the locket. Her expression made Ozzie grimace. Because he instinctively *knew* the answer to Fidget's question.

"He was my . . ."

"Oh," Fidget said. "Your boyfriend."

Ozzie squirmed. It wasn't like he had anything against romance. But it was one thing to gaze longingly at Laurel, the girl who sat across from him in social studies; it was another to have to think about the fact that your *aunt* had those sorts of feelings.

Fidget scrutinized the photo. "He's handsome," she

pronounced, which, for a reason Ozzie couldn't quite explain, bothered him.

"Definitely," Tug agreed, plowing his giant snout between Fidget and Aunt Temperance.

"I don't understand," Aunt Temperance said, rising to her feet to pace across the floor—which wasn't entirely easy with Tug present. "*Save him.* Save him from what?"

"Klaxon and the motos—obviously," Fidget said. "But, um, no offense . . . *everyone* needs saving from the motos. What makes your boyfriend so important?"

"*Old* boyfriend," Ozzie quickly interjected. "Ex-boyfriend."

"Why did you break up?" Fidget asked.

Aunt Temperance exhaled. "Because sometimes the world conspires against you. Or at least your parents do. Mercurio, Zaria, and I . . . those days . . ."

"Those days *what*?" Ozzie prompted.

"If Mercurio's in trouble—"

"*Everyone's* in trouble," Fidget corrected her.

Aunt Temperance nodded. "Mercurio is—I've never met anyone like him. Clever. Kind. If anyone can stop these . . . these . . . motos, maybe it's him. Zaria said to come to Zoone. So that's where I'm going. But I'll go farther if I have to."

Who are you? Ozzie thought, gaping at her. Aunt Temperance wasn't a take-charge type of person. But now she had a glint of determination in her eyes. "You're actually going to do it?" he asked her. "When do we leave?"

"Immediately," Aunt Temperance announced. "Well, as soon as I pack a few essentials. Oh! I'd better grab my blender."

"Your blender?!" Ozzie cried, chasing Aunt Temperance into the kitchen. *I guess she hasn't completely changed*, he thought. Which, in a way, was kind of comforting. But there was also a part of him that was annoyed. What did Lady Zoone expect *her* to do? Most heroes embarked on quests with swords at their sides—not blenders. "You know, Aunt T, I'm not sure the blender's an 'essential.' I'm not even sure it will work in Zoone."

"I guess we're going to find out," she replied, unplugging the blender and wrapping the cord around its glass pitcher. "I'm going to figure this out, Ozzie. I'm going to save my friends."

She whisked herself off to her room, where Ozzie heard her hurriedly yanking out drawers.

"Ozzie," she called, "clean up that knocked-over fern, will you? And put away the groceries. Then you'd better pack a few things, too."

"Like what?" he wondered, going to her doorway.

Aunt Temperance didn't reply; she was burrowed waist-deep in her closet. Ozzie sighed, then turned to the groceries that were still scattered near the front door. Tug and Fidget joined him and together they contemplated the trickle of orange juice meandering from one of the bags. Tug licked it up with a single swipe of his tongue.

"A little sour," he decreed before moving on to snuffle the grocery bags. "I'm not sure what happened to that fern, Ozzie, but I can help with these. Anything good in here?"

"Mostly vegetables," Ozzie said, slipping the bag out of Tug's reach. "You know, healthy stuff. Wait a minute! Aunt T did let me buy chips for a Sunday treat."

He foraged for the bag of chips, then ripped it open and placed it in front of Tug. The skyger sniffed curiously at the bag—then promptly inhaled its contents with all the tact of a vacuum cleaner.

"Sorry," Ozzie told Fidget. "I should have saved some for you."

Fidget waved away the comment, her expression hardening. "Look, maybe I didn't make this clear: Zoone's dangerous. The motos have already replaced the entire security force. Who's next? The kitchen workers? The inn staff—don't sneer at me, Oz. Maybe next will be the *porters.*"

Ozzie shook his head in disbelief. "Look," he said as another loud thump emanated from Aunt Temperance's bedroom, "you're not going to stop her from going." Then he pictured a boy in a Dreerdum's uniform pummeling him against a locker, which prompted him to add, "Or me."

"I'll come with you," Tug announced as he licked a few remaining crumbs from his chin. "Zoone's in trouble. Besides, we're a team."

"I'm not saying don't go," Fidget huffed. "I'm saying we need a plan. And maybe an army. We should go to the Council of Wizardry. Find what's-her-name. Adaryn Moonstrom, the head wizard."

"And how are we supposed to do that without going to Zoone first?" Ozzie demanded. "There's one door here and it only goes to the nexus. So, that's where we're going. Look, everything will work out."

Fidget sighed and crossed her arms. "Says the boy who can't even get his shirt on the right way."

Ozzie stared down at his collar to see the tag sticking out. Backward *and* inside out.

"Just don't blame me if it all goes to quoggswoggle the moment we get there," Fidget said. Then, thrusting a thumb in the direction of Aunt Temperance's bedroom, she added, "How long is she going to be?"

"I have no idea," Ozzie answered. He glanced around the apartment, wondering if there was anything worth showing his friends. Eridea was probably the only world in the multiverse that he knew more about than Fidget. "You guys could check out the TV?"

"What do you do with that?" Tug asked, ears twitching inquisitively.

"You watch it," Ozzie replied.

Aunt Temperance's TV was embarrassingly old, hailing from an era when entertainment units thought they had to disguise themselves as furniture. It didn't even have a remote—though, as Aunt Temperance liked to point out whenever Ozzie complained, at least it was in color.

Tug slumped in front of it. "I'm watching it, Ozzie," the skyger called over his shoulder. "But, just to tell you, I don't think it's going anywhere."

Ozzie navigated his way around the enormous cat and switched it on. "Let me change the channel. This is just a commercial."

"Wait!" Tug cried. "What's a commercial?"

Ozzie's hand paused on the dial. "Just a thing they make you watch to try and sell you stuff between the scenes of the actual story. This one's for shampoo."

"Oh . . ." The skyger was staring at the flashing images, mesmerized. He nudged Ozzie out of the way with his giant snout, then inched so close to the TV that his nose was touching the screen. It was impossible for Ozzie and Fidget to see anything past his mountainous head.

"Just to tell you," Fidget said to Ozzie, "I think Zoonian skygers like TV."

5

PIRATES IN THE PORTAL

An hour later, Ozzie was trekking down the winding set of stairs that led into The Depths, taking up the rear behind Fidget, Tug, and his aunt—though she was hardly recognizable. To begin with, instead of a skirt, she was wearing an old pair of cargo pants (*cargo pants!*), a checkered shirt, and a tall pair of boots. Then there was her hair, which she'd done in two braids. For Aunt Temperance, this was the equivalent of sporting a Mohawk.

Then there was the canvas backpack that she had slung over her shoulders. It contained not only her blender, but a vast assortment of other items mined from the nooks and crannies of Apartment 2B, everything from tea bags to extra underwear for Ozzie (in the end, it had been Aunt Temperance who had made his packing decisions).

"I don't think I'm ready to leave this world," Tug lamented as they neared the bottom of the stairs. "I was right in the middle of this fantastic story on the TV about a place called Burger Empire."

"That wasn't a story," Ozzie said. "That was a commercial. Burger Empire is a real place. It actually exists."

"We can go there?" Tug exclaimed, coming to a halt as his fur rippled tangerine orange. "That would be so cool."

"Cool?" Ozzie echoed. "Where did you get that word? Let me guess—TV."

"Don't they have burgers where you come from?" Aunt Temperance asked.

She had just reached the landing, and Ozzie noticed her looking longingly down the passageway, toward the door to Zoone. *Of course*, he thought. *When I was desperate to go there, it was all about patience and managing expectations. Now that she wants to go, we can't leave soon enough.*

"They don't have anything like Burger Empire in Zoone," Tug protested. "Did you know the emperor is a deluxe burger? The empress is a cheeseburger, the prince and princess are mini burgers, the knights ride these things called hot dogs and—"

"It's not really like that," Ozzie said, trying to push the skyger down the remaining steps. "They just serve food. There're no burgers walking around singing 'long live Emperor Beef.' That's a made-up story."

"I thought you just said it *wasn't* a story," Fidget said.

"Well, yeah, not that kind of story," Ozzie clarified. "It's a special type of story to sell burgers."

"So, they're lying?" It was dark in The Depths, with just a row of bare light bulbs hanging from the ceiling, but even through the gloom Ozzie could see Fidget raise a purple eyebrow.

"Well, not really," Ozzie tried to explain. "I mean, sort of. But everyone knows it's not the truth."

"Your world is confusing," Fidget decided.

"Come on," Aunt Temperance urged, continuing down the corridor.

She had decided to wear the chain with the locket and ring around her neck, putting Ozzie in charge of the Zoone key. As soon as they reached the portal, he inserted it into the lock and threw open the door. There were no bricks now; instead, they saw nothing but the track stretching out into the distance, a vortex of stars spinning gently around it.

"Oh!" Aunt Temperance gasped. "It's . . ."

It wasn't like her to be at a loss for words, Ozzie knew, but then he remembered how overwhelmed he had felt the first time he'd seen this. "Beautiful?" he suggested.

"Ensorcelling," she finally managed.

She adjusted the bag on her shoulders and stepped through the door and onto the track. The instant she did so, she began to trundle away, as if on some invisible conveyor belt. Everyone else followed.

"How are we moving?" Aunt Temperance asked, turning in a slow circle.

"It's magic, Aunt T," Ozzie explained, putting the key back around his neck. "Isn't it amazing?"

"You know what would help us get there faster?" Tug said, sitting on his haunches. "The new Bolt Ultra-ZX. It's a type of car I saw on the TV and, when you're driving it, the wind whips through your hair. 'Freedom at your fingertips!' I don't have fingers, but I think I could steer one with my paws, or my tail, and . . ."

He trailed off, prompting Ozzie to say, "Tug? What is it?"

"Do you hear that?" the skyger whimpered, ears flattening against his head.

Everyone began to glance around nervously. Soon enough, what had already reached the skyger's sensitive ears caught up to everyone else's—a faint but high-pitched squeal coming from somewhere beyond the portal.

"It sounds like a drill," Ozzie said with a shudder. "The type a dentist uses."

"What kind of maniacal dentists do you have in your world?" Fidget said. "They use drills? Remind me to never come visit you again, okay? Especially if I have a toothache!"

The noise continued to crescendo, causing the entire tunnel to shake. Ozzie could feel it vibrate through his heels and up his legs. He reached out to steady himself against Tug, only to find that the cat had crouched to bury his head in his paws. His fur had turned a grisly green.

"What's happening?!" Aunt Temperance cried.

"I don't know!" Fidget shouted over the now-deafening roar. "Things only seem to go wrong on this track when Ozzie takes it!"

The track began to quake so violently that soon everyone was bouncing around like they were on a trampoline. The sky buckled and bulged—and then, suddenly, it ruptured open to reveal the tip of what looked like an enormous mining drill. The machine grumbled to a halt, providing instant relief to everyone's ears. The track ceased to twist and turn—in fact, it ceased to move at all. They had come to a complete standstill.

"The track!" Ozzie yelped, panicked. "What'd they do to it?"

"Is everyone okay?" Aunt Temperance asked, fumbling a few steps forward. Her glasses were askew and one braid had partially unraveled in the ruckus. She looked like she had gone swimming in her own blender.

Ozzie nodded distractedly and turned his attention to the split in the tunnel. Even though the auger was no longer spinning, it was still moving forward, and now he could see that it was actually the business end of a humongous floating ship. At first, he wasn't sure how it was remaining aloft, but once the ship had plowed fully into the tunnel, he noticed a spinning turbine on its back end, gushing clouds of steam amid a cluster of undulating tentacles. This, combined with the drill at its nose, made the ship look like a giant metal squid.

"Are they dentists?" Tug asked worriedly.

Fidget snorted. "I wish. That's a pirate ship."

"There are pirates in Zoone?" Aunt Temperance asked incredulously.

"We haven't actually made it to Zoone yet," Ozzie pointed out as the metal leviathan loomed over them.

"Portal pirates," Fidget explained. "Scavengers, marauders—my grandfather used to tell tales about them. They roam the spaces between portals and slice their way onto tracks to rob and kidnap innocent travelers."

"Spaces *between* the portals?" Aunt Temperance echoed. "Is that even possible? Scientifically?"

"Oh, I don't know," Fidget snapped. "Maybe I'm

just imagining the massive metal monstrosity hovering above us."

A series of hatches clicked open from the undercarriage of the ship. Next, long cables began to unspool toward them. Then came the dark shapes of the pirates, scuttling down the ropes like spiders, hooting, hollering, and brandishing weapons. A loud crack sounded, and something whizzed through Ozzie's mess of hair.

"They have guns!" he exclaimed. "Come on—we have to reach the door, get to Zoone. Tug, can you fly?"

The skyger gave him a trembling nod, so Ozzie clambered onto his back and sank his hands into his thick fur. "Come on, guys!"

"You know, perhaps I'll stick with my feet," Aunt Temperance said hesitantly.

"We don't have time for this," Fidget growled. "Get on the skyger! *Right. Now.*" Without waiting for further argument, she boosted Aunt Temperance onto Tug, then leaped up after her.

Pirates began dropping onto the track—this side, that side, every side, until Tug was surrounded. Aunt Temperance shrieked. Tug yowled—he was as terrified as any of them, but the pirates didn't know that. All they saw were his giant fangs, and that seemed to make most of them pause and reconsider certain life choices. Ozzie could have told them that they had it all wrong. When it came to Tug, you needed to worry about his back end—the one that served as base of operations for the wrecking ball otherwise known as his tail. That tail had now been set to full-anxiety mode, which meant pirates were soon flying through the air like plastic soldiers who'd been introduced to a tornado.

The pirates were hardy, though; Ozzie had to give them that. It took only a moment for them to begin picking themselves up.

"Hurry, Tug—let's get out of here!" Ozzie yelled.

The skyger burst from the ground in a flutter of feathers. Ozzie heard more bullets fly, more pirate war cries. A marauder came swinging toward them from the ship above, one hand clenching a rope and the other a sword with a curve like a malevolent smile. The pirate slashed at them; Tug swooped out of the way just in time, and then Ozzie heard a loud whack. He turned to see the pirate tumbling to the ground and Fidget brandishing a weapon of her own: an umbrella.

Where did she get that from? he wondered, and then remembered the umbrella Aunt Temperance had packed in the side pocket of her bag.

Suddenly, Tug shuddered beneath them. "You okay?" Ozzie asked him.

"Doing . . . my . . . best," the cat replied in a strained tone.

"We're too heavy for him," Fidget realized as more bullets whistled past them. "It's your bag, Aunt T. Stupid blender! You'll have to drop it!"

Aunt Temperance gasped. "It's an *essential*. Can't we drop something else?"

"You?" Fidget suggested.

Ozzie peered around Tug's massive head and focused on the tunnel stretching before them. He could just make out the door to Zoone in the distance. It looked exactly like the one in The Depths: weathered and gray with hints of turquoise.

"You can do it, Tug," Ozzie encouraged. "We're almost th—"

A sound split the air like a cannon shot, followed by the sensation of being walloped by a giant claw. They crashed violently to the ground—though, thankfully, the track was soft, which probably saved them a few broken limbs. Still, it took a moment for Ozzie to regain his wits. He was pressed between the ground and one of Tug's massive wings. He heard the skyger groan, followed by the complaints of Aunt Temperance and Fidget. Ozzie tried to wriggle free of Tug's feathers, only to realize that they were somehow pinned to the ground as part of an immense skygerish heap.

"We've been ensnared in some sort of net," Aunt Temperance announced. "They must have fired it from the ship. No use struggling; it's only going to make things worse."

"How could it be worse?" Fidget grumbled from some far region of the pile.

"Well, for one thing, you might roll onto my glasses! Because I can't—oh, here they are."

Ozzie finally managed to find a vantage point to look down the tunnel. They were so close to the door! He tried to claw his way across the track, as if he could somehow tug the net and everyone in it the last few feet. But, of course, he couldn't.

This isn't fair! he screamed inside his head.

Then the pirates were there, swarming around them like ants on a lump of candy. They didn't exactly look like the pirates Ozzie had read about or seen in movies. Sure, they had some of the usual trademarks—tattoos, scars, and mouths sparsely populated with gray teeth— but many of them were wearing goggles and leather flight caps, while their weapons were a combination of swords and flintlock pistols covered in rusty switches and cogs.

"They look like they're on their way to a steampunk convention," Aunt Temperance commented.

"Really?" Fidget wondered. "Is a steampunk convention a place where pirates stew prisoners in their own juices? Because I think—"

"Steampunk is just a type of look," Ozzie interrupted. "That's what she means."

Fidget grunted. "Yeah? Well, they look mean."

As if to prove her point, one of the pirates came up and delivered a kick to the pile—*Ozzie's* part of the pile. "What do we got here?" the scoundrel snarled as Ozzie massaged his aching ribs. The pirate was short and stout, but he looked menacing enough despite the lack of height. One of the lenses in his pair of goggles was blacked out— his version of an eye patch, Ozzie assumed—and his right hand was missing. In its place was a gun-sword attachment with a double barrel and a gleaming blade. Still, the worst thing about him was his beard. It was gray and greasy; it looked—and smelled—like a rat had clamped onto his chin and died there.

"Not every day you capture a skyger, is it?" Ratbeard boasted with a flourish of his weaponized hand.

The pirate rabble cheered in response. One or two of them even fired celebratory rounds into the air.

Ratbeard knelt to attach a towline to the net. Then, giving it a yank, he yelled up to the ship, "Winch 'em up, boys! Cap'n Traxx is waitin'!"

"Captain Traxx?!" Fidget cried as the net—and everyone inside of it—jerked unceremoniously into the air. "Did he just say *Captain Traxx*?"

"What's wrong?" Ozzie asked, with a creeping sense of dread. "Who's Captain Traxx?"

"Quoggswoggle," Fidget groaned. "Things just got a lot worse."

6

THE QUEEN OF THE COSMOS

"This is bad," Fidget moaned. "Really bad. Traxx is merciless. Get captured by her and you don't come back."

"Just to tell you, I saw this one story on the TV where this woman used a bubble bath to escape," Tug mentioned. "She had all this stress in her life, but she poured this stuff into the tub and all her problems disappeared."

"This is a serious predicament!" Fidget growled at him in frustration. "Bath bubbles can't help us! Like we have any, anyway."

"Actually, *I* do," Aunt Temperance revealed. "Not that I can reach my backpack right now. But we *do* have an enormous raptorial creature on our side."

"Where is he?" Tug asked excitedly. "Can we call him?"

"Er, I think she means *you*," Ozzie told the skyger.

"I don't know how to call him," Tug said.

Ozzie groaned. "No, *you're* the raptorial creature."

"Oh, *raptorial*," Tug said affably. "That's me all right."

"I'm pretty sure that doesn't mean what you think it does," Fidget chipped in.

Tug purred as a response, but then everyone went quiet because at that moment their net was reeled through a hatch in the underbelly of the ship, instantly enveloping them in darkness. They were still being hoisted upward, but they couldn't even see where they were going.

I don't know how we're going to get out of this one, Ozzie thought.

He had faced plenty of dangers on his last trip to Zoone, but there had always been adults nearby to swoop in and help out, like Captain Cho or Lady Zoone. Aunt Temperance was technically an adult, but Ozzie wasn't sure she counted in a situation like this.

Soft light flooded over them as the net rose out of the shaft and they found themselves suspended above the uppermost deck of the ship, surrounded by the starscape of the damaged portal. Ozzie peered down to see two pirates working a crankshaft attached to the towline and net, which they now dangled over an open-roofed cage.

Without warning, the entire net was dropped inside. After some groaning and grunting, Ozzie managed to clamber free of the mesh, along with everyone else. More pirates scrambled forward to slide a grid of iron bars over the top of the cage, completely imprisoning them, and then pulled the now-empty net out from the side—cautiously, Ozzie noticed, keeping well clear of Tug's jaws.

The deck was a clutter of wheezing pipes, flickering control panels, and sagging cables. Ozzie was put in mind of Aunt Temperance's old Volkswagen Bug; each time they parked, they were never quite sure if it would start up again. And, like Aunt Temperance's car, every scrap of metal on the ship seemed scarred and rusted, boasting of adventures past. Even the masts looked slightly askew, though they were draped with beautiful sails made out of some sort of diaphanous fabric. Ozzie wasn't sure why the ship needed sails—there was no wind in the portals— but then he saw them shimmer silver, which caused him to wonder if they were for absorbing some sort of cosmic energy.

Ratbeard appeared from below deck. "All aboard and accounted for!" he shouted, and the ship lurched so violently that Ozzie had to clutch the cage bars to keep his footing.

Aunt Temperance groaned, cradling her pack against her chest. "Now what's happening?"

"I think you're about to discover the vastness of the multiverse," Fidget announced.

The ship pivoted and, after rumbling back through the split it had made in the side of the tunnel, emerged into a fabulous skyscape. All about them were clusters of nebulae colored blue and indigo and festooned with stars. It would have been . . . well, *ensorcelling*, Ozzie thought, to steal an Aunt Temperance word, if their plight wasn't so dire.

"How can we breathe up here if we're in space?" Aunt Temperance marveled.

"We're not in space," Fidget replied. "I don't think we're anywhere. I told you: This is the realm between the portals."

"We have to be *somewhere*," Aunt Temperance insisted.

"Yeah," Fidget retorted. "It's called 'in trouble.'"

"I've been there before," Tug said. "Plenty of times. Usually with Ozzie."

"So, here's our quarry," Ratbeard announced, lumbering to their cage. Still careful to keep his distance from Tug, he reached through the bars and prodded Ozzie with his gun hand. "No worse for wear, I see. Nothin' broken or busted."

"That's more than you can say for our portal," Ozzie retorted.

"The track should repair itself," Ratbeard said. "Most

of 'em do. No reason to get your knickers in a knot. You got other troubles." He allowed himself a chuckle before lifting his chin to shout, "Ahoy, Cap'n! Prisoners ready for inspection!"

Ozzie followed his gaze into the rigging above to see a solitary silhouette darting along one of the mast arms, so high up that it made him dizzy. The figure leaped down from spar to spar to land gracefully on the deck.

"Captain Traxx," Fidget murmured. "Queen of the Cosmos." She almost seemed starry-eyed.

"Ask for her autograph, why don't you?" Ozzie grumbled. "She's kidnapped us, remember?"

But as Captain Traxx marched up to their cage, Ozzie had to admit that she was impressive. Most of her crew seemed scruffy and vulgar, but the captain was extremely elegant. Her skin was smooth and unblemished, except for her cheeks, which were dotted with bright, pomegranate-red freckles. Her thick, luxurious hair was the same color, as were her eyes. She wore a wide-brimmed hat and a long peacock-blue coat, punctuated by a bejeweled belt. She looked like the type of person you might find at a fancy costume ball or a masquerade, rubbing elbows with Sir Pomposity.

"Well, well, Mr. Burr," Captain Traxx addressed Ratbeard. "I see you've captured a family. How brave of you."

Her voice was sharp and eloquent, and though she

paced calmly before them, hands clasped behind her back, Ozzie detected a hint of danger burbling beneath her surface. It made him rethink his original impression of her. *Maybe* she was the type of person you could find at a masquerade, but she'd probably be just as comfortable in the middle of a bloodthirsty pirate brawl. Neither situation would require a change of outfit.

"Well, and a skyger," Ratbeard—Mr. Burr, apparently—replied, cowering sycophantically. "If we can get the beast to the black market, we'll be swimmin' in coin."

"*If,*" Captain Traxx repeated. "Surely, Mr. Burr, you've heard of the Balindor Massacre?"

"Well, they said it was a whole cloud of skygers that attacked them folks in Balindor, but they weren't pirates and—"

"Do you know what I think, Mr. Burr?" Captain Traxx asked, turning swiftly on the cringing pirate. "I think you've made us either very rich or *very dead.*"

Then, without warning, she snatched Ratbeard by the collar, and slammed him against the cage so that his face was pressed against the bars, right in front of Tug's snout.

"Go ahead, beast," Captain Traxx offered. "Have a taste."

Ozzie heard the rest of the crew gasp, but he kept his eyes on Ratbeard, squealing and squirming at the end of Captain Traxx's powerful arm. Tug smiled—or at least appeared to, because it was difficult to tell with skygers. Then the cat cautiously extended his snout to snuffle the man.

"Ew!" Tug moaned, wrinkling his giant nose. "Just to tell you, if you're hiding a snack somewhere in your pockets, I think it's started to rot."

Captain Traxx laughed, revealing a perfect set of teeth. "I think what your keen nose detects is the aroma of Mr. Burr himself."

She thrust the pirate aside, sending him sprawling into a nearby crate. He appeared too weak-kneed to stand up, but Captain Traxx didn't seem to care. Instead, she reached into the cage and scratched Tug's chin with her slender fingers. Ozzie noticed that her fingernails were polished and expertly manicured.

"What kind of skyger are you?" she mused.

"A Zoonian one," Tug declared.

Captain Traxx raised an eyebrow. "No savage temper or ravenous appetite?"

"Oh, he has the appetite, all right," Fidget spoke up.

Captain Traxx turned to the princess. "Is that so? He is clearly a kitten otherwise. We'll have to do our best to conceal his true nature if we want him to fetch a suitable price. And you, my purple-haired girl—you're dressed fashionably. What world do you hail from? A wealthy one, I presume."

Fidget blushed; for once she didn't seem to have a comeback.

"Ah, yes, a world where you sip tea, attend parties, and watch the common folk toil away—that's it, isn't it? A world where you dream of fancy weddings and bat your eyes at boys." Captain Traxx gestured to Ozzie. "Not this one, I hope. He needs a haircut. And I believe his socks are two different colors."

Ozzie checked to see if the captain was right about his socks (she was). Then he glanced at Fidget and found that her cheeks had turned even more purple. Fidget didn't dream of fancy weddings, but that *was* exactly what her parents wanted for her, already having arranged her marriage to the prince of Quogg. Ozzie felt a wave of sympathy for his friend, especially now that his own parents had decided to ship him off to boarding school.

"As for me, I come from no such privilege," the pirate captain continued, her bright freckles flaring with pride. "Yet, here I am, Aurelia Traxx, captain of the *Empyrean Thunder*, the finest ship in the 'verse. And this"—she turned, gesticulating to the multicolored skyscape—"is my kingdom. Out here, we are free of the mundane obligations that plague your pathetic lives. Which, I regret to inform you, are about to become a great deal more pathetic."

At that moment, as if on cue, a bundle of fur shot across

the deck and scampered up the captain's side to perch on her shoulder.

"Shiny stuff! Shiny stuff!" the bundle squawked. It had the voice of a parrot, but it looked more like a lemur, one with reddish fur and a pair of large eyes that were fixed greedily on the chain dangling from Aunt Temperance's neck.

"Yes, my pet," Captain Traxx soothed it, stroking the animal with a delicate hand. "You may fetch the valuables."

The creature bounded into the cage, prompting Aunt Temperance to shriek and hurl her pack at it. She missed; the bag struck the bars, slid to the floor of their prison, and disgorged its assortment of contents, the most embarrassing of which was Ozzie's superhero underwear. He hoped nobody, especially Fidget, was paying close attention. Thankfully, Captain Traxx's pet was causing a suitable distraction.

"Shiny stuff!" it cackled as it leaped onto Aunt Temperance's shoulder and used its nimble fingers to pluck her chain free.

"Horrible little weasel!" Aunt Temperance cried, ripping it from her shoulder and tossing it into the air. The creature deftly caught one of the bars in the ceiling, then hung there, grinning smugly with Aunt Temperance's chain clenched in its tail.

"Weezle-weezle-weezle!" it mimicked.

"Weasel?" Captain Traxx said with some amusement. "Meep is a specimen of the rare Revellian monkey. You should feel privileged to meet him."

"He's not the first monkey I've dealt with," Aunt Temperance snapped. *Of course, the circus*, Ozzie thought, still a bit baffled by that revelation. "He could learn some manners—and so could you."

"Easy, dear," Captain Traxx threatened. Her freckles burned hot and red, like flashing alarm signals. "You are already *plain*—make sure you do not become a *pain*."

Aunt Temperance frowned. Then, as if suddenly recognizing her disheveled appearance, she began anxiously trying to rebraid her hair. Ozzie had never really known her to be self-conscious about her looks, but you didn't normally bump into someone like Captain Traxx in their neighborhood back home. The pirate queen had the type of personality that went after you with a club.

Meep began to search the rest of them. Tug had nothing of value, but Fidget and Ozzie each had something all too precious: their Zoone keys. Ozzie played—and lost—a fierce game of tug-of-war with the monkey for his.

"Keep! Keep!" the creature cackled after returning to Traxx's arm.

"Yes, you may keep the boy's key, my pet," the captain

said, turning her attention to the other pilfered property.

"Thief," Aunt Temperance fumed.

Captain Traxx offered her an apathetic shrug. "Such trinkets will not help you in the slave markets of Kardoome." She gave Lady Zoone's key, with all its gears and cogs, a mere glance before tucking it away in a pocket. Aunt Temperance's necklace was a different story. She lifted it and scrutinized the ring, pulsing with its strange power. "This stone is *amelthium*. How did you come by it?"

"It's none of your concern," Aunt Temperance said.

"Everything on this ship is my concern," the pirate queen responded, though she now turned her attention to the locket. As soon as she opened it, a gasp escaped her. For once, she seemed off-kilter. Glaring at Aunt Temperance, she demanded, "Why do you have a picture of this man?"

Aunt Temperance hesitated. "He was—"

"Her friend," Ozzie quickly intervened. "But you know him, too," he suddenly realized. "How? He's from our world. Eridea."

Captain Traxx threw a hostile glance at Ozzie, then returned her gaze to the picture. "Yes," she admitted eventually. "I knew him."

Aunt Temperance scrambled to the front of the cage. "How? When?"

Captain Traxx trained her pomegranate eyes on Aunt Temperance. "*Knew* him," the pirate queen emphasized. "He was . . . one of mine."

Aunt Temperance gasped. "Your prisoner?"

"One of my crew," Captain Traxx said slowly. "For a short while." She closed the locket with a resounding snap. "We marooned him on the dead world of Creon. He begged us to do so. I could not refuse him."

"Creon?" Aunt Temperance questioned. "Where's that? Why is it dead?"

Captain Traxx flashed them a cryptic smile. "This man," Captain Traxx said carefully, "he was important to you? It—well, it doesn't matter. I assure you, my dear, he would not have survived Creon. He has certainly perished."

"No!" Aunt Temperance cried. She yanked on the bars of the cage, as if she could somehow split them asunder. "You're wrong. He's alive."

Captain Traxx's eyebrows arched. "You do not know Creon."

Aunt Temperance dropped her hands to her sides. "You don't know Mercurio."

The pirate queen stared at Ozzie's aunt with a quizzical expression. She was, Ozzie decided, like a bead of rain meandering down a windowpane—beautiful and graceful, yet slightly erratic at the same time. You couldn't predict which direction she might go—though, if forced to choose, Ozzie would have said ballistic. But, to his surprise, the volatile pirate simply turned away from Aunt Temperance and said to her first mate, "Mr. Burr? Have you quite recovered from your near-death encounter with the skyger? I think it's time you send our prisoners to the brig. They can languish there until we make port at Kardoome."

"Aye, Cap'n!" the one-eyed pirate responded, struggling to his feet. He scuttled over to a control panel and flicked a few switches, and the entire cage began to sink into the deck, on some kind of elevator platform.

Aunt Temperance never took her eyes from Captain Traxx and the chain, containing the locket and ring, that she clutched in her fingerless glove. Even after the imposing pirate queen disappeared from sight, even after the cage lurched to a halt on the floor of some lower deck, Aunt Temperance didn't flinch. She just stared straight ahead into the dim reaches of their prison.

Something's going on here, Ozzie thought. *Something big.*

And it was definitely something he didn't like.

ATTACK OF THE COSMIC STORM

"Well," Tug offered after no one else had spoken, "at least we weren't captured by dentists."

"This isn't funny," Fidget groused.

"He's not trying to be funny," Ozzie said. "You know that."

Fidget rolled her eyes and slouched against the bars. Ozzie stared out into the gloom and sniffed the air. It smelled stale and close, like something gone bad at the back of the refrigerator. Artificial lights ran along the interior of the hull, revealing many other cages crammed into the hold, but they were all empty. Then the muted but raucous sound of pirates singing came from above. It was a sort of call-and-response sea shanty:

"WAY-HO!"
"Do you hear the Thunder?*"*
"WAY-HO!"
"Do you hear the Thunder?*"*
"WAY-HO!"
"Do you hear the Thunder?*"*
"Here we come to plun-der!"

"I don't hear any thunder," Tug commented.

"I think they mean this ship," Ozzie explained patiently. "The *Empyrean Thunder.*"

"They're probably planning to raid more portals," Fidget said. "So they can fill up these cages. And then it's off to the slave markets of Kardoome."

"At least we're together," Tug said as he flopped to the floor with a slumberous yawn.

Then, even though the pirates were still bellowing their song, the skyger curled his tail around his body and fell fast asleep. Ozzie wasn't surprised by Tug's ability to switch off, but he definitely envied it. Tug certainly wasn't "too sensitive." And he didn't get worked up about anything—unless there was food involved.

Ozzie looked over at Aunt Temperance, but she was still staring into nothingness, so he returned his attention to Fidget. "You're a princess of Quoxx. If you tell Captain Traxx that, maybe she'll release us."

"Are you kidding me? She'd just try to ransom me off or something. Then I'm back to . . . all the complications." She looked like she was on the verge of tears.

"Okay," Ozzie said. "I'm sorry, I just . . ."

Fidget turned away and began thumping her head against the bars. "I'm stuck. Stuck, stuck, stuck."

"Stop it!" Ozzie hissed, clutching her shoulders. "I'm stuck, too, you know. My parents want to send me away to boarding school. I won't be able to live at home anymore. I've seen photos of the place, and it's the worst. Everyone wears these navy blue uniforms and—"

"Really?" Fidget interrupted. "You're comparing *uniforms* to my problem? If I go back to Quoxx—I can't marry the prince of Quogg! I can't! And now, not even Zoone's safe. My problem is *forever*, Ozzie. So what if you have to wear navy for a couple of years?"

"Well, navy *is* the weakest of all colors," Aunt Temperance declared, finally rousing from her torpor. "It's not black. It's not blue. Just hides in between."

Fidget wiped a wrist across her eyes. "You're a strange person, aren't you?"

"I'll take that as a compliment," Aunt Temperance said.

"And, just so both of you know, pain is *not* a competition. Listen, things look particularly calamitous right now. But we can't give up."

She began tapping her hands together, up near her chin, which was what she always did when she was formulating a plan—though, usually, the most exciting thing she needed to strategize about was what type of tea to drink. "Don't worry; we're going to bust out of here," she announced.

"How?" Ozzie asked.

"I'm not sure yet," Aunt Temperance admitted. "The truth is, I still don't understand where we are exactly. Explain it to me again, Fidget."

"I just remember what my grandfather taught me," the princess replied. "We're in the interstitial cosmos. It's no different than the track we were on to Zoone, except that track is a specific tunnel between two places. Out here . . . this is just a vast directionless sea."

"So, you can get to any world from out here?" Aunt Temperance asked.

"I think we'd have to find a track," Fidget said, considering. "The pirates bore into them with their drill. But how would we get to one anyway? We're too heavy for Tug to fly us all that far."

"I saw some lifeboats up on deck," Aunt Temperance said. "We can steal one and use it to reach a track."

"We're just going to row across the cosmos?" Fidget asked skeptically. Then she shook her head. "It doesn't matter. In case you haven't noticed, we have another problem. This cage."

"There's a door on this side," Ozzie said, rattling the bars. "We'll have to steal a key or something."

Aunt Temperance dropped to her knees and began sorting through her belongings, which were still scattered across the floor of the cage. "We'll figure something out. We're lucky that Captain Traxx didn't confiscate all our resources."

Fidget guffawed. "This stuff? The reason she didn't take any of your junk is because it's useless." Then, seeing Aunt Temperance's brow knit into a frown, she added, "Oh, sorry. I meant, entirely essential supplies. Shall we *blend* our way out of here?"

"First, it's time to bolster our attitudes," Aunt Temperance lectured as she began organizing her supplies. "We'll escape this pernicious predicament, you'll see. We just have to find the right moment."

As it turned out, that moment didn't come until a few days later. Until then, they idled in their cell with little to do. Once or twice a day, the pirates brought them watery gruel to eat. Ozzie and Fidget complained about the taste. Aunt Temperance complained about the questionable nutritional value. Tug complained about there not being enough of it.

The bathroom was a bucket in the corner. Thankfully, they could use Tug as a giant blue wall to give them a modicum of privacy during these awkward moments and, perhaps more thankfully, Aunt Temperance's pack included a bottle of hand sanitizer and a roll of toilet paper. Even Fidget begrudgingly admitted that these *were* essential.

The hardest thing to deal with, in Ozzie's opinion, was the boredom. They couldn't get much exercise in the cage, and the portholes in the brig were tiny, which meant they couldn't even gaze out at the cosmic vistas. Aunt Temperance had brought a copy of *The Tempest*, and she often read sections of it aloud, but it just made Ozzie feel even worse. He was used to the old-fashioned language—Aunt Temperance often read Shakespeare to him in Apartment 2B—but it needled him to hear about a magical island when the magical place he kept trying to get to seemed so far out of reach.

"Lots happens in Shakespeare's story," he griped on the third night of Aunt Temperance's reading. "But nothing is happening *here*."

"Bad things have happened," Fidget pointed out.

Ozzie kicked at the bars of their cage. "We almost made it to Zoone," he moaned. "Just a few more steps, and we would have been through the door."

Aunt Temperance lowered her book. "If there's one thing I've learned, dwelling on what could have been isn't helpful. We—"

"We're farther away from Zoone than ever!" Ozzie interrupted. "And now—"

Suddenly, there was a loud, rumbling boom from outside, causing the entire ship to tremble. Anxious shouts came from above.

"Oh, good," Tug said.

"What's good?" Fidget snapped.

"Something's happening," the skyger replied.

Fidget fired a glare at Ozzie. "Yeah, be careful what you wish for. You wanted *Tempest*-level excitement? Looks like we got it."

The ship shuddered again. One of the pirates—his name was Skelly—was just descending the stairs with their nightly gruel when he slipped, dropped everything with a clatter, then slid the rest of the way down. The ship tilted and he ended up tumbling right up against the bars of their cage, a look of terror in his amber eyes.

"It's just a storm, isn't it?" Aunt Temperance questioned Skelly. "Surely, a crew of your ilk isn't afraid of a little inclement weather?"

"Cosmic storm," Skelly mumbled feverishly as he pulled himself to his feet.

"What's that?" Ozzie asked.

Skelly didn't answer; he simply turned and scrambled up the stairs, leaving them alone in the brig with a slick of gruel trickling into their cage.

"Is he going to bring more?" Tug asked, cleaning up the slop with his blue tongue.

"I think we have bigger problems," Ozzie said as the ship jerked in the other direction, sending everyone staggering to the far wall of the cage. They heard more panicked screams from above.

"This isn't a problem," Aunt Temperance declared, straightening her glasses. "This is an *opportunity*. While the pirates are distracted, we'll make our escape."

"You do realize that we're still in a cage, right?" Fidget pointed out.

"We need a Zitro Kitchen Knife," Tug suggested. "I saw one story on TV where they used it to cut through metal. So cool."

Aunt Temperance was on the floor, rooting through her pack. "I don't have a Zitro Knife, but—ah, here!" She produced a hairpin from the depths of her bag and, because the ship was rocking so violently, she crawled on her hands and knees to the cage door.

"What are you doing?" Ozzie asked.

"I'm going to pick the lock."

"You can do that?"

"There was an escape artist in our circus," Aunt Temperance answered, jiggling the hairpin in the door's keyhole. "She taught me a trick or two."

"You mean, you could have busted us out of here three days ago?" Fidget cried in exasperation. "I've been peeing in a bucket all this time for nothing?"

"We've all had to pee in a bucket, *Your Highness*," Ozzie retorted. Fidget swung at him, but the ship lurched and she missed.

"I was waiting for the opportune moment," Aunt Temperance explained. "Besides, I'm not sure if I actually can do thi—wait, there it goes!"

There was a click and she swung the door open.

"Ta da!" she sang as they scrambled out of the cage. "Once we reach the deck, we steal that lifeboat and soar away from this dreadful ship." She hefted her canvas bag over one shoulder and began climbing the stairs. "Everyone stay together!"

She led them through the door, then up another flight of stairs, before arriving at a hatch. They could hear wind howling above them—and the pirates. It sounded to Ozzie like they were about to have front-row seats to absolute chaos—but the instant they stepped onto the deck, he realized he had gotten it slightly wrong. It was chaos all right—but they weren't in the audience. It was more like being center stage to a riot.

Gale-force winds mercilessly pummeled the ship. Pirates were everywhere, buzzing back and forth across the deck like manic bees trying to save their hive. Some were clutching rigging lines and tying down sails. Others were cranking flywheels and banging fists against reluctant control panels. They rushed past Ozzie and his friends or, in some cases, between them, as if they didn't realize—or care—they had escaped.

Ozzie stood there, gaping, until a swell of wind blasted across the deck with such vigor that it ripped him from his feet. He clamped onto Tug and managed to steady himself, but it felt like his stomach had scampered up and decided to hide in his throat.

"Is that all you have, beast?!" Ozzie spotted Captain Traxx standing on a spar halfway up a mast, shaking a fist at the sky. Then, to her crew, she bellowed, "Skelly! Rosa! Xango! Fire, you weak-kneed knaves! FIRE!"

A cluster of pirates rushed to the side of the ship and began discharging their pistols and muskets, though at what, Ozzie couldn't tell. It looked like they were trying to battle the cloud cluster.

Then it dawned on Ozzie.

They *were* attacking the storm—because it was attacking them. The sky was alive; Ozzie couldn't see eyes or a face or any kind of body, but there was no doubt that the tempest was a living, thinking entity. He watched, stupefied, as a claw of lightning materialized in the sky and reached down with electrified fingers to pluck an unsuspecting pirate—it was Skelly—from his feet. The crackling hand sent him sprawling across the deck and crashing into the base of one of the masts, where he crumpled into a motionless heap. His body was covered in scorch marks. Black wisps of smoke curled from his hair.

Another rope of lightning struck; this one swiped across the deck, sending an entire row of pirates tumbling over the side.

Where do they go? Ozzie thought, heart pounding in his ears. *There's no water overboard! Do they just fall forever?*

"DO SOMETHING!" Captain Traxx roared, prompting Ozzie to jump into action. An abandoned sword was lying on the deck, so he snatched it up and charged toward the railing. Drawing upon all his best imaginary ninja skills, he hurled the sword toward the storm.

And missed.

Which basically meant he had missed hitting *the entire sky.* But he didn't miss everything. The blade *did* manage to slice through a rope that was stretched taut between the railing and the lifeboats on the deck.

Ozzie watched in despair as the rope uncoiled. Next came the boats, breaking free and being sucked into the sky, one by one. They ricocheted off each other, clanking as they swirled in the gale around the *Empyrean Thunder.*

"Great job!" Fidget hissed, dashing to his side. "There goes our escape."

"Come on!" Aunt Temperance hollered, her hair blowing wildly in her face. "We can fly up there and snatch one!"

Determined to make amends for his clumsiness, Ozzie quickly scrambled onto Tug's back. He hoped that the skyger would have enough strength to carry them all to one of the lifeboats. Fidget and Aunt Temperance climbed on behind him and Tug began bounding across the chaotic, badly listing deck in an attempt to take flight. His runway came to an end all too quickly; Tug reached the edge of the ship and was forced to leap over the railing and into the cosmos. Down they dropped, plunging like a stone.

"Come on, Tug!" Ozzie encouraged. "You can do it!"

The skyger managed to get his wings working. He veered toward the lifeboats, but it was like the storm knew they were trying to escape. Whips of lightning began snapping at them from every direction. Tug juked and dove to avoid the savage attacks, which only managed to take them farther and farther away from the lifeboats.

As they flapped alongside the *Empyrean Thunder,* Ozzie could see the beating the ship was taking. Its carapace was dented and one of the masts had crashed across the deck. Two or three of the tentacles at the back end had been severed, leaving amputated stumps that glowed with raw heat. The ship still looked like a squid, but it was a squid in distress.

Suddenly, Tug jerked backward. One of the storm's claws had managed to snag him by the tail. Ozzie clutched at Tug's fur and he felt Fidget's arms wrap tighter around his torso. But the monster must have let go, because the next thing Ozzie knew, they were spinning wildly through the forest of masts and rigging jutting from the deck of the *Empyrean Thunder*. Tug struck one of the horizontal spars belly first and, for a brief moment, they were stapled there. The skyger clawed desperately at the air until he was able to find purchase on the pole and heave his body up onto an unsteady perch. He slumped against the mast, breathing heavily. The tips of his normally sky-blue wings were seared black. Ozzie didn't even want to know what his tail looked like.

"OZZIE!"

He swiveled to see Fidget staring at him with wide, terrified eyes.

"What is it?" he cried into the wind, only to realize that there was no one sitting behind her. "Where's Aunt T?"

Fidget slowly shook her head and pointed to one of the spars below them. There was Aunt Temperance's canvas bag, dangling precariously by one strap. But there was no sign of Aunt Temperance herself. Not on the mast, not on the deck—not anywhere.

The storm had taken her.

8

AN UMBRELLA, SOME NERVE,
AND A BOTTLE OF BUBBLE BATH

The sky was booming and pulsing, but to Ozzie everything seemed suddenly distant and muted. It was as if
someone had pulled the plug on all his senses, leaving him
feeling numb. He had wanted so badly to share Zoone
with Aunt Temperance, to show her the wonders of the
nexus, to introduce her to all his friends there, to—

He suddenly realized that Fidget was shaking him.
"Ozzie! Look!"

She pointed past his shoulder and he noticed that the
storm was morphing. The cosmic clouds were drifting
apart, a dark void forming between them. Then those same

clouds began to swirl, faster and faster, like a whirlpool—or something even more ominous. Because even though the cosmic storm didn't have eyes, a face, or even a body, it had a mouth—and this astral maelstrom was it.

Where there's a mouth, there's a stomach, Ozzie thought as a thunderous rumble reverberated across the sky.

Two massive tentacles of lightning reached out from the storm, grasped the ship by its drill nose, and began reeling it toward its maw. The ship lurched, causing Tug to tighten his grip on their spar, even wrapping his tail around the mast. The engines of the *Empyrean Thunder* screamed, fighting to pull away, but the cosmic creature held fast. The entire ship was about to become its dinner.

A scattering of pirates led by Captain Traxx charged onto the drill nose and began firing their weapons into the cavernous mouth. Fingers of lightning crackled around them; more pirates were snatched up and tossed as appetizers into the storm's stomach. Soon, only Captain Traxx remained, brandishing something that looked like a harpoon.

Ozzie couldn't help imagining what it would be like to be digested in the beast's belly. It made him queasy—and worried. "We have to find Aunt T and get out of here!" he yelled at his friends.

"I don't think we can escape this thing," Fidget shouted

in response. "We're going to have to beat it! Tug, I need Aunt T's bag."

"Oh, sure," the skyger said.

He fluttered toward the spar where the bag was snagged. Just before he reached it, a bolt of lightning struck the mast. There was a devastating crack; then the whole structure split and tipped toward the deck. Aunt Temperance's bag slid off the spar and began to tumble away. Fidget stretched out and managed to grab it, though Ozzie wondered how it didn't rip her arm right out of its socket. That bag was heavy—like, deluxe-kitchen-blender heavy.

"What now?" Ozzie asked as she hauled the bag onto Tug's back.

"Just circle, Tug!" Fidget directed. "And try not to get swallowed by that vortex. Here, help me, Oz."

As the skyger swooped around, dodging the storm's claws, Ozzie lifted his legs and carefully swiveled to face the princess. Fidget thrust Aunt Temperance's bag into Ozzie's arms, then began rifling through it.

"Need to find something to knock the slippers off that thing, something to—aha!" She yanked Aunt Temperance's bottle of bubble bath from the depths of the pack and held it up like a trophy.

"Seriously?" Ozzie said. "What's that going to do?"

"Oh! Need this, too," Fidget added, plucking Aunt Temperance's umbrella back out of the side pocket. She quickly unscrewed the cap on the bubble bath, then, with a flash of her periwinkle eyes, warned, "Don't follow me. Got it?"

"Follow you where?"

Fidget's only answer was to fling herself off Tug's back, into nothingness. Well, not quite nothingness, Ozzie realized as he lugged the canvas bag onto his shoulder and turned the right way around on Tug's back. The deck of the *Empyrean Thunder* was below them, and Fidget was hurtling toward it at an alarming speed. Before she struck it, she clicked open the umbrella and jerked to a halt, floating gently downward like some sort of purple-haired Mary Poppins—that was, until the breath of the storm grabbed hold of her and began sucking her toward its churning cavity.

"She's brave," Tug remarked.

Ozzie rolled his eyes. "Or crazy."

The storm still had its fingers wrapped around the *Empyrean Thunder*, hauling it ever closer to its stomach, but it soon seemed to comprehend that Fidget was up to something. It turned a claw on her.

"We have to distract it," Ozzie told Tug, directing the skyger toward the storm mouth.

They were too late. Fidget's makeshift parachute took a direct hit from a bolt of lightning. The umbrella disintegrated into ash, leaving the princess holding only the handle—and her bottle of bubble bath—as she plunged toward the whirlpool's greedy gullet. She pitched the bottle into the swirling black hole, but whatever she had expected to happen . . . didn't. Instead, she was sucked into the vortex, completely disappearing from sight.

"Go after her!" Ozzie screamed.

Tug banked toward the astral whirlpool, following in the wake of the *Empyrean Thunder*. The ship had finally succumbed to the gale and was spinning around the void, its front end pointed toward Ozzie and Tug. There was Captain Traxx, still clinging desperately to the drill nose of the ship, but only by the fingers of one hand. Ozzie could see her white teeth as she grimaced in determination—and then she went pinwheeling free.

Ozzie didn't even think about what he did next. As the pirate spun past him, he instinctively leaned out and snatched her by the belt, which was when he realized that he probably *should* have thought about it. Captain Traxx was heavier than he was, and he nearly ended up getting pulled right off Tug's back. Thankfully, he managed to clumsily hoist her atop the skyger, facing him. She immediately began yelling at him, but they were in the jaws of the storm now and he couldn't hear her over its booming wail. She certainly didn't look very grateful; her freckles were flashing like sirens.

Tug was fiercely beating his wings, but they were still

wheeling wildly around the maelstrom, as if circling a bathtub drain. The *Empyrean Thunder* went down first, and Ozzie heard the clouds release a satisfied boom—like some kind of cosmic burp, he thought. Then the vortex unexpectedly swirled shut.

The sky was instantly empty and silent. Tug banked in a circle, above where the mouth had been only moments before. Ozzie and Captain Traxx were still sitting face-to-face on the skyger's back.

They're gone, Ozzie thought, dazed. *Fidget, Aunt Temperance . . .*

"Fool of a boy!" Captain Traxx snarled, seizing him by the neck of his shirt. "You robbed me of a captain's death. It was my duty to go down with the *Thunder*! Why did you do that?!"

Her freckles were burning so hot and bright that Ozzie had to close his eyes. He had no idea why he had saved her life. Aunt Temperance had always taught him to help others, but he was pretty sure she hadn't been talking about cutthroat portal pirates.

The entire sky suddenly shuddered—and the vortex opened back up, frothing and gurgling white foam.

"Is that soap?" Ozzie asked as Captain Traxx released him.

"No," Tug said confidently, "that's bubble bath."

The maelstrom rumbled and quaked, vomiting bubbles

like a laundry machine gone crazy. There was a loud retching sound, and out popped the *Empyrean Thunder.* The swirling void closed again; this time, it seemed, for good.

"That thing just threw up the ship," Ozzie realized.

"Take me to her, beast," Captain Traxx commanded. "*Now.*"

Tug lugged them to the deck, and Ozzie and the pirate queen clambered from his back. The ship was a disaster, listing slightly to one side, with mangled masts and scorched sails drooping precariously overhead. Smoke billowed from various hatches and control panels. Snapped and severed cables snaked across the deck. Pirates, many of them groaning and moaning, were strewn about like toys after a two-year-old's tantrum.

Ozzie dropped Aunt Temperance's canvas bag to the deck and turned his attention to Tug. The skyger's bushy tail was singed black and he was missing large snatches of fur. "Are you okay?" Ozzie asked, gently touching his coat.

"I *am* a little hungry," Tug confessed between panting breaths, "but other than—oh!"

Aunt Temperance and Fidget suddenly plopped onto the deck in front of them.

"And my father said being a trapeze artist would be a

waste of my life," Aunt Temperance announced, brushing her hands together.

Ozzie gaped at her. "What just happened?"

"When I fell off Tug, I snatched a rigging line to save myself," she explained. "I was actually aboard the ship the whole time—above you. After we got sucked into the belly of that beast, I spotted Fidget floating around, so I called upon my old skills to swoop down and rescue her." She paused to massage her shoulder. "I'm going to be sore tomorrow."

Ozzie shook his head in disbelief. People always said things like, "I wouldn't have believed it if I hadn't seen it with my own eyes." But Ozzie *hadn't* seen Aunt Temperance's heroics, which meant his mind was swirling with an extra dose of doubt. Swinging on a rope across a pirate deck?

"Curious," Captain Traxx declared, breaking his train of thought. The pirate queen had collapsed onto a nearby crate and was staring at Aunt Temperance with an indecipherable expression.

The surviving pirates began to slowly gather around. Meep scampered out from some hidey-hole and perched on the pirate queen's shoulder, making her wince. It was only then that Ozzie noticed that her left arm was dangling limply at the side of her body.

"I think your arm is broken," Aunt Temperance told her.

"It's nothing." Captain Traxx's gaze flitted toward Fidget. "You, girl. You defeated the beast."

"I remembered something my grandfather told me," Fidget explained. "He said those creatures are made up of bits of cosmic dust, fused together by magic. I thought, what better way to clean up dust than with a bit of soap? Well, I only had bubble bath. But, same difference."

"I told you bubble bath is good for escaping," Tug purred proudly.

"Evidently," Captain Traxx grunted. She rose to her feet and, looking to her crew, bellowed, "Enough lingering, you knaves! Take the wounded to the surgeon and get the *Thunder* moving again. Where's Mr. Burr?"

"Can't find 'im anywhere, Cap'n," one of the crew said sullenly. "Storm musta snatched 'im."

Captain Traxx grimaced, but otherwise showed no emotion. Even with her arm dangling at her side, she continued to comport herself as a queen. "It seems I'm in need of a new first mate," she mulled. She scanned the crew with her pomegranate eyes, then announced, "*You.*" She had raised her one good arm. It was pointing directly at Fidget. "Now the rest of you, get to work!"

"Are you crazy?" Fidget growled as the crew scattered. "I'm no pirate."

"You could be," Captain Traxx said with a glint in her eyes. "It's a good life. A life of freedom. You're young. Good in a fight. And a little insane. All qualities I admire."

"Go to Quogg," Fidget retorted, her cheeks flushing as purple as her hair.

"You really are that type of girl, aren't you?" Captain Traxx snapped disdainfully. "Dreaming of pretty balls and handsome suitors. You'd rather be a princess."

"Actually," Tug said, "she's already a"—Fidget delivered a sturdy kick to his leg, but he registered it the same way a windshield does a bug—"princess."

"Really?" Captain Traxx said, with obvious interest. "From which world?"

"I'm *not* a princess," Fidget snarled. "He's got it wrong."

"Who do you think you are?" Aunt Temperance demanded of Captain Traxx. "You can't encourage children to become murderous marauders!"

"I can do whatever I please," the pirate queen retorted. "Miserable old maid! What did *you* want to be when you were her age?"

"I wanted to join the circus," Aunt Temperance replied, raising her chin defiantly. "And I did, if you must know."

"You quit that life, though, didn't you?" Captain Traxx accused.

Aunt Temperance cringed.

"Yes. You have that look about you," Captain Traxx

said. "The look of someone who gave up. Why? Was it for a man?" She reached into her coat, pulled out the locket, and clicked it open to reveal the photo. "This man?"

"No," Aunt Temperance said immediately.

Captain Traxx raised a reddish eyebrow. "A different man, then?"

Aunt Temperance didn't say anything.

That means there was *someone else*, Ozzie thought. *Who?* What kind of complicated life had Aunt Temperance led, anyway? It was hard enough to imagine her with one boyfriend, let alone multiple ones.

"You've thrown your life away for others," Captain Traxx told Aunt Temperance angrily. "You've let them make the decisions for you. Life isn't about being a passenger!"

"Oh, it's about being a pirate, is it?" Aunt Temperance retorted. "You're very good at throwing around your opinion—but that's all it is. *Your opinion*. That and a quarter is worth twenty-five cents to me."

Captain Traxx erupted into laughter. "Good! Some passion. Now we're getting somewhere."

"If you're just going to sit there and extoll the virtues of freedom, then I suggest you let us go," Aunt Temperance said, brushing her silver lock of hair out of her face.

Captain Traxx put her good hand on her hip and

scrutinized them. "Yes," she said after some consideration. "I owe you that much. You saved the entire ship. So, name your port and I will take you there."

"Zoone," Ozzie said immediately. He had been quiet up to this point because the pirate queen had seemed so annoyed with him. Now Captain Traxx leveled a scowl at him that made him want to take three steps back. And possibly dive overboard.

"Not Zoone," she decreed. "Anywhere but there. The nexus does not welcome pirates."

Ozzie's ears prickled hot. "But that's where we need to go. You can just take us back to our track and we'll get there ourselves. The station's in trouble. We need to save—"

"Actually," Aunt Temperance interrupted, "we need to go to Creon."

"What?!" Ozzie cried.

"What?" Captain Traxx repeated.

"Creon! Creon! Creon!" Meep squawked.

"Yes, Creon," Aunt Temperance said again. "You said Mercurio was there."

"No!" Ozzie blurted. "We need to go to Zoone. That's where we were headed when all this started. We need to save them, remember?"

"Yes, exactly," Aunt Temperance said. "Zaria said if

we saved Mercurio then we could save Zoone. And he was last seen on Creon. Correct?" She looked critically at Captain Traxx.

"Well, well, well," the pirate queen said, returning to her seat on the crate. "It seems I have the self-appointed defenders of the nexus standing before me. An unlikely bunch. But still . . ." She leaned back, contemplatively stroking Meep's fur. Then, looking directly at Aunt Temperance, she said, "Yes, your sweetheart is on Creon. Or he was. As I told you before, it's a dead world. He could not have survived. And if I take you there, neither will you."

"I think we've proven we can look after ourselves," Fidget said.

"You're agreeing with this plan?!" Ozzie cried, grabbing her arm. "Don't you want to go to Zoone?"

"Actually, what I want is to *save* Zoone," Fidget said. "You haven't seen it, Oz, not the way it is now. There are curfews. Restricted areas. It's like . . . it's like we have a dictator."

Captain Traxx snorted. "Sounds like an improvement to me."

Ozzie shook his head. He didn't want to believe Fidget. Things couldn't be *that* bad. Besides, he had saved Zoone once; he could save it again. He looked desperately at Tug because if there was anyone he could count on, it was the giant blue cat. "Tug? You want to go home, right? To Zoone."

Tug's first answer was a thoughtful twitch of his burnt tail; it nearly took Ozzie out at the knees. "Lady Zoone gave Fidget and me a mission, to deliver a message to Aunt T," the skyger said eventually. "And that message said to save Mercurio. So, I think we need to do what Lady Zoone says. Just to tell you, she's usually right."

Ozzie felt his gut swirl like the maelstrom they had just escaped. With each step of the journey, they were just getting farther away from Zoone. It was true what Tug said—Lady Zoone *was* usually right. As the steward of the station, she had the best interests of the nexus at heart, so if she said that the key to helping it was saving Mercurio, then that's what they had to do.

But how did Aunt Temperance really know that Mercurio was on Creon? Shouldn't they go to Zoone first, just to be sure?

"What if she's not telling the truth?" he asked his aunt, jerking a thumb at Captain Traxx.

"I am many things," the pirate queen said, "but a liar is not one of them."

A gurgle came from below deck, followed by a sputter of smoke from a nearby exhaust pipe. The pirates were already making progress in their repairs. It would not be long before the *Empyrean Thunder* was able to set sail again. Captain Traxx rose steadily to her feet, her arm still hanging limply at her side.

"It appears the decision has been made," she said. "We set course for Creon."

THE PIRATE QUEEN GRANTS A GIFT

Now, instead of being the pirates' prisoners, they were
their guests. Captain Traxx even gave them their own
cabin, but just between him and himself, Ozzie had no
desire to hang out with his aunt or his friends. He was
so bitter about the travesty of justice he'd dubbed the
"Creon Decision" that he decided to give everyone the
silent treatment.

Which was particularly difficult when it came to Tug.

"Oh, there you are," the skyger announced one evening, padding up to sit alongside Ozzie at the bow of the
ship. "You always disappear after dinner."

Ozzie shrugged, but didn't say anything. He kept his

eyes fixed on the skies, hoping Tug would take the hint.

He didn't. "I'm glad the pirates are giving us something other than gruel to eat," the skyger continued. "It's not as delicious as the grub Miss Mongo makes at Zoone, but they probably don't have the ingredients for her famous snirf and snarf. Right, Ozzie?"

Ozzie sighed and finally cast a sidelong glance at the cat. He wished he could be like Tug. Give him a bowl of something to eat, a place to sleep, and he was content. Not Ozzie. His emotions were always so intense and heavy, like stones in his pockets.

"Aunt T said she's going to read from that *Tempest* book again," Tug went on.

Ozzie shook his head. "I think I'll just stay here."

"Okay," Tug said. "I'm going to go listen to some more. Though I think I'll swing back by the galley first. Just in case they have dessert."

Maybe my mom's right, Ozzie thought as the skyger whisked away. *Maybe I am too sensitive.*

How had Aunt Temperance defined it? Having good instincts. Awareness. But what use was that when all it did was make him feel miserable? Still, it wasn't like there was anything he could do about it. He couldn't just switch on and off—though, sometimes, he wished he could.

"Mine! Mine!"

Meep was scuttling along the railing, straight toward

him. Captain Traxx had returned their possessions, which included the key to Zoone, but the decision had sent her pet into a permanent tantrum. The monkey pounced into the shaggy rain forest that was Ozzie's hair and began yanking at the cord around his neck.

"Mine! Mine!"

"No!" Ozzie growled, batting at the creature. "Scram!"

"Scram! Scram!" Meep parroted.

"That is enough, my pet."

Ozzie turned to see the elegant pirate queen striding across the deck. As she reached the railing, Meep launched himself off Ozzie's head and onto her shoulder. Her injured arm was now in a sling, but she appeared no less formidable. Her mere presence sent a shiver scampering down the back of Ozzie's neck—either that, or the monkey had given him fleas. He turned away from her, hiding his gaze in the sky, where a magnificent cluster of rainbow-colored clouds had appeared. A sound reached Ozzie's ears, like the cooing of birds. Despite wanting to keep to himself, he cast a questioning glance at Captain Traxx.

"The Singing Nebula of Starsea," the pirate queen supplied, idly petting Meep. "One of the great wonders of interstitial space. And a sign that we are nearing the track to Creon."

Ozzie grimaced.

"You seem as sullen as a Zelantean slug," Captain Traxx observed. "Tell me, boy, what makes you so desperate to return to Zoone?"

What do you care? Ozzie thought. But he decided that telling her might encourage her to leave him alone, so he said, "Because I love it there. I was happy there."

Captain Traxx laughed, in that hearty, slightly frightening way that revealed her white teeth and scarlet tongue. "Foolish boy," she said. "If you can't be happy in your heart then you won't be happy anywhere in the 'verse—and that includes Zoone."

Lady Zoone had once said something similar to him, Ozzie recalled. But she was the steward of the nexus, one of the most important people in the multiverse. Aurelia Traxx was a pirate. Yes, she was tough as a bag of bolts and, yes, she spoke with the sort of confidence that could send thunder slinking home with its tail between its legs, but that didn't make her *right*. At least not the sort of right that Ozzie was willing to accept.

"You know where I *won't* be happy?" Ozzie snapped, keeping his eyes fixed on the nebula. "Creon. That's for sure. It's a dead world. I've been to a dead world before, you know: Glibbersaug. It wasn't good."

He could feel Captain Traxx's gaze boring into him. "You? Glibbersaug? And you survived? There *is* more to you than meets the eye. Still, Glibbersaug is not Creon. I assure you, boy: Creon is worse."

"How do you know?"

"Because," the pirate queen replied, "Creon was once my home."

Ozzie turned and stared at her anew: her tall countenance, her brightly freckled face, and her pomegranate hair. If everyone from Creon was as intimidating as her, then they really were going to be in trouble.

"Yes, I am Creonese," the pirate continued. "At least, I *was*. My family, my entire people, were forced to leave that desolate world in order to survive."

"Really?" Ozzie asked in spite of himself. "What happened?"

"For centuries, Creon prided itself on its industry. We built machines to improve our quality of life. To do our manual labor. To harvest resources and expand our cities." She tapped her fingers against the railing, stewing. "That ring I gave back to your aunt. The amelthium stone. It comes from Creon."

"It does? How did she end up with it?"

Captain Traxx grunted. "That's a question for her. I doubt she knows what it was used for: a power source for those . . . those *machines*. The machines that decimated Creon."

Ozzie shrank away from her. "How did it happen?"

"The Creonese—and their machines—just kept

building, building, building . . . until it was too late. The machines took over, and by the time I was born, Creon was already descending into environmental collapse."

"You could have turned off the machines. Cleaned up the world."

Captain Traxx rapped her fist gently against the railing. "My father was an idealist, like you. My brother, too. Thought they could stop the machines and save Creon. And what did they get for their idealism?"

Ozzie tugged uneasily at his key. Captain Traxx banged again on the railing, so hard that her knuckles split and began to bleed. Meep huddled in a sheepish ball on her shoulder.

"They broke my family," she growled.

"The machines?" Ozzie asked cautiously.

Captain Traxx sneered. "We survived Creon. We survived the machines. It was the heartless treatment by the multiverse that destroyed us."

"Wh-what do you mean?"

"I was still a girl when my family escaped Creon. We were one of the last families to do so, left to the end because we were poor. Just the rabble. Who cared if we escaped? But we did escape and . . ."

Her words floated away into the nebulae. Ozzie worried that she would turn and leave. Only a moment ago, he had wanted to be left alone, but now he was desperate for her to finish her tale. He stared pleadingly at the imposing pirate.

Captain Traxx sighed. "We tried to settle in other worlds, only to be rejected. Time after time. We were not considered 'desirable' citizens, because of where we had come from. I was only a child, but I felt their hate. I spent years in a refugee camp on Lattharyn before finally running away."

"What about your family?" Ozzie ventured.

"All gone," Captain Traxx said. "My parents, my brother . . . the 'verse chewed them up, crushed their spirits more heartlessly than any machine, and spat them out." She whirled on Ozzie then, as if, somehow, *he* was the one responsible for their deaths. "Now do you understand?" she asked, brandishing her bloody fist in his face. "I bow before no nation's whimsy. I am a citizen of the 'verse and I make my own way."

"B-but you harm others," Ozzie stammered. "You're doing the same thing they—"

"I care for the citizens of the 'verse as much as they cared for me and my family."

Ozzie scowled. That was the sort of logic that Aunt Temperance called a good excuse to behave selfishly. But it was hard to say this when he could so clearly hear the pain and anger vibrating in the captain's voice.

"See them?" Captain Traxx continued, turning toward

the deck. "They're like me. Come from every corner of the 'verse. Rosa over there is from Innishu. Vindu escaped the genocide on Baelzadra. The late Mr. Burr? Found him in the labor camps of K'thung. Castoffs, exiles, refugees. With me, they've found a crew. A purpose. As I said before, this is our kingdom, boy. We do not need a world to call our own. And neither do you."

"I don't want one world," Ozzie grumbled, toying again with his key. "I want *Zoone*. It's the world between worlds. Kind of like this place. But instead, we're going to Creon. You're going to abandon us there."

"That was your choice," Captain Traxx said icily.

"Not mine," Ozzie insisted. "I got overruled. Everyone gets to choose except me. That's my life. The entire multiverse is against me."

"Feeling sorry for yourself is not an admirable quality," the captain chided. "If you don't like the rules, then fashion your own. That's what I say. Still, it seems to me your companions are willing to do the hard thing. I don't agree with their choice to go to Creon, but I respect it."

Ozzie frowned. "Why?"

"They're thinking of Zoone—or, to put it another way, their crew. You should always look after your crew. Because, trust me, no one else will." She stared at him intently. "Though . . ."

"What?" Ozzie asked.

"*You*," she said emphatically. "You saved my life. Me, your enemy. I can understand the girl fighting the storm—that's saving *herself*. Why did you save me? I intended to sell you as a slave!"

She had asked him that before, right after he had done it. He hadn't known the answer then, and he didn't know it now. He finally settled on saying, "It's not like you wanted to be rescued. You were angry afterward. So, I'm pretty sure it doesn't count."

"It counts," the enigmatic pirate told him. "The things you do without thinking about them are the truest of all things." She jabbed a finger at his chest. "Trust your instincts, boy. But I'm not here to give you the gift of a traveler's wisdom. I'm here to give you something else."

She reached into the pocket of her long peacock-blue coat and produced a small metallic orb. "Take it," she commanded.

Ozzie did—cautiously, because it reminded him of the robotic flying death bug. The orb had a tiny antenna, and a seam around the middle, as if it were capable of opening.

"You saved my life," Captain Traxx said. "Whether I wanted it or not, that puts me in your debt." She scowled, causing her freckles to flicker like embers. "I do *not* like to be in debt."

"What is this thing?" Ozzie wondered, turning the orb over in his palm.

"A beacon," she answered. "Flip it open, hit the switch, and the *Empyrean Thunder* will heed your call. But only once, which means you must use it only when you are in the most desperate danger. If you use it the moment you land on Creon, I promise you: I will not come. Or if I find that you have misused it, then I will make you walk the plank and you can float here, in the heavens, until you starve to death or find yourself in the belly of a cosmic storm. Is that clear?"

Ozzie looked up into the pair of lasers she called eyes and nodded.

"Good," the pirate queen said. She began to saunter away, only to turn and offer him one last piece of advice. "Stick with them."

"Who?"

"Your crew," Captain Traxx replied. "Everyone needs a crew, boy. And that includes you."

There was nothing sentimental about the farewell with the pirates. The *Empyrean Thunder* found a track leading to Creon and simply dropped Ozzie and his companions off. The ship didn't even have to bore into the tunnel; it was already ruptured open, offering up its quiet and motionless track without protest.

Not a good sign, Ozzie thought as Aunt Temperance led the way along the desolate path. Her hair was now tied into two tight ponytails; Ozzie noticed that they were both infused with gray, as if her one silver strand of hair had decided to multiply. *That's what stress will do to you*, he grumbled to himself.

Though, he had to admit, Aunt Temperance didn't seem stressed. If anything, she had a determined glint in her eyes. In one hand, she clenched her locket and ring, while the other was gripping the strap of her canvas bag, which had swollen in size and weight as a result of the pirates providing them with canteens of water. If the burden bothered Aunt Temperance, she didn't show it.

They heard Creon long before they saw it. From the end of the tunnel came the faint clamor of machinery.

"What's going on over there?" Aunt Temperance wondered. "I thought Creon was supposed to be a dead world. I assumed that meant desolate and quiet."

"It doesn't sound quiet," Tug remarked, his ears flattening.

With a shudder, Ozzie remembered Captain Traxx's words: *The machines took over.*

They can't still be in operation . . . can they? Ozzie wondered.

But there was no denying the mechanical din—it was growing louder with each forward step. They arrived at a gaping doorway that clung desperately to its frame by one mangled hinge. The door itself was made of thick metal with giant cogs and gears adorning its surface. Ozzie paused to spin one of the gears, but it was so rusted that it wouldn't even budge.

He followed the others through the doorway and into an abandoned station house. It was nothing like the cavernous and beautiful complex of Zoone Station. This place was tiny and dingy by comparison, the walls pitted with holes and the floor littered with rubbish. There were many empty archways, leading to bricked walls— dead doors, Ozzie knew. There were only three intact doorways: the one they had come through, one that was shut with a padlock, and one other that had been thrown open, a pair of conveyor belts trundling in and out of it.

"It's the conveyors making all the noise," Fidget said. "Must be a loop."

She was right, Ozzie realized. The conveyor entering the door carried large, empty crucibles, but the ones on the outbound conveyor were filled with rock.

"It's ore," Aunt Temperance observed. "For smelting into metal."

"Where do you think this track leads?" Ozzie asked as he wandered over for a closer look. "It has to be another world, right?"

The door was made of weathered stone and featured a carving of a peculiar creature that looked like a bear with enormous teeth. Ozzie craned his neck to stare past the conveyors but could only make out a long black tunnel.

"We don't want another world," Aunt Temperance reminded him. "We want this one. We'll follow the conveyor belt into Creon."

"Is this really a good idea?" Ozzie asked.

"I don't think we have a choice," Aunt Temperance said.

Ozzie watched her tramp away, her bag bouncing on her back. *I know I sure don't*, he thought. Sure, it was great to have a crew (to use a Captain Traxx phrase), but sometimes he wished he could just do things his own way.

10

A MAZE OF MACHINERY

The conveyor belt led them across the station, through an archway, and to the top of a wide staircase. There was no smelter to be seen, just the landscape beyond—or at least, Ozzie decided, what passed as landscape.

The ground stretching ahead of them was tiled with rusted metal plates, while above them, the air was so choked with ash and noxious green clouds that the sky was more or less a rumor. There wasn't a speck of life— not even a weed poked through the seams in the metal tiles. The only movement was the pair of conveyor belts they had followed out of the station, vanishing into the hazy horizon.

Tug instantly began coughing and wheezing.

"Creon is even worse than Glibbersaug," Ozzie quavered.

Fidget scuffed her toes across one of the metal plates on the stairs, dislodging a cloud of rust. "W-we survived Glibbersaug. We can survive this place."

But Ozzie detected the uncertainty in her voice, teetering on the edge of panic—and he felt the same way. "Captain Cho rescued us from Glibbersaug. This time . . ." He shook his head, then turned to Aunt Temperance. "It's not too late to turn around."

"Yes, it is," Fidget said. "The pirates are gone."

"There's that other door in the station," Ozzie said. "It might lead to a safer world. One that can take us to Zoone."

Aunt Temperance sat down on the steps and grimaced at the landscape in silence.

"My grandfather always said Creon was polluted," Fidget said. "But I didn't know it was going to be like *this*."

"The air here is terrible," Tug moaned, his fur paling to a dull blue.

"How are we going to survive here if we can't even breathe?" Ozzie asked, seizing the opportunity to make his case. "We need to go back."

"We have to save Mercurio," Fidget argued. "That's

what Lady Zoone said. We have to search this place, see if he's here."

Tug purred in agreement. "Hey! I know—do you have any Breathe-Eazzy in your pack, Aunt T?"

"Breathe-Eazzy?" Fidget echoed. "What's that?"

"There was a story about it on the TV," Tug explained. "All you have to do is spray it and it freshens the air. It's really cool."

"The stuff you're talking about is just simulated fragrance," Aunt Temperance told the skyger, snapping out of her thoughts. "I don't think spraying *more* chemicals into the air will help this place." She began digging through her bag. "I brought some headscarves. We can tie them around our faces."

Ozzie swelled with anger. "Are you guys serious?! We're actually going through with this?"

Aunt Temperance began tying a headscarf around his neck. "I won't let anything happen to you, Ozzie. I promise. But I—I have to do this. If there was someplace safe for you to wait, then I'd leave you there. All of you."

"We have to stick together," Fidget declared. "If we learned anything from our last dead world, it's that. Right, Oz?"

Ozzie only grunted in response. *Overruled again.*

It took three headscarves knotted together to fit over

Tug's enormous snout, but eventually everyone was ready, and they began trudging across the dismal landscape, following the conveyor belts. There was no question of flying; the poisonous clouds were so thick and low that they wouldn't be able to see a thing.

"You could always lose some stuff," Fidget suggested when she saw Aunt Temperance struggling with her bag. Aunt Temperance responded with a swift glare, prompting Fidget to quickly add, "Yeah, I know—everything's essential. Here, I'll carry the blender for you—at least the pitcher. That'll lighten the load."

By a ton, Ozzie thought as the princess took the appliance. He knew the real reason Fidget wanted the blender—it would be as good as a club if they encountered danger.

After an hour's trek, shapes began to appear out of the gloom in front of them: industrial silos, gigantic pipes, and more conveyors, producing a clamorous racket. The thrum was so loud that Ozzie could feel the metal plates vibrate beneath him. As they pressed forward, the equipment became more concentrated until they found themselves in some kind of dense, open-air (or, as Ozzie thought of it, open-smog) factory city.

The buildings were tarnished tanks, charred smoke-stacks, and cement towers streaked with grime. The streets were assembly lines and conveyor belts that criss-crossed in every direction, some of them suspended high above their heads. The sidewalks were narrow aisles that snaked through the maze of machinery.

But there were no people.

It sent a shiver down Ozzie's neck. Even though Captain Traxx had described Creon to him, he hadn't really understood until seeing the world for himself. As he glanced around, he couldn't detect the slightest trace of human life—it was just the machines, running as if on automatic. Mechanical arms tipped cauldrons of hissing molten ore into molds. Giant rivet guns fired bolts into metal plates. Saw blades chopped through iron rods.

"The machines really did take over," he said with a gasp.

"Don't let your imagination run wild," Aunt Temperance said with a frown. "These are just mindless machines. They're not sentient. They have no will or purpose."

Ozzie wasn't convinced, not based on what Captain Traxx had told him. "Something's in control here," he said.

Even through his headscarf mask, he could detect the pervasive stench of oil, and that, combined with the whirring machinery, was giving him a headache. He slumped against the nearest wall, only to feel something buzz against his shoulder. He turned and found that the wall was actually a massive control panel, its surface animated with rattling gauges and flickering sensor lights.

"Ouch!" Tug suddenly screamed, tossing his head and sending his headscarf mask flying. "Something just bit my tail!"

"That *something* was a giant cleaver—be careful!" Aunt Temperance warned.

Ozzie watched in horror as the skyger's tail thrashed dangerously close to a line of overenthusiastic chopping blades.

"TUG!" Ozzie cried. "Get out of the way!"

Tug jumped—backward, *closer* to the machinery. Down came the ax blade, slicing off half the bushy tuft at the end of his tail. With a yowl, the skyger catapulted forward, bowling over Ozzie and slamming into the wall of control buttons. The whole structure crumpled with a sputter of sparks and steam. In a panic, the skyger sprang into the air, wings aflutter, only to immediately smash into an overhead pipe. Tug sank to the ground with a groan. All around them, like a giant ripple, machines began fizzling to a halt.

"I told you this was a bad idea!" Ozzie growled in frustration as he climbed to his feet. He had to watch his step; the pipe that Tug had crashed into was spewing green liquid.

Fidget shrugged. "If you ask me, the score's Tug: one, factory: zero."

An earsplitting alarm bell began blasting through the city.

Tug crouched close to the floor and tried to cover his ears with his enormous paws. "Just to tell you," he mewled, "this is not my favorite world."

Aunt Temperance succeeded in grabbing his tail. "You're okay, Tug; looks like just a bit of a haircut." Then, handing the tail to Ozzie, she added, "Here, you better hold on to this the rest of the way. And tie those shoes! This is *not* the sort of place where you want to trip. Come on. I'll get us out of this."

"Out of this?!" Ozzie cried as his aunt turned and began walking again. "You're the one who got us *into* it! We could be in Zoone right now, enjoying a cup of—"

Fidget slugged him in the shoulder, which made him drop Tug's tail. "You just don't get it, do you? You keep thinking Zoone is just like you left it. I've been telling you—it's not. So, *come on.*"

Then, snatching Tug's tail and tilting her chin high, she marched after Aunt Temperance.

"Princess," Ozzie muttered as he rubbed his shoulder and reluctantly set off after them.

They left the circle of dead equipment and eventually arrived at a wall of rough and weathered stone. It was too high to see over, but they only followed it for a short way before they came to a rusted wrought-iron gate, hanging apologetically from its hinges. It looked like a relic from a forgotten time—*a time of people*, Ozzie thought. But when he peered through the gate's bars, all he could see were mounds of metal debris.

"Looks like the place where old parts of the factory come to die," Fidget said.

Aunt Temperance tugged on the gate until it opened on its protesting hinges, then led them through. "Might be safer, if there are no working machines here—but remain vigilant. The last thing we need is someone stepping on a rusty edge and getting a tetanus infection."

They followed a twisting path through the heaps of junk, the alarm bell still ringing faintly in the distance.

"Hey, look," Fidget said. "There's no metal or concrete on the ground here. It's dirt."

With the toe of his shoe, Ozzie maneuvered a jagged end of a pipe out of the way so that he could get a closer look at the ground. He wasn't sure if you could call it dirt. Perhaps once, but now it was a dull and powdery white, as if all its nutrients and moisture had been leeched away.

Then he realized there was something on the other end of the pipe he had just moved, a sort of squat metal statue. It was so stained and rusted that he could barely discern what it was. But, if he had to guess, it was in the shape of a bird with some kind of saddle on its back.

Aunt Temperance leaned over his shoulder. "That

looks like it belongs on a seesaw—oh."

She was slowly turning around, as if taking everything in for the first time, and Ozzie followed her lead. It was only then that he noticed familiar fixtures poking out of the heaps of industrial refuse. There were park benches (most of the wooden parts had rotted away), an old water fountain (thick with grime), and what looked like a large rubber cog with a frayed piece of rope tied to one end.

Creon's version of a tire swing? Ozzie guessed. He wondered if Captain Traxx had ever swung on it, but it was hard to imagine her as a kid, having fun.

"This was a city park," Aunt Temperance murmured. "Now it's just a junkyard. A garden of rust."

They wandered farther ahead, climbing over a massive steel girder that was lying haphazardly across the path, until they arrived at what might have once been a duck pond. Now? It was a swamp, with all sorts of things half sunk in the stagnant muck: bloated garbage bags, corroded oil cans, the arm from a plastic doll. A film of grease coiled around everything.

"This is water in Creon?" Tug asked, wrinkling his nose. "What are we supposed to drink?"

"The water in our canteens," Aunt Temperance advised. "We'll have to drink cautiously and conserve our supply if we—where's Fidget?! She's the one who said to stick together!"

Ozzie cupped his hands to his mouth. "Fidget? Where'd you go?"

"Quoggswoggle!" came a reply from somewhere beyond a colossal pile of scrap metal. "I'm over here. Come see what I've found."

11

THE GARDEN OF RUST AND RUIN

Ozzie led the charge around the heap of rusted metal to find Fidget standing in front of something that looked completely out of place in the desolate ruins.

"A tree!" Tug exclaimed.

Or what's left of one, Ozzie thought.

The tree looked like it had once been strong and beautiful, maybe hundreds of years ago, before the pollution of Creon had sunk its claws into it. Strips of gray bark were peeling off its trunk, revealing patches of raw, exposed wood. The branches drooped solemnly and were completely bare of leaves. The roots were gnarled and twisted and pulling up from the ground, as if the tree was trying to stand on tiptoe on the toxic soil.

"It's dying," Aunt Temperance said forlornly. "Too many contaminants have leached into the soil and the water. Now there's nothing good for the tree to draw from. Only poison."

Fidget sighed. "I bet there were a lot of trees here before."

"Perhaps," Aunt Temperance said. "Back when this park was alive with people. With children. Everything must have died."

"It's the first scrap of life we've seen in this entire world," Ozzie said as he stared at the tree's stark branches. "Maybe this is it. The last tree of Creon."

"Why would Mercurio choose to be left in this dreadful place?" Aunt Temperance wondered as she slowly circled the dying tree. "It makes absolutely no sense. I think there's something that pirate wasn't telling us."

Maybe, Ozzie thought. But he also figured Aunt Temperance was just trying to blame someone else for them ending up in the middle of a wasteland.

He watched her wander away from the tree, back to the path, where she dropped her canvas bag to the ground and sank onto it. "I could use a cup of tea," she murmured.

Uh-oh, Ozzie thought as he and the others gathered around her. He had been ready to rub an "I told you so" in her face, but he couldn't do that now. Not with her staring blankly into space, teetering on the edge of an emotional cliff.

The alarm bell, which had been ringing in the distance the entire time, abruptly turned off. Somehow, that didn't seem like a positive turn of events.

Tug nudged Ozzie with his huge snout. "Ozzie? I think someone's coming."

"Where?" Fidget asked, turning with the blender raised above her shoulder like it was a weapon.

Tug's fur turned even paler than before. "Everywhere."

"Hello?" Ozzie called out, lowering his headscarf mask. The sting of gasoline was so strong it made him cough.

Aunt Temperance rose shakily to her feet. "Anyone there? Mercurio?" Her tone was crisp with hope.

But when a reply came, it wasn't a human one. It was a chorus of mechanical voices, all speaking in unison, reverbing through the garden of rust: "Do not worry, friends. Help is on the way."

"Help?" Ozzie wondered. "What kind of help?"

Robots began emerging from behind the scrap heaps. They all looked completely identical, with multiple legs and burnished cylinders for bodies, covered with lights, switches, and gauges. There were more lights on their heads, along with gyrating scopes and antennae.

"Motos," Fidget gasped as the robots began forming a circle around them. "Just like the ones patrolling Zoone."

"What are they doing *here*?!" Ozzie cried.

"I don't know!" Fidget told him.

The motos began to close in. Their hands were large and shaped like clamshells, without individual fingers, and they were tilted upward at their wrist joints, as if offering a sign of peace.

"Do not be afraid, friends," they said. They spoke flatly, without fluctuation in tone, but Ozzie immediately had the impression that they were trying to sound kind and caring, maybe even compassionate—if that was something robots could do.

"We're looking for someone named Mercurio," Aunt Temperance said. "Do you know where he is? We were told he came here. To Creon."

"Creon is no more, friends," the machine men answered as they continued to approach. "Now there is only Moton."

"Moton?!" Aunt Temperance cried. "I knew it; that pirate took us to the wrong place! She betrayed us. She—"

Ozzie cut her off with a gasp. "They're the same!" he exclaimed as the realization struck him. "Creon and Moton. This *used* to be Creon, but now . . ."

"You mean the motos came from here—like, originally?" Fidget asked.

"They . . . they must have," Ozzie said as the truth sank its teeth deeper. "The motos are the ones running this world. Machines running machines! They took it over, they . . ."

"Poor friends, you are only flesh and bone," the motos droned, inching ever closer. "We will save you."

Their clamshell hands clicked open, revealing all sorts of sinister attachments: flashing scalpels, whirring saw blades, and two-pronged forks with arcs of electricity between them. The motos were basically life-sized robotic flying death bugs—well, if your life happened to be sized six feet tall. Which, incidentally, Ozzie's was not.

"Where is Mercurio?!" Aunt Temperance implored as they all huddled together in the middle of the quickly closing moto circle.

Suddenly, something hot and wet sizzled against Ozzie's arm. He rubbed frantically at his skin, then peered upward. The toxic clouds were spitting bullets of green water. "What the . . . ?"

"Acid rain!" Aunt Temperance gasped.

"We've really got to get out of here," Fidget said, pushing her scarf over her head. "This whole world is trying to kill us."

"Do not worry, friends," the motos chorused. "We will save you."

"Do not worry, friends—we will *run away*," Fidget mimicked, brandishing the blender.

"Maybe we should try escaping on Tug," Ozzie

suggested. "You know, before you do anything rash."

"I don't think I can fly in these clouds," Tug whimpered, nudging his enormous head into Ozzie's armpit, as if he might somehow hide there. His fur had turned a sickly green.

Even as the skyger spoke, another drop of acid rain splattered against Ozzie's ear, and he winced. "Yeah, you're right," he agreed.

He closed his fingers around the beacon in his pocket. Was this the time to call Captain Traxx for help? She had warned him not to use the beacon unless the situation was absolutely desperate, but what could be worse than being surrounded by an army of psychopathic robots with can openers for hands? But he realized just as quickly that calling the pirate queen would be useless. By the time she arrived, the only thing left for her to do would be to mop up the mess.

"I've got this," Fidget said.

With both hands wrapped around the blender handle, the brazen princess stepped forward, swung, and clobbered the nearest moto so hard that its head whirled clear off its shoulders. The other motos didn't even react. They just kept clicking systematically forward—except for the decapitated moto; without visual sensors to direct its course, it veered and took out the moto next to it, leaving a wide gap in the circle.

"Hmm," Fidget grunted, lifting the blender to examine it with sparkling purple eyes. "Maybe this thing *is* essential."

"Run!" Aunt Temperance yelled.

They dashed through the newly cleared opening in the moto circle and down the nearest path winding through the junk. They couldn't go back to the entrance of the park—it was blocked by motos—so they went straight ahead, deeper into the scrapyard. As he ran, Ozzie glanced over his shoulder and found the motos in pursuit, though they were moving at the same slow, consistent speed.

"I don't get it," he said. "They'll never catch us going that slow."

"Good!" Fidget said.

They had soon left behind the motos, as well as the last remnants of the park. Now it was just more garbage, mountains of industrial scrap that seemed to have no end: tangles of wire, abandoned control panels, twisted rods of iron sticking out of crumbling slabs of cement, like hands waving for help in the drizzle of acid rain.

Unfortunately, that drizzle was quickly maturing into a shower. Soon, each drop felt like the peck of a sharp beak.

"We need to find shelter!" Fidget cried.

There was still a pathway ahead of them, but it was narrow and meandering. Suddenly, they arrived at a junction. The path branched in three separate directions.

"It's like a maze in here," Ozzie complained. "Which way do we go?"

"I pick this one," Fidget said. With her free hand, she pushed aside a sheet of scrap metal to reveal the mouth of a giant industrial pipe poking out of the nearest mound. "Come on," she said, scurrying inside.

Everyone followed; the pipe was so big that even Tug could fit.

"We can't stay here," Ozzie warned. "The motos will find us."

"We can't go out there," Fidget countered. "We'd get melted alive."

Ozzie couldn't really argue with her. The rain was now pounding the metal outside, causing a racket. Water, red with rust, was spilling over the opening of the pipe.

Aunt Temperance sighed. "I could *really* use a cup of tea." In the darkness, the pulsing of the stone on her chain was even more pronounced, casting a flicker of light on everyone's faces.

"This pipe keeps going," Fidget said, probing ahead. "Maybe we can follow it."

"Just wait!" Aunt Temperance called, but the princess had already disappeared into the darkness.

"Someone's back there," Tug mewled, his ears twitching.

"Motos?" Ozzie asked in alarm.

"No," Tug said. "I think it's—"

Fidget shrieked from the depths of the pipe. Ozzie tore after her, but a loud thump brought him to a halt. Then a light switched on behind him—Aunt Temperance had brought a flashlight, he remembered—and there was Fidget, standing with the blender raised above her head, ready to swing again. A giant shape was stirring on the floor in front of her.

A *human* shape.

"Who are you?" Aunt Temperance demanded.

The figure groaned, then rolled over to reveal his face.

"Quoggswoggle," Fidget gasped.

Lying at her feet was none other than Cho Y'Orrick, the captain of Zoone.

12

NO SORT OF WORLD
FOR SLEEVES AND SWORDS

"Ch Cho?" Fidget stammered, quickly thrusting the blender into Aunt Temperance's arms. "I'm sorry—really sorry."

"It's okay," came the wheezing reply. "You just knocked the wind out of me, lass."

"You're Captain Cho?" Aunt Temperance gasped as the titanic man slowly sat up, massaging his stomach. "I thought you would be more . . . *captainish*."

Ozzie understood what she meant. Cho didn't look like the strong and vigorous man who normally patrolled Zoone. He seemed a mere specter of his former self—

gaunt, pale, and bedraggled. Gone was the long turquoise coat of his uniform; in its place, Cho wore a stained undershirt. His hair, usually styled into a tidy topknot and two braids, was hanging loose and wild around his shoulders. Black bags sagged beneath his eyes, obscuring his scar and tattoo.

It was only those eyes that gave a hint of the noble man Ozzie knew so well. There was still a flicker of warmth in them. It was the type of warmth you wanted to huddle around on a cold winter's night—or when there was poisonous rain hammering down outside. Ozzie and Fidget dropped to their knees and hugged the fallen man, while Tug gave the captain a sloppy lick with his blue tongue.

"You're here!" Ozzie exclaimed. "How did you find us?"

Cho tousled Ozzie's hair. "I heard the alarm going off, then I spotted you from my lookout, fleeing the motos. I didn't mean to startle you, Fidget."

"It's okay," the princess said. "But how did you get here to begin with? To Creon?"

"Creon?" Cho echoed in surprise. "This is Moton."

"That's just what the motos call it," Ozzie said.

Cho exhaled. "Let me guess—you've already been figuring out the mysteries of this place. Just like old times, hmm? A skyger, a purple-haired lass, an Eridean traveler—"

"And an aunt," Tug interjected.

"Ah, yes," Cho said, rising to his feet and holding out one enormous hand. "You must be the infamous Aunt Temperance. You have a whiff of magic about you."

Aunt Temperance wrinkled her nose at him. "I don't know what *that* is supposed to mean, Captain. *You* have a whiff about you—but I wouldn't describe it as magical."

"No," Cho conceded. "I'm afraid I've not had much opportunity to bathe in this wretched world."

"Cho can smell magic," Ozzie told his aunt. "That's what he means."

"I smell like magic?" she said skeptically.

She looked to Ozzie, but he only scratched his head. Cho had said something similar to him when he had first arrived at Zoone, but he had always assumed it was because he had been carrying his aunt's key—in fact, he was still carrying it. As for Aunt Temperance? Well, she *was* wearing a glowing orb around her neck. Maybe it was magical, too.

"The nose does not lie," Cho said. He was still holding out his hand, but Aunt Temperance had yet to take it. Ozzie knew that his height, along with the scar on his cheek and the two missing fingers on his left hand, could make him seem intimidating.

"Captain, may I inquire . . . are you okay?" Aunt Temperance asked, the beam of her flashlight wandering over the captain's body from head to toe.

Cho dropped his hand and chuckled because, well, that's what Cho always did. Pain, disaster, dire predicaments—it didn't seem to matter; he faced all situations with a sprinkling of mirth. "This *is* a dangerous realm, madam," he said. "But I didn't lose my fingers here. This is an old injury, from when I was a lad in my home world of Ru-Valdune."

Aunt Temperance's face contorted as if several emotions were competing for real estate all at the same time. "Madam?" she said sourly. "I'm pretty sure I'm younger than you."

Cho chuckled again, his dark brown eyes glinting in the beam of her flashlight. "That's most likely true. Though I'm not as old as you think. Being stranded here all these weeks has taken its toll."

Aunt Temperance gasped. "You've survived here for weeks?! How—"

A loud clang broke through the rain, causing everyone to instantly freeze.

"That's the motos catching up," Cho whispered, and Fidget wrested the blender back from Aunt Temperance's hands. "They never hurry, but they always come. We can't linger here any longer." He turned into the darkness of the pipe and beckoned everyone to follow.

"Wait a minute." Aunt Temperance balked. "Where are we going?"

"To my hideout," Cho answered. "Now, hurry!"

He led them deeper into the pipe, which let out on the other side of the junk heap. Once through, they darted into the rain, crossing the rubble to reach the mouth of another gigantic pipe half-hidden in a pile of scrap. Cho moved confidently through the tunnel—he knew the way by heart, Ozzie realized. The end of the second pipe jutted out over a wide canal of sludge. Ozzie guessed it had once been a proper river, but now it was gray, thick, and oozing like wet cement. On the opposite side were more hills of abandoned metal, stretching into the haze of rain, as far as Ozzie could see. Black garbage bags pockmarked the heaps like painful sores.

"The motos don't recycle or reuse," Cho explained, gesturing at the pitiful landscape. "They simply dump whatever they can't use anymore into this ever-expanding scrapyard. Maybe this was once the center of the city, but now it's dormant and dead. Which means it's the safest place in this desolate realm. My hideout's just on the other side of the river."

The mire was bubbling in certain spots, issuing plumes of yellow smoke. It was one giant toxic soup. Ozzie gave it a dubious look. "How do we cross?"

"We swing," Cho replied.

He grasped a heavy metal chain that was dangling down in front of the pipe. The other end of the chain was attached to the arm of an ancient crane perched on the opposite side of the sludge.

Aunt Temperance threw the captain a reproachful glare. "Are you sure it's safe?"

Cho chuckled. "Nothing in this world is safe, my lady. If you're scared, perhaps Tug can fly you over."

Aunt Temperance's eyes narrowed into slits as she tucked away her flashlight and adjusted the canvas bag on her back. "Do *not* call me 'my lady,'" she said indignantly, silver strands of hair dangling at her cheeks like a pair of exclamation marks. "*Or 'madam.'*"

Then, snatching the chain from Cho's hands, she leaped from the lip of the pipe and swung across the river of gunk to land gracefully on a block of concrete on the other side.

Cho's jaw dropped. "Is this the same aunt you used to tell me about?" he asked Ozzie. "I always had the impression that she was feeble. *Delicate.*"

"To be honest with you, Cho, me, too," Ozzie said.

Cho's sanctuary turned out to be nothing more than a cave hollowed out in the junk, with a makeshift roof of corrugated tin. It rattled in the rain, but at least it kept the area beneath dry.

"My humble home," Cho announced with an apologetic smile as he led the way inside.

Ozzie could see the evidence of the captain's habitation over the past few weeks. A couple of cement slabs had been arranged into a hard bed, with only Cho's long turquoise coat to serve as a blanket. Nearby, on top of an old oil drum, were Cho's hat and his gloves, while on another was his belt, carefully laid out with all the tools of his trade, including his hunting horn, his handcuffs, his canteen, and—most important, in Ozzie's opinion—his Valdune sword.

"Aunt T!" Ozzie said excitedly. "This is Cho's blade. The one I told you about—it can transform depending on who he's fighting."

Aunt Temperance scowled. "And whom do you like to fight, Captain?"

Ozzie was mortified by her response. Cho was a hero—a real hero, one who charged into danger and repelled glibber hordes with a magical sword. But Cho merely said, "I don't care to fight at all. Only when it's necessary."

"If it wasn't for him, we would have been worm meat back on Glibbersaug," Ozzie added. "Cho, how come you don't use the sword now? Or at least carry it around? You could defeat the motos."

Cho shook his head. "The blade has no effect on those mechanical men, lad. They are not living beings, so the steel doesn't respond to them. It merely clanks off their metal bodies. It's useless in this pitiful place." He slumped onto a crumbling cement block and gestured for everyone else to find similar seats in the rubble. "And all my belt and coat ever seem to do is get snagged on the junk here, or the equipment in the factories. Better to sneak through this world without sleeves and swords."

"No kidding," Fidget said. "Tug nearly lost his tail."

Cho ran a hand through the skyger's scruffy and scorched fur. "Poor cub," he said. "Your coat has seen better days."

"All I need is some Luxuria," Tug told him. "Then my coat will get back its natural sheen."

"Luxuria?" Cho echoed.

"It's a type of shampoo," Tug explained. "There was a story about it on the TV in Ozzie's world. If we had some, it could help renew my hair's natural gloss. Oh, and it would prevent split ends." He looked hopefully at Aunt Temperance.

"Sorry, Tug," she said. "I have a lot of things in my pack, but no Luxuria. Split ends are the least of our problems."

"What's a split end?" Cho asked. "Actually, what's a TV?"

"It's a place where everything is amazing," Tug raved.

Cho's brow furled. "Where is this land? I've never heard of it."

Fidget snorted. "That's because it's not a real place."

"I wish it was," Tug said. "TV Land would be so cool. All your problems would get solved in, well . . . I would say thirty seconds. My favorite stories are the ones about food—by the way, what do you have to eat around here, Cho?"

"There is nothing to eat in this wasteland," the captain answered. "Thankfully, though, I had this when I arrived." He leaned over to retrieve his canteen. "Arborellian nectar. There's a bottomless well of it in this magical container. I've grown a little weary of the taste, but it's kept me from starving."

"I'm not weary of it," Tug promised, licking his lips.

Cho laughed as he undid the stopper and held it over the skyger's gaping mouth. The skyger happily gargled down a stream of syrupy liquid. Ozzie knew Tug could have kept drinking for ages, but Cho cut him off and passed around the canteen.

"It *is* delicious," Aunt Temperance acknowledged after taking a sip, "but I'm sure it plays havoc with one's dental hygiene. And I'd like to know about its nutritional value."

Ozzie rolled his eyes. "It comes from Arborell, Lady Zoone's home world, you know."

"It's said to be the lifeblood of the Arborellia," Fidget added. "So, I'm pretty sure it's good for you."

Aunt Temperance didn't seem convinced. She passed

the canteen to Ozzie, but he waved it off. "Tell us what's going on, Cho," he said. "How did you end up here?"

"I came from Zoone," the captain replied. "Same as you, I assume."

"No," Ozzie said with an irritated edge. "I haven't been back since I last saw you."

"Actually," Tug said, "Captain Traxx dropped us off."

"Captain Traxx!" Cho exclaimed. "*The* Captain Traxx?! The pirate?!"

"She's pretty cool," Tug informed him. "Well, cooler than dentists."

"It's a long story," Aunt Temperance cut in. "And we're happy to tell it to you, but first—"

"Wait a minute, Cho," Ozzie said excitedly. "If you came from Zoone, that means there must be a portal here that will take us back to the nexus! Is it in the station house?"

"There's a station house here?" Cho asked in surprise.

"On the outskirts of the city," Fidget told him. "We came through one of its doorways after the pirates dropped us off. But we didn't see a door to Zoone there."

"That's not a surprise," Cho said pensively. "The magic in this world has all but died, and with it a connection to the nexus. If there are tracks, they will lead only to other dying or less magical worlds."

"Then how did you get here?" Ozzie pressed.

Cho sighed. "The portal I used is different. The motos built it on the terrace at the top of Zoone Station. I snuck through because I thought Lady Zoone was here. But it was a mistake. Once I was here, I couldn't get back." The captain stared forlornly at the ground. The rain had tapered off, turning the world quiet again, with just the soft sound of water dripping off the edge of their tin roof. "I failed Lady Zoone," he said, just above a whisper.

"I don't know about that, Captain," Aunt Temperance spoke up. "But Zaria sent a message to me. To seek her out, and to help her save our friend."

"Friend?" Cho asked, eyes flitting up. "What friend?"

"Well, he's my old . . ." Blushing, she fingered the locket around her neck. "We were all in the circus together," she said. "And the truth is—"

Suddenly, a deafening, terrifying scream ripped across the scrapyard and reverberated through the hideout. It was impossibly loud, so loud that it even caused the tin roof to tremble. But the shriek didn't sound as if it was coming from close by—Ozzie had the sense that it was somehow being amplified from far away.

Cho erupted to his feet. "That's no moto!" he exclaimed as soon as the sound had ceased. "Someone's out there!"

Aunt Temperance was on her feet, too, her eyes wide and her hands trembling as she shouldered her canvas bag. Ozzie knew exactly what she was thinking: Maybe, just maybe, they had found Mercurio. Cho led them outside, and up the side of the nearest mound by way of an improvised set of steps. Even though the rain had stopped, water still dripped from every edge of metal, making the climb extra precarious. Ozzie slipped more than once; it didn't help that his shoelaces had come untied.

The sky was bleary and yellow, but the rain had caused the haze to lift, meaning the top of the heap provided them a good view of the inhospitable world in every direction. Behind them was the entrance to the park, and the factory sector that they had navigated when first arriving. In front of them was more junk, stretching toward a horizon that was dominated by a massive dome of metal. It was covered with blinking lights and antennae. If a robot could get a pimple, Ozzie thought, that's what it would look like.

"What is that thing?" he asked.

"That's where I ended up when I came through the door from Zoone," Cho replied, staring earnestly ahead. "Some sort of moto base or headquarters. The only reason I escaped is because it's still under construction. I jumped through an open section of wall and made my way into the scrapyard."

The scream sounded again, so loud and agonizing that it caused Ozzie's skin to prickle.

"It's coming from the base," Cho declared as he began

descending the hill. "I'm going to help that poor soul!"

"We're coming with you!" Ozzie called, chasing after the captain.

"No!" Cho insisted. "It's too dangerous."

"Captain," Aunt Temperance said forcibly. "The children can remain, but I'm—"

"Listen up!" Fidget interrupted with all the authority of a princess. Everyone turned toward her, still standing at the top of the junk, still clutching Aunt Temperance's blender. "No one goes *anywhere* alone. We all stick together."

"I agree," Tug added with a twitch of his tail that nearly sent Ozzie tumbling down the slope. "We're a team."

Another shriek sliced across the wasteland.

Cho shook his head in defeat. "Hurry, then."

They scrambled to the bottom of the pile, back into the hideout, where Cho quickly donned his long turquoise coat and buckled on his belt.

"Didn't you say those got in the way?" Ozzie asked.

Cho cast his gaze about the hollowed-out hole in the junk, as if to bid it farewell. "They might. But I won't be coming back here. One way or the other, it's time to leave this world."

SOMETHING IN BETWEEN

Even though the base had appeared enormous from Cho's lookout, it took them nearly an hour to reach it. The screams had long since stopped by then. Ozzie didn't want to think about what that meant. Aunt Temperance had a look about her that seemed to waver somewhere between absolute determination and complete and utter breakdown.

Cho brought them to a halt at a ridge of junk on the outskirts of the dome and they peered over to survey the situation. Now that they were closer, Ozzie could see that the structure consisted of thousands of plates of metal bolted to a skeleton of curving iron girders, many of which were exposed because the dome was midconstruction. Down on the ground, motos calmly patrolled the perimeter.

"We need a distraction," Cho said.

Ozzie thought of the old throw-a-rock trick that heroes always used in movies, but he realized they would need a better plan if they were going to ninja their way inside. He wandered over to the nearest pile of garbage bags and nudged one with his foot, making it tumble down and split open. It was full of reams of paper, like old computer printouts.

"These will burn!" Ozzie said excitedly. "Aunt T, did you pack any matches?"

"Of course," she answered. "And candles."

Ozzie was soon positioning a candle at the base of the garbage pile. After a couple of attempts, he lit it, then gestured for everyone to scurry back to their hiding place.

"Just to tell you, that candle smells delicious," Tug announced, his fur turning an optimistic orange.

"You can't eat it," Aunt Temperance said. "It's just scented. Lavender and vanilla."

The enticing smell didn't last long; as soon as the garbage bags caught on fire, it turned to an oily odor, and a column of black smoke began gushing into the sky. Once the paper was burning, the entire pile soon followed.

An alarm began to blare from the base. Peeking over the junk, Ozzie saw the moto guards abandoning their posts, antennae telescoping and lights flashing. They were soon followed by scores of motos emptying out of the base.

"It worked," Cho said, patting Ozzie on the back. "Let's go!"

The first door they found in the side of the dome was locked. It had no handle or keyhole, just a pad of toggle switches and buttons. Cho didn't even try to break in. He just kept sneaking along until they reached a part of the dome where its shell was not yet completed.

"We're in luck," Cho said, leading them inside.

They began creeping down a long straight corridor, gleaming with brand-new metal walls. There was no decoration, only functional lighting and evenly spaced access panels.

"Where to now?" Ozzie asked.

"I'm not sure," Cho answered. "This place was only girders and half-finished floors the last time I was here."

They came to many junctions where they were forced to choose which way to go. In some cases, they climbed ramps to higher levels, but to Ozzie, every corridor looked the same as the last.

"Should have left a trail of bread crumbs," he grumbled to Fidget.

She arched a purple eyebrow at him. "Who carries bread crumbs around with them?"

Ozzie shrugged. "Aunt Temperance might."

"True. But it wouldn't matter. Tug would just lick them up."

"Quiet," Cho warned. "We're coming to some sort of control room."

He was right. The next room appeared to be a large command center. It was lined with control panels, with another corridor leading off from a gap on the opposite side. But the room's most prominent feature was a large archway with a sheet of buzzing static across it.

"I know this place!" Cho announced excitedly as he pointed at the archway. "That's the door I came through from Zoone."

"That thing leads to Zoone?!" Ozzie exclaimed. He charged to the door and immediately tried sticking his hand through the opaque static, only to receive a shock so violent that it sent him tumbling to the floor.

"Are you okay?!" Aunt Temperance cried, racing over to him.

Ozzie managed to nod, but the truth was that it felt like he had stuck his hand into a beehive.

Tug licked Ozzie's cheek. "Hmm—tingly," he remarked. Then he snatched Ozzie by his collar and lifted him to his feet.

"You won't get through, lad," Cho said. "Not without the passcode."

"No motos around here," Fidget observed. "I guess every tin can in the vicinity left to investigate the fire."

"They'll return before long," Cho said. "Everything looks different from when I last came through. None of these instrument panels were here. Seems like the motos have made a great deal of progress in building . . . whatever this is."

Massaging his hand, Ozzie turned to examine the command center in more detail. He now noticed two closed doors, one labeled *Operations*, the other *Simulations*. He had no idea what that meant—he wasn't sure he *wanted* to know. The control panels were covered with switches, gauges, and rows of screens—though none of them were activated.

"Are those TVs?" Tug purred, his fur turning a vibrant ultramarine. "That means they'll show stories!"

"Not likely," Ozzie told him.

Fidget suddenly shrieked, causing everyone to turn.

"Sorry," she said, blushing purple. "But . . . look."

Everyone joined her at the instrument panel where she was standing. Ozzie could see a number of gauges, like the ones you'd find in a car for fuel, except these ones were divided into percentage points. They were labeled *Motonization Levels.*

"They've got world names next to them," Fidget pointed out. "Look at the first one. *Creon: one hundred percent motonized.*"

"Motonized? What does that mean?" Aunt Temperance wondered.

"The motos converted Creon to this . . . to Moton," Fidget stammered. "And now they're working to do the same to other worlds." She kept reading: "*Untaar: ninety-two percent motonized, Yo-Kando: twenty-one percent motonized, Ru-Valdune—*" She abruptly stopped.

"Ru-Valdune?!" Cho gasped. He shuffled the princess out of the way and scrutinized the panel. "*Seven percent motonized . . .*" There was no mirth now in his expression, not even a glint. "The motos are in Ru-Valdune," he murmured in comprehension.

"Ru-Valdune?" Aunt Temperance asked. "Your home world? The violent place?"

Cho bristled. "It's still a *place.* Untaar, Yo-Kando, Ru-Valdune. I know *all* these worlds. They border one another—they're known as the wild lands."

Ozzie's imagination churned. Cho had mentioned the wild lands before; they had always made Ozzie think of bloodthirsty dragons and inhospitable landscapes.

"The wild lands are on the perimeter of the 'verse," Cho continued, tapping the control panel pensively. "Cut off from the nexus . . . no doors to connect them directly to Zoone." He looked at the group, his face drawn with worry. "The 'verse largely ignores them, which probably means no one knows what's happening there. That they're being devastated by the motos."

"Not just the wild lands," Fidget added. "The entire multiverse. That must be why the motos want to take over the nexus. They'll spread like a virus—look at this!"

She had moved over to the adjacent control panel. It had only one giant gauge, labeled *Zoone.*

"*Five percent motonized,*" Ozzie read in shock. There was a bank of switches next to the display. Ozzie pushed one and a screen at the top of the terminal flickered to life, revealing a view of the station grounds. It was the north platform; Ozzie recognized some of the doors in the picture, plus the view of the station behind them. Travelers were hustling back and forth. "I think this is a live feed," he said.

He flipped more switches, and more screens came to life, displaying different scenes throughout the station. Ozzie's eyes danced from picture to picture; some of the cameras showed wide views, but others were more focused—like the one trained on a boy sitting on an upturned crate near one of the information booths in the station hub. The boy had light blue skin and shabby clothes.

"That's Scuffy Will," Ozzie said. "The shoeshine boy."

As he said it, two motos marched into the picture and began hassling Scuffy. There was no sound coming from the screen—Ozzie desperately searched for a knob to control the volume, but there wasn't one.

"They want to see his work permit," Cho deduced. "Lady Zoone hasn't required one from Will in the past, but . . ."

One of the motos clamped onto Scuffy with metal pincers. As he tried to wriggle free, the other moto jabbed him with his forked hand. A crackle of lightning rippled across Scuffy's body, causing him to spasm, then go stiff and collapse to the ground. The motos picked him up and carted him away, trampling his shoeshine kit in the process. They left it behind, busted on the ground.

"Where are they taking him?!" Ozzie cried.

"Oh no," Fidget murmured.

She was pointing at yet another screen. It showed the Infinite Wood of Zoone—only a giant swath of it had been cut down. A machine rumbled out of the forest, equipped with a giant blade.

Ozzie gasped. "They're cutting down the trees!"

"They're motonizing Zoone," Fidget moaned. "They want it to look like *this* place! No world in the entire 'verse will be safe. The motos control *everything*."

"How could Lady Zoone let this happen?" Ozzie demanded. "Where is she? Why isn't she stopping this?"

"I told you!" Fidget said. "She's under a spell or something. Or the motos tricked her."

"Zaria's not the type to be easily fooled," Aunt Temperance said.

"No," Cho agreed, pacing back and forth in front of the monitors. "But one thing is certain: Watching these pitiful images will not help us—or Zoone. We need to keep moving."

Everyone began filing out, down the corridor they had come from, but Ozzie lingered a moment longer, gazing at the place he loved, a place now being slowly destroyed. Even as he stood there, he saw the needle on Zoone's meter tick upward.

Six percent motonized.

He turned to catch up with the others. Tug had been right: There *was* a story being told on the screens. A story of devastation.

They had only made it halfway down the corridor when they heard the sound of returning motos.

"They're done with the fire," Fidget surmised, raising her blender. "We'll have to bash our way through."

Cho gently lowered the blender with one of his giant

hands. "No, lass. We'll find another way out."

He led a retreat back to the command center and across to the corridor on the opposite side. They only made it a few steps, however, before everyone instantly froze. The left wall of the corridor featured a long window, and it was impossible to ignore what was on the other side of it: an operating room.

There was a table in the middle, with a patient strapped to it, though from their vantage point, all Ozzie could see of him was a pair of boots sticking out. What he *could* see clearly were the moto surgeons. There were three of them, with scalpels and saw blades for hands, though one had what looked like a blowtorch. All of them were splattered with blood.

"That door in the command center said *Operations*," Ozzie whispered.

"Oh," Aunt Temperance murmured in realization. "I thought it meant industrial operations. Not the . . . *medical* kind."

Fidget waved her hand in front of the window. "I don't think the motos can see us. It's a one-way window. The patient must have been the one who we heard scream. At the beginning of his . . ."

Torture, Ozzie thought. *What else would you call being operated on by a moto?*

They could still hear the moto guards approaching

from the other side of the control hub, but no one moved, transfixed by the scene in front of them. Then one of the moto surgeons activated a pedal and the operating table tilted upward to reveal the patient.

Ozzie would have screamed, but the sound stuck in his throat. Because the patient wasn't a person—not really. If anything, it looked as if someone had mashed together a human and a moto, but had decided to skimp on the human. He watched in horror as the lurching, jerking monster of a man was released from his restraints and slid off the table to begin staggering across the room.

Fidget gasped. "That's Klaxon! But he's missing an arm . . ."

It took a moment for Ozzie to digest her meaning—because the man *did* have two arms. It was just that one of them was fully robotic. It was skinny and made of metal, with pincerlike fingers at the end. As Ozzie stared at him, Klaxon raised his metal arm jerkily upward and wriggled the pincers, as if trying them out for the first time.

"They amputated his real arm," Fidget thought aloud. "They replaced it with a moto one."

"Wh-why w-would they do that?" Ozzie stammered.

"It's not just worlds they want to motonize," Fidget said slowly. "It's people, too. And he's patient zero! The first experiment. I think they've been doing it to him all along. Bit by bit. Because . . ."

She trailed off, as if overcome with disgust. Ozzie couldn't blame her. Klaxon's head was encased in metal—it looked like a helmet covered with switches and antennae, but riveted directly to his head. He was also wearing goggles, but Ozzie could see nothing behind the lenses; they must have replaced his eyes, too. The bottom part of Klaxon's face was flesh, but it was chalk white. His body was encased in thick armor with hoses, like the ones on a scuba tank, protruding from his sides.

The doorway slid open and Klaxon staggered into the command center. As distressing as it was to watch him, Ozzie found himself creeping back to the opening of the corridor to continue spying upon the half-moto man.

He's not a machine or a human, Ozzie thought. *He's something in between.*

At that moment, the moto guards entered the command station from the opposite passageway, but they immediately halted when they saw Klaxon. There was a clamor of banging and clinking as they raised their metal hands in salute.

"All hail Friend Klaxon!" they droned. "Friend, it is time to continue your mission."

Klaxon lumbered across the chamber toward the door of static. He used his new metal claw to begin flicking a series of switches on the nearby control pad. "Yes. I have a mission to complete," he said inexpressively.

"Motonization must continue."

His voice blared from all directions at once, causing Ozzie to realize that it was being amplified through speakers in the base—and beyond. *That's why we heard his scream from across the scrapyard*, Ozzie thought.

Klaxon pressed a switch on his chest plate and the archway's curtain of static shivered away, revealing the world beyond.

Zoone.

Ozzie's heart leaped—and so did his legs, straight toward the door. But Cho reeled him back into the corridor with one mighty hand and clutched him against his side. The other hand clamped over Ozzie's mouth.

Zoone was there. *Right there.* Ozzie could see through the archway and onto the terrace at the top of Zoone Station. He could smell the night air. He could hear the flutter of the station's banners in the breeze. He could see the nexus's many moons smiling in the sky.

Ozzie thrashed to break free of Cho's grasp, but it was already too late. The moto guards had spotted them and now they rolled into the middle of the command center, blocking Ozzie and his friends from the door to Zoone. Klaxon stepped through the archway and clicked a switch on his chest, and the door shut.

Zoone was gone in an instant.

There was no sound, no slamming of a door. The

archway simply returned to a buzzing sheet of static. Ozzie sagged in Cho's arms. He had been so close!

As one, the motos opened their clamshell hands to reveal their menacing weapons. "Do not worry, friends," they announced, scuttling forward. "We will save you."

"Time to go," Cho declared. He finally released Ozzie from his grip, but Ozzie remained where he was, eyes fixed on the door. That's when he realized Aunt Temperance was still standing there, too. This whole time, she had said nothing. She was just frozen, staring into the command center.

Ozzie reached for her hand and wrapped his fingers around hers, but she didn't squeeze them back in response.

"Aunt T?" he asked. "What is it?"

"That wasn't Klaxon," she whispered. "That was Mercurio."

REMNANTS OF THE PAST

"Wh-what?!" Ozzie spluttered. "That's . . . that's impossible."

He couldn't reconcile Klaxon with the picture of the man in Aunt Temperance's locket. How could she tell it was him through all the metal and machinery?

"It was him," Aunt Temperance said. Her voice was quiet but full of certainty. Even though the motos were still approaching, weapons whining and whirling, she was looking past them, toward the door to Zoone. Where Klaxon—*Mercurio!*—had gone.

"We don't have time for this!" Fidget snarled. There was a control panel on their side of the door; she bashed the blender against it and a metal panel slid down, block-ing off the motos. The robot in the lead had been so close, with its buzz-saw hand extended, that the door sliced its arm right in two. The limb clattered to the floor at Ozzie's feet, its blade still spinning.

Aunt Temperance didn't even notice. She just contin-ued staring ahead, except now at the closed door. Then sparks began flying from the seams.

"They're cutting through!" Cho cried. "We must flee."

Ozzie twisted Aunt Temperance around to face the corridor, but she didn't move. He locked his hand onto her wrist and began tugging her through the maze of ramps and hallways.

"They hurt him," she murmured over and over again. "They hurt him. Why are they doing this?"

Ozzie remembered what Lady Zoone had said about Mercurio in the memory marble: *He's in trouble—terrible trouble.*

No kidding, Ozzie thought. But Aunt Temperance was in trouble, too, he realized. She was the one he was really worried about.

At least the motos were slow, same as always. By the time they made it outside, there was no sign of them.

"We have to stop," Ozzie told Cho as they entered the scrapyard. "Aunt T needs to rest. She needs—"

"Not yet," Cho said over his shoulder. "We must stay

one step ahead of the motos."

"Or a lot more steps than that," Tug added. "Just to tell you, those motos have pretty long arms."

"One of them doesn't," Fidget said as she tapped her fingers on the blender. "Not anymore."

"Mercurio's arm," Aunt Temperance murmured, as if she was clinging vaguely to the conversation.

"Cho, we really need to stop," Ozzie insisted.

The captain glanced back and seemed to take in Aunt Temperance's condition. "I know a place," he conceded. "This way."

He guided them through the heaps of junk until they arrived at a gutted-out warehouse. It had a roof, but most of the walls had rusted or fallen away over the years.

"There's a second story," Cho told them. "Let's catch our breath there. We'll be able to see when they're getting closer."

They climbed to the top to find still more junk—but, strangely, there was also furniture. Human furniture: chairs, shelves, and a table with three wooden legs, the fourth being an improvised rod of metal.

"What is this place?" Ozzie wondered.

"I'm not sure," Cho replied. "I've taken refuge here before, during my explorations, but I never felt it was safe to stay for very long. Too close to the base."

"People must have lived here," Fidget said, glancing

around. "Maybe at the end, in the last days of Creon."

"Maybe," Cho said. He took a seat on one of the chairs and passed around his flask of Arborellian nectar. Ignoring the offer, Aunt Temperance dropped her bag and meandered over to the open wall of the building, which offered a view of the debris field and the moto base.

"Aunt T?" Ozzie said, following her. She still seemed in a daze, and it was a long way down to the ground. "Are you okay? Are you sure—was it really him? Mercurio?"

"Yes," Aunt Temperance said, her eyes planted on the base. "You don't forget the first person you fall in love with. No matter what they try to cut away. But why . . . why are they hurting him?"

Ozzie shifted uncomfortably. "It's like Fidget said, I guess. They're trying to make everything, everyone—"

"But *him*. Why him?"

Ozzie didn't have an answer for her. He just stood there, awkwardly.

"Zaria said we have to save him," Aunt Temperance murmured. "How?"

Ozzie didn't know that, either.

Aunt Temperance finally turned around and shook her head, as if to clear it. She marched back to the others with considerably more purpose in her steps. "We need to rescue Mercurio," she declared.

"The thing is," Fidget said, "I don't think that's Mercurio anymore."

"It's him. I told you—"

"He's more moto now than man, that's what I mean," Fidget interrupted. "It's too late to save him. How much is even left of Mercurio when he's half machine?"

"They can't turn his soul into a machine," Cho said pensively.

"Or his heart," Tug added.

"There's no way I'm going back there," Fidget said. "We'll be the ones who end up on the operating table. Aunt T, you'll just have to . . ."

"Have to what?"

Fidget shrank back. "Find another boyfriend?" she suggested quietly.

"You don't have the faintest clue of how love works!" Aunt Temperance exploded. "Do you?"

Fidget snorted, but Aunt Temperance was right, Ozzie realized. Fidget's parents had arranged a marriage for her without giving her any say in the matter. She hadn't even met her husband-to-be. That kind of match definitely had nothing to do with love.

"Mercurio wasn't just some boy I had a crush on," Aunt Temperance said. "We loved each other. We were engaged."

"What?!" Ozzie burst out. He still hadn't gotten used

to the idea of Aunt Temperance having a boyfriend. But a fiancé? *Who are you?* he wondered, for what felt like the zillionth time in the last few days.

"We need to rescue Mercurio," Aunt Temperance repeated.

She had that steely glint of determination in her eye again, which, Ozzie had to admit, was a relief. She might be springing news on him left, right, and center, but he much preferred this version of her to the silent one.

Ozzie turned to his friends. "She's right. We need to follow Mercurio to Zoone."

Fidget scowled. "You saw how that door worked, right? You need to know the code."

"I don't get it, anyway—you can't just manufacture a portal," Ozzie said. "They're magical. The tracks have been here since forever. Right?"

Fidget nodded. "The tracks to the nexus are natural. Zephyrus Zoone—Lady Zoone's ancestor—was the one who discovered them. The Council of Wizardry eventually added doors to regulate them, but you're right, Oz. You can't just *build* your own track."

Cho shook his head. "Somehow, the motos did just that. But they must originally have reached Zoone a different way—through a regular portal. And that means we can, too." He looked intently at Ozzie. "You said there's a station here, with a door that led somewhere else. What did it look like?"

"It was stone," Ozzie explained. "It had this creature on it. Like a bear with giant teeth."

Cho's eyebrows arched in surprise. "That's Unta, the tusk bear! Which means that's a door to Untaar!" He stood up and punched his fist into the palm of his three-fingered hand. "Of course! That's how the motos have begun taking over the wild lands. There's a portal that leads straight there."

"We don't need to go to the wild lands, Cho," Ozzie said. "We need to go to Zoone."

Cho was walking in a circle, scratching his beard. "I know the wild lands. How to cross them. I know where we can find another door, one that will lead to the nexus."

"And how long will that take?" Aunt Temperance wondered. "Is it safe?"

"It's *possible*," Cho said emphatically. "Unlike using the door in the base."

Aunt Temperance grimaced. "What if Mercurio comes back here, to Moton?"

"What if we're all dead by then?" Fidget countered.

"I don't think we can stay here any longer," Cho said. "If there's a way out of this desolate realm, then we should take it."

Aunt Temperance exhaled. "I agree. Which means the sooner we leave, the better."

Everyone began collecting their things, but Ozzie just stood there, dumbfounded. "Wait a minute," he said. "That's it? We're leaving?"

Fidget goggled at him. "Aren't you listening? We've got a death army of tin cans marching toward us and—"

"We're so close to Zoone," Ozzie interrupted. "We can't give up this easily!"

Aunt Temperance's face pinched like a knot. "We're not giving up at all, we—"

"We need to go back to the base!" Ozzie growled, stamping his foot. "Start another fire, distract the motos, get back to the door. We can hack in, we can—"

Cho dropped to one knee and put a heavy hand on Ozzie's shoulder. "Listen, lad—don't you think I would already have gone through that door if there was a way?"

Ozzie twisted away, toward Aunt Temperance. She *had* to take his side. Now that she knew where Mercurio was, now that she had found him . . . "You want to go to Zoone," he said. "Right?"

"Desperately," she said. "But we have to—"

Ozzie didn't want to hear any more excuses, any more rationalizations. "Yeah, I get it," he snarled. "Overruled again."

He turned away from her. *I'll just go back myself. I defeated the glibber king! I can deal with some motos . . .*

He stormed off into the junk. He heard Tug start after

him, only to be followed by Aunt Temperance saying, "Leave him, Tug. Let him cool down."

Cool down, Ozzie thought as he disappeared around a junk pile. *Cool down* this.

He wound up and kicked the nearest oil drum. It had already been lying on its side, but now it began to roll ponderously across the floor.

Right into a stack of metal bins.

Ozzie winced as the whole tower crashed to the floor, stirring up a cloud of dust.

"Ozzie!" he heard Aunt Temperance shout. "What happened? Are you okay?"

"Ugh!" That was Fidget. "Are you *trying* to get us captured? Maybe you could, you know, make *more* noise?"

"I wouldn't do that," came Tug's reply. "The motos might hear us."

"We're coming, lad!" Cho called. "Where are you?"

Ozzie didn't answer. He was staring into the bin that had crashed to the floor in front of him. Its lid had popped off and Ozzie could just make out a peculiar shape inside. He took a tentative step forward and peered into the darkness.

Ozzie's heart skipped a beat.

Staring right back at him was a moto.

15

THE MISFIT MOTO

Ozzie's immediate instinct was to turn tail, race through the warehouse, and hide behind the nearest skyger, but . . .

But.

There was something about this moto, something that beckoned him like a magnet to metal. Instead of retreating, he crept *toward* it.

It was inactive, which meant it was about as threatening as a teapot. And that was just it, Ozzie realized as he scrutinized the moto. It *looked* like a teapot—at least, one without a spout. It was bulbous and squat, even its head, which was capped by a metal hat in the shape of an upside-down flowerpot. Several crooked antennae jutted from the top.

Ozzie grabbed a nearby rod of scrap metal and used it to prod one of its thick hands, checking to see if it had any dangerous weaponry. Instead of saw blades or knives, it had chunky three-fingered hands. Its fingertips looked like they were supposed to plug into something.

"Ozzie?" came Aunt Temperance's voice from over his shoulder. "Are you all right? What are you doing?"

Ozzie whirled around. Everyone was hovering behind him in concern. "Look what I found," he said. "Can you help me pull it out?"

"That's a moto!" Fidget exclaimed.

"It's not working; it won't hurt us," Ozzie assured her. *At least, I hope not*, he added to himself.

He began tugging on the plump mechanical figure. That was when he realized it had no legs; instead it had a single wheel attached to its base. Still, it was so heavy that he had trouble shifting it.

"Let me try, lad," Cho said.

Ozzie stepped out of the way so that the captain could maneuver the moto out of the bin and into the light. Now that Ozzie could see it better, he noticed how old and rickety it looked. The other motos had looked, for lack of a better word . . . perfect. This one, though, was a patchwork of dented scraps that had been crudely bolted together. Ozzie could see seams crisscrossing its rotund belly.

"What a hunk of junk," Fidget pronounced.

"I don't know," Ozzie said, scratching his chin. The moto had large round eyes and the shape of its head gave the impression of chubby cheeks, in between which was the mouth. But instead of the featureless slit that Ozzie had seen on other motos, this one had four large teeth, like piano keys. "I think it looks kind of cute."

"And cool," Tug added agreeably.

"You're joking, right?" Fidget protested. "It's a *moto*. You know. The things that want to hack us to pieces? To '*save*' us?"

Ozzie ignored her. He had circled around the moto to discover a bank of switches on its back, five in total, and next to that a large round cavity. He began flicking the switches up and down, but nothing happened.

"Ozzie?" Aunt Temperance asked warily. "What are you doing?"

"I want to see what's wrong with it."

"It's a metal murderer, that's what's wrong with it," Fidget griped.

Ozzie glared at her. "I don't think so. It doesn't look dangerous. I . . . I just have this feeling."

"Oh, that explains everything," Fidget scoffed. "You have a *feeling*. Well, so do I—which is that this thing is going to turn on at any moment and start trying to grind me into purple powder."

"You know, people are always saying that skygers are ferocious killers—and look at Tug," Ozzie said. "He's not dangerous."

"Actually, that's because I'm a Zoonian skyger," Tug declared, sitting down on his haunches. He playfully swished his tail—and both Fidget and Aunt Temperance quickly scrambled out of the way to avoid being slammed into the nearest wall.

"Not dangerous?" Fidget snapped, snatching Tug's tail out of midair and shaking it at Ozzie. "He just about brained me with this thing."

"You know what I mean," Ozzie told her.

Cho chuckled. "Ozzie makes a good point. Zoone is full of our kind—misfits. Perhaps this moto is one, too."

Ozzie ran his fingers over the rough surface of the moto. He *did* have a feeling about it. His mom might call that being too sensitive, but Aunt Temperance had said that meant having good instincts. And Ozzie's instincts were telling him to switch on this moto.

"All we need to figure out is how to power it up," he said, studying the panel on the back of the moto.

"Try kicking it," Fidget suggested. "Actually, I'll do i—"

"Wait," Ozzie said. "There's a slot next to these switches. It's round—like for a battery."

"Oh!" Tug purred excitedly. "I saw this one story on the TV where they used Power-X batteries. Just to tell you, they last forever." His fur turned a hopeful purple as he looked at Aunt Temperance.

"Don't look at me that way," she told the skyger. "The only batteries I have are in my flashlight and I'm not letting you use those."

But Ozzie barely heard their exchange. He was staring at Aunt Temperance's ring, dangling on the chain next to her locket. As usual, the stone was pulsing with an electrical charge. "Captain Traxx told me your stone came from here."

"Really?" Fidget asked. "When did she say that?"

Ozzie ignored her question. He hadn't told any of them about his heart-to-heart with Traxx because he had been so angry with them. And he was still angry with them, so he definitely wasn't about to get into it now. "She said the stones are what the Creonese used to power their machines."

Aunt Temperance stiffened. "Mercurio did *not* give me a battery for an engagement ring."

"That's an engagement ring?!" Ozzie exclaimed. It did make sense. If there was an engagement, there had to be a ring. But why was it a stone from Creon?

Aunt Temperance seemed to have the same thought. "How would Mercurio have gotten it? He's . . . he's from our world. He told me he came from Hungary!"

"Just to tell you, that sounds like a *terrible* place," Tug said.

"Maybe Lady Zoone got the ring for him," Ozzie said. "Let's just try it, Aunt T."

He could see the curiosity percolating inside of her; she wanted answers, too. Which meant it didn't take her very long to make a decision. She removed the ring from the chain and passed it to Ozzie. "Be careful," she warned.

Ozzie plugged the ring into the socket on the back of the moto and gave it a twist. There was a quiet click, and a loud hum instantly began reverberating throughout the moto's metal body.

"It worked!" Ozzie exclaimed.

Fidget glanced at Aunt Temperance. "Looks like Mercurio *did* give you a battery. That's romantic."

Aunt Temperance didn't respond, mostly because the moto was now loudly vibrating. Electricity crackled across its surface. Suddenly, it stood erect, and its eyes began to glow.

"Watch out!" Cho cried.

The moto lurched.

"It's trying to kill us!" Fidget shrieked.

"If you ask me," Ozzie said, "it's trying to dance."

The moto was rolling in a tight circle with one hand curled near its mouth, as if it was holding an imaginary instrument. A peculiar noise burbled out of it, sort of like a trumpet—or a kazoo with an inflated sense of self-esteem.

The moto came to a halt, as did its fanfare. "Up-down-up-up-down!" it trilled, its head shooting up on a long rodlike neck.

"Do you think it's malfunctioning?" Aunt Temperance asked.

"I told you this was a bad idea!" Fidget shouted.

The moto's head slid back down into place. "Up-down-up-up-down," it repeated. Then, without warning, it zoomed forward and wrapped its spindly arms around Ozzie.

"Um, what are you doing?" Ozzie wondered.

"I think she's trying to hug you," Tug said.

"She?" Fidget said skeptically.

"I don't know," Tug said with a carefree flick of his tail. "I just think she's a she."

The moto rolled backward; then, after its head spun fully around, it began to shout, "I want to be a she! Creator, can I be a she?" It—or she, Ozzie supposed—was staring directly at him.

"I . . . I . . . ," Ozzie mumbled.

"Pleasey-please, Creator?" the moto begged, clasping her hands together.

"I don't mind if you want to be a she," Ozzie told her

truthfully. "But why do you keep calling me your 'creator'?"

The moto began wheeling around again. "You *are*. You built me. Don't you remember, Creator? Up-down-up-up-down."

"I didn't build you," Ozzie told her. "Why do you think that?"

"You look like Creator!" the moto replied. As she spoke, her teeth wiggled as if they really were piano keys.

Fidget arched a purple eyebrow and looked Ozzie up and down. "What, your creator wore his shirt inside out?" she asked.

"Ha ha," Ozzie retorted. "I don't think that's what she m—"

"Yes, yes, yes," the moto said. "Creator dressed the same. Plus, Creator was the same heighty-height."

"Heighty-height?" Aunt Temperance said disapprovingly.

"Hmm," Cho murmured, contemplating the moto. "Do you mean, perhaps, that your creator was a child?"

"That's right! Same shirty-shirt. Same hair."

Ozzie reached up and self-consciously ran his fingers through his hair. It was wilder than usual, all knotted and tangled. That wasn't exactly his fault, either, he consoled himself. They *were* trapped in an industrial wasteland crawling with killer robots.

"Did this creator have a name?" Aunt Temperance asked.

"Yes! Creator."

"That's not a name," Fidget said. "That's a job."

"What about you?" Tug asked the moto. "Do you have a name? Just to tell you, most people call me Tug. And this is Ozzie, Fidget, Aunt T, and Captain Cho."

"I'm 'She,'" the moto declared proudly.

"That's not a name, that's a gender," Fidget told her crossly. "And I don't think you can have a gender because . . . because . . . well, you're a moto! You can't just choose what you want to be."

"Why not?" the moto asked, staring inquisitively.

Fidget's only response was to cross her arms.

"I want a namey-name!" the moto blared. She began careening around again, zigzagging in between the bins and barrels, stirring up the dust.

"She can really scoot," Tug remarked.

"Scoot! Scoot!" the moto cried, screeching to a halt. She reversed and twirled around in front of the skyger. "I want to be Scoot!" Then, turning to Ozzie, she added, "Can I be Scoot, Creator?"

"Yes, of course," Ozzie replied in exasperation. "But I told you, I'm not your creator. Just call me Ozzie."

Aunt Temperance's eyebrows angled so steeply and sharply they could have knitted wool. "Scoot," she said, "how long have you been here?"

"I don't know," the moto replied, pirouetting on her wheel. "Creator said, 'Up-down-up-up-down. Be ready.' Then he put me to sleepy-sleep in the bin."

"You mean he removed your battery?" Ozzie asked.

Scoot threw her hands in the air and twirled. "I don't know. That's the last thing I remember."

Cho stroked his scruffy beard. "You are a curious design, Scoot," he remarked. "You don't look like the other motos, you don't speak like them, and you certainly don't behave like them. It's a mystery."

"Mystery, mystery!" Scoot cheered. "I want to be Mystery! Can I be Mystery, Creator?" she asked, wobbling in front of Ozzie.

Ozzie sighed. "I told you—look, let's just stick with 'Scoot.' Okay?"

"Okeydokey, Creator," Scoot said. "But—oh!" She came to a sudden halt. Two of her antennae shot upward and her eyes began flashing as her head swiveled 360 degrees.

"That's not a good sign," Fidget said. "What is it now, Glitch-Bucket?"

"Oh! Glitch-Bucket!" Scoot chirruped. "Can I be Glitch-Bucket, Creator?"

"No!" Ozzie replied adamantly, throwing an irritated glance in Fidget's direction. "What's going on?"

Scoot tilted forward intently. "Don't you hear it?"

"I do!" Tug cried with a whimper, his ears flattening.

"Motos are mobilizing," Scoot announced. "I can hear their signals. Uh-oh!"

She began buzzing around in a frantic circle—she reminded Ozzie of a bumblebee. "What now?" he asked.

Scoot braked to a halt and held up one of her chunky fingers in a gesture of warning. "They've discovered our spot," she said gravely. "And now they're coming straight-straight-straight toward us. *All of them.*"

THE FACTORY FIGHTS BACK

"All of them?" Ozzie asked the moto. "What do you mean, *all of them*?"

"Ninety-nine thousand, three hundred and seventy-eight motos," Scoot relayed. "That's every moto in Moton. Unless you count me. Then it's ninety-nine thousand, three hundred and seventy-nine."

"How did they detect us?" Aunt Temperance wondered.

"They detected *me*," Scoot said. "They're not very pleasey-pleased that you switched me on."

"We could always switch you off," Fidget grumbled.

"I think it's time we find that door to Untaar," Cho

announced. "Scoot, do you know the way to the station?"

"Nope," the moto replied, her head swiveling around on its base. "But all I need is to find an interface terminal, pluggy-plug in my connectors, and I will."

An alarm began to blare, prompting everyone to rush to the edge of the building—even Scoot. Every light on the dome was flashing red. If it had looked like a pimple before, now it was one bursting with motos. They were coming in endless columns, clicking and clacking through the scrap from every direction, filling the junkyard with a thunderous din.

Ozzie shook his head in disbelief. He had been contemplating the idea of using Captain Traxx's beacon, but now, staring at the approaching army, he knew there was no way they'd be able to survive until her arrival. The motos might be slow, but they were also relentless.

"And now there's thousands of them," he thought out loud.

"Ninety-nine thousand, three hundred and seventy-eight, actually," Tug supplied helpfully.

Cho craned his neck for a clearer view. "I've never seen them behave like this." He turned back to the group. "Our escape just became a lot more difficult." He pinched the bridge of his nose in thought. "We need a change of plan. Ozzie and Fidget, you can fly out on Tug. We'll meet—"

"No way," Fidget interrupted. "I thought I made it

clear: We stick together." She shook her blender at them. "I have my essential item. I can handle these oversized tin cans."

"You can't fight the entire moto army with just a blender," Ozzie argued.

"We need something more practical," Aunt Temperance agreed. "Not even the rain seems to slow them down."

"Motos can handle rain," Scoot explained. "But thicky-thick is terrible."

"Thicky-thick?" Ozzie said. "What do you mean? Like mud?"

"No, like cement or glue," Scoot replied.

"Oh!" Tug exclaimed, his fur turning an excited blue. "We need Gonzo Glue. It's so cool. I saw a story about it on the TV, and—"

Aunt Temperance cut him off with a groan. "It doesn't matter. I didn't pack any glue."

"Hmm," Cho murmured, fishing his canteen from his belt. "What about Arborellian nectar? It's pretty sticky."

"Let's see!" Scoot said. After taking the canteen from Cho, she undid the lid and poured some on the floor. "It's going to work okeydokey!"

"So, what are we going to do?" Fidget wondered crossly. "Pour our way out of here?"

"Oh—I know!" Scoot whooped, pirouetting with the

canteen. She rolled over to Fidget and stuck out a hand toward the blender. "May I take a looky-look?"

Fidget glanced skeptically at Aunt Temperance, then passed over the appliance. Scoot plugged one of her hands into the base, and the blade instantly began to whir.

"You can power my blender?!" Aunt Temperance exclaimed.

"To be precise," Fidget said, "it's your engagement ring that's powering the blender. It's powering Bucket-Brain here, so . . ."

"Just need to make some adjustments." Scoot hummed as she clicked open a panel on her belly—*she has secret compartments!* Ozzie marveled—and reached inside to pull out a length of hose. Then, using her surprisingly dexterous fingers, she set to work on the blender.

"What are you doing?!" Aunt Temperance shrieked. "That's a hundred-dollar appliance you're destroying!"

"Aunt T, if we don't bust our way out of here, it won't matter how expensive your blender is," Ozzie said.

"Besides," Tug added, "you can get a better blender. I saw this one story on the—"

"Not now, Tug!" Aunt Temperance scolded.

Scoot extended one of her fingers and the tip began to glow hot and orange. Then, using it like a torch, she melted a round hole in the side of the pitcher and inserted the canteen so that its endless supply of nectar could spill inside. After briskly adding a switch to regulate flow, Scoot raised the blender triumphantly into the air.

"Doo-do-do-doo!" she kazooed.

"Did you just turn my blender into . . . a gun?!" Aunt Temperance cried.

"Ooh! Try testing it on me," Tug said.

"You're not a moto," Scoot told the skyger.

"Try it anyway," Tug implored.

Scoot obliged, firing a blast of nectar in Tug's direction. The skyger opened his giant maw and gulped it down. "Delicious," he purred, his fur turning a satisfied orange.

Cho chuckled. "We might have a chance now. Come on, everyone." He led them to the stairs, but he came to a halt before taking the first step. There were motos heading up from below.

"Action time!" Scoot proclaimed. She gave her blender gun a theatrical twirl, then bumbled down the steps on her wheel, firing and squealing in delight the whole way down.

Fidget rolled her eyes. "She's enjoying using that blender way too much."

"Oh, and you didn't?" Ozzie asked.

"Whatever," Fidget said. "Come on!"

They raced down the stairs to see every moto in the vicinity coated in a thick layer of nectar, their eyes flickering in distress and their limbs twitching like dying insects.

"A-lert! A-ler . . . ," came their gargled speech—then they sputtered to a stop.

"It worked!" Ozzie cheered.

"Six motos sabotaged," Scoot reported. "Ninety-nine thousand, three hundred and seventy-two remaining."

"Good work, Scoot," Cho congratulated her as he used the tip of his sword to prod a sticky moto out of the way. "Now, let's find that station."

The misfit moto gave a salute, then began zipping through the debris, Ozzie and the others hard on her trail. At first, motos attacked them from every direction, but Scoot never stopped firing.

"Ninety-nine thousand, three hundred and forty-two motos remaining," she called out. "Ninety-nine thousand, three hundred and forty-one! Ninety-nine thousand, three hundred and forty! Ninety-nine thousand, three hundred and thirty-nine . . ."

"That canteen really better be bottomless," Ozzie said between panting breaths.

"Yeah, or we're dead meat," Fidget added.

They were soon able to outpace the motos, leaving behind the scrapyard and returning to a functioning part of the city, where the factories still rumbled in ceaseless operation.

Scoot braked in front of a large console. "I can connecty here!" she declared. She plugged a finger into a socket and her eyes started flickering rapidly, as if she was downloading information. "Oh! I found a shorty-short!"

"Do you mean a shortcut?" Aunt Temperance asked, but the moto had already raced off.

They bolted through the labyrinth of machines, Scoot taking every turn with purpose—until she rounded a silo and screeched to a halt.

"Motos!" she shouted.

Ozzie grimaced. The robots were attacking from everywhere. It was like Scoot had said; every single one of them had zeroed in on their location. But why? What had upset them so much? Not even entering their base had provoked this sort of response. Ozzie's gaze wandered toward Scoot. The only thing that had changed was that they now had a moto on their side. A very particular moto.

It's you, he realized as he chased Scoot down a different aisle. *Why are* you *so important to them?*

Every path, every attempted escape route, led to the same result: more motos. Scoot and the blender simply couldn't keep up. Suddenly, there was nowhere else to run. They were cornered against a conveyor belt, a whole new set of motos closing in on them. Ozzie could tell they were new—they had strange attachments at the ends of their arms, like pipe barrels.

"Wait a minute," Ozzie said. "Are those—"

"Duck!" Fidget screamed, grabbing Ozzie by the top of the head and forcing him down. An enormous bullet whistled overhead.

"We're in trouble," Cho uttered, sliding beneath the conveyor belt as more bullets began to fly. "Everyone, under here!"

But Ozzie didn't follow him, despite the flying bullets. He had suddenly noticed something about the conveyor belt: It was carrying heavy crucibles full of rocks. Enormous metal pincers were reaching down to unload the casks of ore—then, once relieved of their burden, the empty crucibles were placed back on the conveyor, which then curved and headed in the opposite direction.

"I think this is the same belt we followed into the city!" Ozzie said excitedly. "We can just climb aboard and ride it all the way to the station—too bad it isn't quicker."

"You want me to juice it up?!" Scoot asked, her eyes flashing excitedly. "No problem!"

She reared to her full height, fired a stream of nectar at the approaching motos to provide cover, then zipped over to the control panel at the side of the conveyor. She brought the belt to a stop, then vaulted herself into the nearest crucible. She was close enough to the console that her long arms could still access it. "All aboard!" she directed. "We'll be out of here in a whirly-whirl."

Ozzie and Fidget clambered into the crucible in front of Scoot, but there was no room left for Tug, so he bounded into the one ahead of them.

Scoot wiggled her chunky fingers over the control panel like a magician preparing to perform. "I'll program it not to stop until we reach Untaar—and plug in a little cheaty-cheat so the motos can't turn it off."

"Are we sure this is a good idea?" Aunt Temperance asked, even as the next wave of motos began firing.

Cho had already climbed into the crucible at the head of the line. "I don't think we have a choice," he told her, extending her a hand.

Aunt Temperance slung her bag into the crucible and, ignoring his hand, leaped gracefully inside.

"Start us up, Scoot!" Ozzie cried.

"How fasty-fast?"

"Moderate but expedient!" Aunt Temperance replied.

"Unless there's a setting for 'get us out of here,'" Fidget quipped.

More bullets soared, puncturing a tank overhead that began hissing hot yellow steam.

"Just punch it!" Cho shouted.

"Okeydokey!"

The conveyor shot off like a roller coaster at top speed—except in roller coasters, Ozzie thought woozily, they buckled you in. His eyes teared up as the factory world whipped past them. They took a corner so quickly that the crucible he and Fidget were in tilted up on one edge, like a car on two wheels, then rocked to the opposite edge before slamming back down on the conveyor. Ozzie managed a glance at Fidget; her fingers were white at the knuckles as she held on for dear life. She leaned over the edge as if she was about to puke herself purple, but Ozzie threw his arms around her waist and reeled her back inside just as a giant mechanical arm zoomed past, narrowly missing taking her head off.

They didn't even have time for a sigh of relief—they were tossed against the far wall, and Ozzie realized the conveyor had started going upward, but without losing any speed. Once it flattened out, they were so far up that Ozzie couldn't even see the factory floor beyond the haze and layers of machinery.

More mechanical arms thrashed around them, as if purposely trying to snatch them. Then it occurred to Ozzie that was *exactly* what they were trying to do. *Maybe the motos can't shut down the conveyor,* he thought, *but they've mobilized the factory against us!*

Ozzie saw Tug's crucible whip around a corner in front of them—but then he lost sight of him completely. It took a moment for Ozzie to register that the container he and Fidget were in had sailed right off the belt.

"Hang on!" he screamed as they plummeted downward.

They crashed onto another conveyor belt and continued trundling along. Ozzie exchanged a terrified glance with Fidget before looking up. Somewhere up there in the green smog was the conveyor that they were supposed to be on with Aunt Temperance and the others.

How are we going to find them again? Ozzie worried.

"Ozzie!" Fidget shrieked.

A giant metal hammer was roaring toward them. It clobbered the side of their crucible, sending it spinning off the conveyor belt. Down they plunged, through the network of machinery. Ozzie squeezed his eyes shut, bracing for impact—but instead of hitting rock-solid ground, they landed with a soft plunk.

"Huh?" Ozzie groaned. He was completely disoriented, flipped upside down in the crucible. Fidget pulled him to his feet, and he saw her face twist in an expression of disgust. "What is i—"

The stench walloped him like a fist: a mixture of hard-boiled eggs, burnt hair, and gasoline. He peered over the edge of the container and saw that they had dropped into a gray channel of wastewater. Though, Ozzie considered, you really couldn't call it water. It was so disgustingly thick that their heavy crucible hadn't even sunk.

Yet.

"I think this is the same gunk that we crossed to reach Cho's hideout," Ozzie said.

"Well," Fidget said, "right now the only place we're going is *down*."

Already, the crucible had started to tip, one side of its rim dipping below the surface and allowing a chunky burble of sludge to ooze inside. It continued to tilt, so precariously that they were forced to scramble over the edge and find safety on its exterior side, which had now become the top.

"It's going to be like drowning in cement pudding," Ozzie said as they shuffled about, trying to balance their weight and slow their descent.

"*Toxic* cement pudding," Fidget added. "Look on the bright side. We might die from the smell before we drown."

Ozzie desperately surveyed the banks of the channel, which were smooth slopes of asphalt. "Maybe we can try to swim for—"

He saw the mechanical arm at the very last minute. It swung down and plucked him from the top of the crucible like he was a toy in a machine at an arcade.

"Hey! Don't leave me!" Fidget shouted.

The robot claw dropped Ozzie and he landed on his back, so hard that it knocked the breath out of him. When he groggily lifted his head, it was to find himself on a conveyor belt running parallel to the river. This one was made of grooved metal, like the stairs of an escalator, and it was carrying heaps of rock rubble. Ozzie pulled himself to his elbows and saw Fidget in the distance, still standing on the crucible—though there was hardly anything left of it. She was dancing on her tiptoes, trying to avoid the ravenous sludge.

Have to help her! Ozzie thought. He tried scrambling to his feet, only to be tugged back down with a jerk—his shoelace had gotten snagged in the toothy metal slats beneath him and now he was being reeled along like a fish on a hook. As he frantically tried to kick himself free, he managed a desperate glance toward Fidget, but she was even farther away now—and up to her ankles in gunk. What was worse, he wondered: Having your feet devoured by a conveyor belt or by acid?

Then something sharp slammed into his shoulder from behind, causing him to spasm in pain. He twisted around.

And screamed.

He was staring straight into a set of metal jaws, grinding everything into oblivion. Pebbles and grit—the spit-back from the rocks being pulverized—were pelting him. He yanked even harder on his foot and threw one last look at the river—only to see that Fidget's crucible had sunk.

She's gone, Ozzie thought. *And so am I.*

17

CROSSING THE WILD LANDS

Suddenly, Ozzie's shoelace snapped. He toppled backward into the toothy throat of the grinder and—felt himself flying through the air.

Something had him by his shirt collar, but only for a moment before it hurled him forward and he landed atop a gigantic pipe. He nearly slid right off its rounded surface, but then, somehow, Aunt Temperance was right beside him, steadying him with a firm hand. Her other hand clutched the frayed end of an electrical cable, which stretched into the mechanical clutter above.

Ozzie gaped at her. "Did you just save me? Fidget's—"

"Safe, too. Get on my back—now!"

That was the last thing Ozzie wanted to do. It was embarrassing enough to have been rescued by an aunt who, up until recently, had been known mostly for her ability to dispatch a cup of tea, but now she expected him to ride piggyback like a three-year-old?

"I said NOW!" Aunt Temperance commanded.

Ozzie looked up to see an enormous mechanical blade slicing toward them, and every self-conscious thought evacuated his mind like water down a drain. He leaped onto Aunt Temperance's back and she launched into the air, barely avoiding the ax. She swung them to a nearby catwalk, snatched another cable, then vaulted onward, like an orangutan through an industrial jungle.

Before long, they were dangling over the original conveyor. Ozzie could see the empty crucibles zooming along below them, but the conveyor was moving so fast, the casks were spaced much farther apart.

"Get ready!" Aunt Temperance warned—and then, after taking a moment to gauge the timing, she dropped them into one of the empty vessels.

Ozzie stared at her in bewilderment. He had spent his life thinking Aunt Temperance was the type of person who was hanging by a thread. But it turned out she had actually been hanging by a trapeze swing, ready to perform death-defying stunts with perfect timing. "How . . . how can you do that?" he asked.

"More practice than you can imagine," Aunt Temperance told him. Her hair was wild, sticking out in every direction.

"Fidget—"

"Tug snatched her from the sludge, and I snatched you," Aunt Temperance told him.

"You flew through the air," Ozzie said. "Like a superhero."

Aunt Temperance coughed. "I don't think that's what makes you a hero."

"What, being able to *fly*?" Ozzie countered. That was exactly what made someone a superhero. He felt the sudden need to apologize to her, to tell her he was sorry for underestimating her. Even though he had seen her swing over the river to Cho's hideout, even though he knew she had rescued Fidget in the cosmic storm, he hadn't quite believed it until now.

"Why didn't you tell me?" he asked.

"About what?"

"Anything!" Ozzie blurted. "About the circus. About Mercurio. Why didn't you guys get married?"

Aunt Temperance swallowed. The conveyor had finally exited the city and now she turned her gaze to the vast landscape of rusted metal plates whipping past them. "My parents were against it," she said at last. "We planned to elope, but . . ."

"What?" Ozzie prodded.

"My father came and stole me away. Mercurio and I were supposed to meet at a prearranged place, but by the time I managed to escape through a window and get there, I . . . I . . . I was too late. Mercurio was gone." Aunt Temperance released a long sigh. "He must have thought I changed my mind."

"Didn't you ever try to find him?" Ozzie asked.

"He vanished," Aunt Temperance said simply. "And I had . . . other things to deal with. Life."

Ozzie pondered her explanation, but it didn't make much sense to him. Why had she given up? Or, at the very least, why hadn't she gone back to her job in the circus? It would have been way better than her tedious office job. He had so many questions, he didn't know which one to ask first. He settled on, "What do you mean, Mercurio vanished? Why didn't he come looking for *you*?"

"I don't know," Aunt Temperance admitted. "I spent a long time asking myself that very question. Then a longer time trying to ignore it. But . . ."

"But what?"

Aunt Temperance was still staring out at the metal landscape. "What if pain is important?" she asked.

That made zero sense to Ozzie. "Aunt T, maybe—"

The conveyor abruptly sputtered to a halt. Ozzie and Aunt Temperance looked at each other in surprise.

"I guess the motos figured out how to stop this thing after all," Ozzie said.

The conveyor juddered and started rumbling backward.

"Get out!" Aunt Temperance exclaimed, heaving Ozzie over the side of the crucible. "Hurry!"

Ozzie landed roughly on the metal ground, followed by Aunt Temperance, who arrived with considerably more grace. Ozzie stared at her, so many questions still percolating inside of him. "Aunt T," he began, "why didn't you—"

"Come on," she cut him off. "I guess we'll have to walk the rest of the way."

Ozzie knew that tone. It meant she didn't want to talk about her past anymore—and he knew better than to push it. She had already turned and set off across the desolate landscape, so he squared his shoulders and followed her.

When it comes to Aunt T, every answer just leads to more questions, he pondered.

Only fifteen minutes later, the station came into sight, and there were the others, waiting on the steps.

"Creator!" Scoot squealed, wheeling up to Ozzie. "I thought I lost you again."

"Are you okay?" Tug wondered, after licking Ozzie's cheek with his sandpaper tongue.

Ozzie nodded as Fidget came over and punched him in

the shoulder. "Ow! What was that for?"

"Why didn't you take your shoe off?" she demanded.

Ozzie glanced down at his shoe and its frayed shoe-lace. She made a good point, but he wasn't about to tell her that. "I didn't want to lose it?" he replied somewhat lamely.

"You nearly lost a lot more," she retorted. Then she hugged him—which, Ozzie thought, kind of defeated the purpose of the punch.

"Hey, what happened to *your* shoes?" he asked, staring down at Fidget's feet. They were bare and blistered.

"That gunk ate right through them," she said.

"I have a spare pair of flats in my bag," Aunt Temperance told the princess as she began digging through her things. "Our feet are close to the same size, so they should fit you. And let's get some salve on those sores."

"Thanks, Aunt T," Fidget said, sitting down on the steps.

As soon as Aunt Temperance's ministrations were complete, they climbed the stairs and entered the abandoned station. It had been less than a day since they had arrived here, Ozzie realized, but it sure felt longer than that. They followed the path of the conveyors through the open doorway and into the tunnel beyond. Unlike most of the portals Ozzie had seen during his time at Zoone

Station, this one was somber and quiet; the only sound came from the conveyor belts. The track itself wasn't moving at all, and the skyscape was a swirl of unusually dull colors.

Fidget caught Ozzie scowling. "What did you expect? It leads to the wild lands."

After a half hour's trek, they saw a light shining from the end of the tunnel. The door was propped open, just like the one on the Creon side, so that the conveyors could trundle through.

"Do you smell that?" Tug declared, inhaling deeply. "Fresh air!"

The skyger bounded ahead, through the doorway. Ozzie and the others followed to find him sitting on a wide plateau of rock, gulping in breaths of air.

"This must be what it's like to smell Breathe-Eazzy," Tug announced as he flexed his wings, then bounded off the ledge.

Tug circling against a backdrop of blue sky should have been a joyful sight, but Ozzie couldn't help frowning. Yes, the skies were clear, but the landscape below was devastated. Round hills stretched into the horizon; they might have once been beautiful, Ozzie thought, but now they were gray and pocked with tree stumps.

"There used to be trees here," Cho murmured, coming

up behind Ozzie. "So many trees. It's been wiped clean."

"They're not quite done with this place yet," Fidget said.

She gestured to the conveyor belts and Ozzie's gaze followed their route down a slope and into a gaping hole in the ground.

"It's a mine shaft," Cho said. "The motos have harvested the forest; now they'll take the minerals."

"Fifty-eight motos in this world," Scoot reported, her antennae rising and retracting. "But they're all deepy-deep."

"You mean underground?" Fidget asked.

"That's right! Up-down-up-up-down."

"Why do you always say that?" Fidget grumbled. "You really do have a loose circuit in your head."

"It's a signal," Scoot said. "Creator told me never to forget it." She swiveled her head expectantly toward Ozzie.

"Don't ask me," Ozzie said. "I keep telling you, I'm not the one who built you."

"The motos have detected me," Scoot said, her antennae cycling again. "But they move slowy-slow. They're hours away."

"Let's keep it that way," Cho advised as he began down the slope. "We head due east. Come on, everyone; at least the empty hills will make it easier to chart our way."

"Da-dah-da-dooo!" Scoot trumpeted.

"Keep it down, Sprocket-Brain," Fidget snapped as she picked her way down the hill.

"Oh!" Scoot cried. "I like that! Can I be Sprocket-Brain, Creator?"

"NO!" Ozzie said firmly.

Ozzie was not used to trekking through the wilderness. He and Aunt Temperance had once walked twenty blocks after her car had sputtered to a halt on the way home from an art gallery, but that journey had involved paved sidewalks lined with cafés, benches, and shady trees. In Untaar, there were just cleanly shorn stumps and a sun that beat down on him like it had a personal grudge to settle.

They traveled for three days across the bleak landscape. Every time they rounded a hill, Ozzie thought they might see an end to the clear-cut and find the start of untouched forest. But the motos' destruction reached across the entire land. They encountered no animals or birds, just the odd butterfly that decided that Ozzie's hair was the perfect place to perch.

They scavenged for mushrooms or berries when they could, but mostly they survived by drinking from Cho's canteen. They spent their nights beneath rocky overhangs or in caves carved into the hills.

It was in one such cave that they found the message.

Using the wood litter left behind by the lumber operation, Scoot had built a small fire in the opening of the cave, and the flames picked out a few lines etched into the rocky walls.

"Hieroglyphs of some sort," Aunt Temperance guessed. "I wonder what they say." She fished her flashlight from her pack and shone it directly on the words.

"A message from an Untaari clan," Cho said, tracing his hand along one of the lines.

"You can read this language?" Aunt Temperance asked in surprise.

Cho nodded. "My homeland borders Untaar; our languages are similar."

"What does it say, Cho?" Ozzie asked.

"It speaks of a great tragedy," Cho translated soberly. "A 'metal scourge.'"

"The motos," Fidget gasped.

Cho nodded. "According to this, many of the Untaari were taken by the metal men. Stolen. In desperation, those who remained—the survivors—went into hiding. I'm not sure what became of this clan. There's no more to the message."

"The people are gone," Fidget murmured. "And the animals, too."

"Even the tusk bear," Cho added mournfully. "They

used to roam these hills. I've seen them; magnificent creatures."

Tug slumped to the ground. Even in the faint light, Ozzie could see his fur fading to a gloomy gray. "Just to tell you," the skyger said, "on the TV, the stories have much happier endings."

"Yeah, well, those stories aren't real," Fidget retorted.

"I know," Tug admitted with a woeful twitch of his tail. "But I wish they were."

18

HUNTERS OF MAGIC

They set out early the next morning, all of them irritable after another night on the hard ground—all of them except Scoot, who didn't require sleep, and Tug, who didn't seem to care where he snoozed.

"The hills are flattening out," Aunt Temperance observed an hour into their trek. "The trees have been harvested here, too, but the stumps are thinner. They must be a different variety."

"How fascinating," Fidget remarked sarcastically. "Look, everyone. This type of dead tree is different than the other dead trees."

"She's just trying to point out that the landscape is changing," Ozzie said.

Fidget snorted. "And I'm just trying to point out it doesn't matter."

"It mattered to the trees," Tug chimed in.

That put an end to the argument, and Ozzie was left alone with his thoughts. They weren't exactly good ones. With every step, they were getting closer to Ru-Valdune, the place he had heard so much about from Cho. The place where the captain had lost his fingers. Gotten his scar. And been expelled by his clan. Ozzie could sense that these things were on Cho's mind, too. The normally jovial captain didn't utter a word until they arrived at a wide and roaring river, late in the morning.

"The boundary between Untaar and Ru-Valdune," Cho said grimly.

Ozzie stared at the bleak landscape on the other side of the river. Ru-Valdune looked like a desert, sparsely covered with trees, scrub vegetation, and towering rock formations that jutted upward like crooked bones.

"Did the motos get their claws on it already?" Ozzie wondered.

Cho gave him a mirthless smile. "It's not the motos' doing, lad. Rocks and cacti: That's Ru-Valdune. We'll follow the river north, to Yo-Kando. We can safely pass through its mountain valleys, then snake back down to the Land of Thrak. That's where we'll find a doorway out of the wild lands."

"Wouldn't it be quicker to cross here?" Ozzie asked.

Cho emphatically shook his head. "Ru-Valdune is too dangerous."

"It can't be more dangerous than Moton," Fidget argued.

"That's the territory of the Nedra across the river," Cho said with a passionate gesture. "If their sabermage—"

"Sabermage?" Aunt Temperance cut in.

"The member of the clan who hunts magic," Ozzie explained.

"He will smell your magic," Cho told her.

Aunt Temperance stiffened. "I don't have any magic."

"I can smell it," Cho insisted. "On you, on Ozzie—all of you."

"Cho," Ozzie began, "why—"

"I can't tell you why," the captain said with an uncharacteristic hint of frustration in his voice. "Just that I can smell it. And if I can, so will the Nedra's sabermage."

Aunt Temperance crossed her arms. "Can't you negotiate our way across?"

"I am Y'Orrick," Cho said quietly. "Banished."

"Why?"

Ozzie groaned at her bluntness. "I've told you before,

Aunt T. Cho abandoned the ways of the Nedra. They think a sabermage gets his magic by stealing it from others."

"Oh," Aunt Temperance said, slowly comprehending. "What you really mean is by *killing* them. The sabermage would kill *us*." She narrowed her gaze at Cho. "Your people are barbarians!"

"No, they're not," Fidget spoke up. "Most of the Valdune clans changed their customs eons ago."

"But not the Nedra," Aunt Temperance said.

"No," Cho conceded. "Not the Nedra. Which is why we must take the long way."

"But, Cho," Fidget said, "shouldn't we try warning your people? Or help them? They can't defeat the mo—"

"They will not accept our help," Cho cut her off. "Let's remember: We're trying to save Zoone. If we can do that, we save the entire multiverse—and that includes Ru-Valdune."

He turned and began marching north along the riverbank. Aunt Temperance hesitated, arms still crossed.

"It's not true, you know," Ozzie told her. "A sabermage *doesn't* need to kill anyone. Cho has magic in his sword, but he doesn't hunt for it. He never has. He just is . . ."

"What?" Aunt Temperance prodded.

"Magical," Ozzie finished. "That's what I think anyway."

"Me, too," Tug added. "Just to tell you, I've known him my whole life."

Aunt Temperance stared at Cho for what felt like an interminable moment before finally exhaling a long breath. "I guess we've got another long march ahead of us. But, *just to tell you*, I could really use a cup of tea."

Near midafternoon, they came upon a wooden bridge stretching across the river. It had no rails or ornamentation, but it did look sturdy. And new.

"I don't remember this being here," Cho said, tentatively stepping onto the bridge. "That's Yo-Kando on the other side, but . . ."

"The motos built it, didn't they?" Ozzie guessed.

Cho slowly nodded. "This looks like machine-made construction. Motos can't swim; perhaps they built this bridge to aid their invasion."

Scoot's antennae telescoped up and down. "Zero motos in the vicinity," she reported.

"Good; let's cross," Cho decided.

He led the way onto the bridge and Scoot brought up the rear. Ozzie kept to the center of the planks, away from the open sides. He had been known to trip—literally—on a dime and, even though it wasn't a long drop to the river, the water was swift and swirling. Plus, he could hear the telltale rumbling of a nearby waterfall.

"It's called Unta's Roar," Cho said when he saw Ozzie's expression. "You don't want to go over it."

"Ozzie?" Tug said, ears twitching. "Someone's coming."

"Motos?" They weren't even halfway across the bridge.

"No, I think it's people!"

A gigantic rock hurtled from overhead and crashed into the bridge, splintering the wood at Cho's feet. For a moment, the captain teetered at the edge of the gaping hole in front of him, arms flailing and reaching in vain for the nonexistent railing. Then he toppled through and into the rapids below.

Ozzie watched in horror as the captain was swept toward the falls. There was nothing for Cho to cling to—not a rock, a branch, not anything. Ozzie turned to Tug, but the skyger was already in a crouch, preparing to launch.

That was as far as he got. Something whipped past Ozzie's head; he saw a flash of metal, then heard Tug caterwaul in pain. The skyger collapsed, one of his wings pinned to the deck of the bridge by a long spear. Screaming, Ozzie rushed to the cat's side, wrapped his hands around the shaft of the weapon, and began trying to frantically yank it free.

"You're okay, you're okay," Ozzie murmured. But there were feathers everywhere—and blood. Lots of blood.

"It's the Nedra!" Fidget screamed.

Ozzie jumped to his feet and whirled to see a pack of men emerge out of the landscape. They were carrying an assortment of weapons, including boulder-sized rocks. Ozzie couldn't even comprehend how much strength it would take to throw one of them so far. That was super-hero strength.

But the Nedra looked more like Vikings than super-heroes. Some of them were bare-chested, with muscles bulging across their limbs and torsos and, as they approached, Ozzie could see that they wore their hair in topknots and braids, like Cho usually did. But that was where the similarities ended. They radiated hostility, the exact opposite of the captain.

"How—why are they here?" Ozzie panicked. "This isn't Ru-Valdune!"

"Look out!" Aunt Temperance cried as the warrior in the lead hurled another rock. Ozzie ducked, but the rock sailed over his head, striking Scoot in the belly with so much force that she went flying backward with a metallic scream. She spun off the bridge and back onto Untaari soil, where she slammed into a tall boulder.

"Ouchy . . . ouchy . . . ," the moto groaned, clutching at the giant dent in her body. Then her voice warbled to a halt and her eyes fizzled out. Ozzie could just make out her battery—Aunt Temperance's ring—sitting on the parched ground next to her. It had been knocked right out of her socket.

"W-we have to run," Aunt Temperance stammered. She was shaking like her blender on full nutritional-vitamin-shake mode.

But it was too late to run—the Nedra were already upon them. They pulled off Aunt Temperance's bag, kicked it aside, and quickly bound her wrists and ankles. Two others handled Fidget and Ozzie, tying them up and throwing them over their shoulders, while the rest of the warriors converged upon Tug. Ozzie watched helplessly as they wrenched the spear from the skyger's wing—causing the cat to wail in agony—and bound him to a long pole.

Ozzie managed to steal a last look behind him before they were ferried into the scrub. Scoot was lying against the boulder, rigid and dormant. And in the roiling river beyond, there was no trace of Cho.

I'm never going to complain about walking again, Ozzie thought as he bounced on the shoulder of the warrior spiriting him through the wilderness.

The Nedra were moving at such a hurried pace that Ozzie's stomach was in the air half the time—the other half, it was smacking against the warrior's shoulder. Ozzie knew that part of the shoulder wasn't called the blade—but as far as he was concerned, it should have been. Each time he landed against it, he felt like he was being stabbed in the gut.

Still, it was nothing compared to the pain he felt every time his mind wandered to thoughts of Cho. Ozzie could imagine finding his way back to Scoot and plugging in her battery to bring her back to life. But Cho had disappeared over the waterfall. There was no sort of battery to bring him back.

The Nedra didn't stop to rest, not even when they crossed into the deserts of Ru-Valdune. They simply carried on beneath the shadows of the towering, bone-shaped rocks. Eventually, they arrived at a mountainside with a peculiar cave mouth at its base. And "mouth" was the key word; the entrance had been skillfully carved into the enormous skull of a dragon, with blunted rock teeth jutting from the top and bottom. They were so realistic that they made Ozzie shiver as he was carried beneath them and into the winding slot canyon beyond. Strange pillars curved up on each side.

It's like entering a dragon's throat, Ozzie thought.

It was a long throat—so long that Ozzie drifted off. The next thing he knew, he was being lashed to some sort of column. The men prowled away, leaving him to blink and look around.

They were in an arena, and not the good kind where

players kick a ball back and forth. This was more like a gladiator pit. The ground in the middle was sand, but beyond was a ring of steps hewn from the rock and radiating outward. More warriors were standing at the perimeter, like guards. Beyond the steps was a continuous wall of rock, dotted with doorways and windows. A line of more pointed columns, like the one Ozzie was tied to, curled up the rock face.

Is this where Cho grew up? Ozzie wondered. It was hard to imagine children in a place like this, though; as he glanced around, he realized there were no children about—no women, either. *Maybe the Nedra keep them hidden away*, Ozzie thought. *So they won't see what's going to happen to us.*

He turned his attention to the others. Aunt Temperance and Fidget were bound to the pillars on either side of him, while Tug was sprawled on the ground in front of Ozzie, his feet hobbled by rope. The skyger's fur was a sickly green color, matted with prickly burrs and thorns. His wounded wing, crusted with dry blood, hung awkwardly at his side.

"Tug?" Ozzie asked hoarsely, his throat dry as sand. "Are you okay?"

"I think my wing is broken," the skyger mewled.

"I wish I could help you," Aunt Temperance said sympathetically. "I have a first aid kit in my bag, but those troglodytes left it on the bridge."

"What now?" Ozzie wondered.

"The ritual will start soon," Fidget replied. "You know, the one where the sabermage siphons the magic out through our nostrils and we all die an excruciatingly painful death?"

"Let's try to be positive," Aunt Temperance recommended.

"Fine," Fidget retorted. "I'm one hundred percent positive that we're going to die in this pit of death. Don't you think it's kind of hard to be upbeat when we're surrounded by petrified bones?"

Ozzie grimaced. "Bones? What bones?"

"We're tied to them, Quogglebrain."

"What?" Ozzie cried. "That wasn't a carving where we came in? It was an actual skull?"

"Yes," Fidget insisted. "And the bones here are part of the animal's rib cage. Those ones going up the wall? That was the tail. This entire complex was built around the skeleton."

"That's . . . impossible," Aunt Temperance stammered. "These can't be rib bones. Nothing is that . . . *gargantuan.*"

"Not even dinosaurs," Ozzie added.

"I don't know what a dinosaur is," Fidget said, "but legends say that dragons the size of mountains used to roam Ru-Valdune. They were peaceful creatures. Herbivores. Until the sabermages hunted them to extinction."

"Cho was a sabermage," Tug spoke up. "But he wouldn't do that."

"No," Fidget agreed. "Not Cho."

Ozzie didn't say anything. There was a question hanging heavy in the air, one he still didn't want to consider.

Aunt Temperance addressed it anyway. "He's okay. He survived the river. He'll come for us."

"What does it matter?" Fidget lamented. "Cho can't fight a whole clan."

Ozzie tugged again at his bindings. Deep down in his front pocket was the beacon given to him by Captain Traxx. If this wasn't the time to call her, then he didn't know when would be. But unless he could free himself, there was no way to reach the device.

This is why we should have just gone to Zoone, like I wanted, Ozzie thought, which only sent him further into a downward spiral. If everyone had listened to him, done things *his* way, then Tug wouldn't be injured, Scoot wouldn't be lying in a heap, and Cho would still be . . .

A thunderous cacophony blasted through the arena: a mixture of beating drums, clashing gongs, and deafening horns. Ozzie suddenly realized the sun was dipping behind the wall of the city; the arena was growing darker by the minute.

More clansmen began to emerge from the doorways in the rock, striding down the steps to join the other warriors in the arena. Some of them carried torches, while others were playing the instruments causing the riotous din.

When the noise finally came to a reverberating stop, every man turned toward a large archway in the rock face. A figure appeared, prompting the warriors to hoot and cheer: "Ku T'en Nedra! Ku T'en Nedra!"

Even in the faint light, Ozzie could see that the man was old. The top of his head was bald, shining with skin that was mottled bleach white and livid red. Below, gray hair fell upon his shoulders in long shanks and braids. His nose was pierced with large white tusks that protruded at right angles from each nostril. There was little to be seen of his body; it was obscured by a cloak of black, red-tipped fur.

"He must be their chieftain," Fidget said. "*Ku T'en Nedra*. But I think he's their sabermage, too. And that means . . ."

"The ritual is about to start," Ozzie finished for her.

Ku swept down the steps and sprang into the arena like a leopard. He prowled in front of Ozzie's bone pillar, eyes darting between him and the others. Now that he was closer, Ozzie noticed that he was wearing a necklace of teeth. Some were long and sharp, like those of a wolf or a dragon. But some, Ozzie realized queasily, were human.

His gaze wandered up to the chieftain's face, and he was startled to see just how similar to Cho he looked. He was older, more haggard, and his skin was pale as chalk, but he had the same chiseled cheekbones, the same strong chin. The difference was in his eyes. Cho's eyes were soft and brown, like a warm cup of cocoa on a winter's morning; Ku's were gray, like hard slate.

The chieftain strutted up close, narrowed those eyes at Ozzie, and inhaled deeply. "Ah," he murmured in satisfaction. Lifting his chin high, he began to speak to his warriors, his voice rumbling across the arena like a roll of thunder. "Nedra, clan of Valdune, children of steel!" he boomed. "How many weeks and months have we yearned for the precious nectar of magic? The drought of enchanted creatures has sent us spiraling into desperation. Into starvation. But, at last, Valdune smiles at us from the heavens."

"Well, not *all* of us," Ozzie heard Fidget mutter as an excited stir emanated from the assembly of clansmen.

"Tonight, we shall taste the blood of magic," the chieftain continued, licking his lips. "Tonight, we shall not know thirst. We shall not know hunger. We shall not know weakness. TONIGHT, WE FEAST."

The clansmen erupted into a raucous cheer, hammering their drums and smashing their gongs.

"What's going on?!" Aunt Temperance asked desperately after the warriors' clamor had faded. "I thought only the sabermage consumed magic. Not the entire clan!"

"That's what Cho told me," Ozzie managed to reply. "This isn't right!"

Ku whirled on him with a brandished fist. His hand and wrist were ornamented with jewelry, though it definitely wasn't the kind you'd find lying around your aunt's apartment. This jewelry was savage, consisting of knife rings and a bracelet edged with blades. The chieftain's hand was as weaponized as a moto's.

And now that hand was raised above Ozzie, ready to slice him open.

THE DUEL OF THE VALDUNE

All the blood rushed to Ozzie's head. He couldn't explain what his legs were doing—maybe an impression of a pair of wet noodles. If not for being tied to the bone pillar, he would have collapsed. He squeezed his eyes shut, heard Aunt Temperance scream—and then the chieftain started laughing.

Ozzie opened his eyes and stared in bewilderment at the chortling man.

"You?!" Ku heckled. "You're the man of this group? Not much of one."

Ozzie blinked. He had heard similar insults from the boys at school—hearing it from Ku snapped Ozzie out of his terror, at least momentarily. Because Ku might have the slice-and-dice costume, but when you stripped it all away, he was basically just another bully, the kind who thought you were only a real man if you swaggered, spat, and punched.

How did Cho ever fit in here? Ozzie wondered. Just the thought of the captain filled Ozzie with despair—but it also served to remind him of courage. Emboldened, Ozzie drew a deep breath, fixed his eyes on Ku, and said, "What about you?"

The chieftain glowered. "The *man* speaks. What did you say?"

"What about you?" Ozzie repeated. "You're going against the laws of the Valdune—"

"What do you know of the laws of my people?" Ku spat. "The law is *my* law, the law is—"

"I know enough!" Ozzie cried. "I know Cho Y'Orrick."

Ku's face flushed hot and red. "Do you? Then you know what his name means: Lost. Alone. *Without clan.* He should have taken my place as sabermage long ago. Instead, he abandoned us. Now these *metal* men are coming, encroaching upon our territory. More than ever, we need magic. Our survival depends upon it."

"You're wrong," Ozzie said, wriggling in his restraints. "Killing us won't help you. The motos aren't alive. Your sword won't stop them, no matter how much magic it has."

"He's right," Fidget added. "We've seen them. We know how they work."

Ku pointed at Fidget with his bladed hand. "Silence your tongue, girl. Lest you want me to slice it from your throat."

Tug whimpered. Aunt Temperance gasped. As for Fidget, she turned bright purple, but it wasn't from fear, Ozzie knew. It was anger. She looked like she was about to berate the sabermage, despite his warning. *She's such a princess!* Ozzie thought. *Not used to being ordered around.* He needed to jump in—quick.

"You're wrong!" he challenged, and Ku spun back toward him. "The whole point of a sabermage is to defend the people from *magic*. You're not under attack from magic! You—"

"Enough talk!" Ku growled, his eyes bulging with rage. "I will suck out your magic like marrow from a bone, I'll . . ."

He trailed off. There was a trilling in the distance, causing the chieftain's brow to furl. Ozzie glanced about in surprise; the noise sounded like a sick trumpet. Or maybe a dying accordion.

"It's Scoot!" Tug purred in recognition.

It was the most beautiful ugly sound Ozzie had ever

heard. He could see the uncertainty in Ku's face, a look that transformed into complete stupefaction when, a moment later, Scoot trundled through the opening of the dragon's throat and into the center of the arena. She was still issuing her kazoo sound, with one hand curled up to her mouth, but when she saw Ozzie, she raised it to give him an overly exuberant wave. She still had the dent in her belly, but Ozzie had to admit it wasn't out of place on the mishmash of scrap parts that made up her body. He noticed that she had found Aunt Temperance's bag—it was hanging off her round back.

"Hi, Creator!" Scoot called out cheerfully. "I'm here to rescue you!"

"Oh, great," Fidget muttered. "We're all going to die."

Ku thrust off his cloak, revealing arms taut with muscles and a chest crisscrossed with jagged, violent scars. He unsheathed his Valdune blade and charged toward the moto, only to stop after a few steps. A murmur of confusion rippled through the clansmen—everyone was staring at the chieftain's blade. It wasn't changing shape, like it was supposed to when brandished before an adversary.

"I told you," Ozzie called to Ku from his pillar. "Your sword has no power over motos."

Ku frowned, then continued approaching Scoot. The moto herself seemed nonplussed. A pipe telescoped out of the top of her hat and began gushing a thick cloud of white smoke, quickly obliterating the light of the Nedra torches. Ozzie couldn't even see Aunt Temperance or Fidget on either side of him. The next thing he knew, Scoot was right in front of him with her large, unblinking eyes and ever-present smile.

"Do you like my tricky-trick, Creator?" the moto asked. Using one of her welding fingers, Scoot started to burn through Ozzie's ropes. "Up-down-up-up-down! As soon as I free you, we need to skedaddle-daddle."

"The Nedra aren't going to just let us prance out of here," Ozzie heard Fidget say through the haze.

"Don't worry," the moto chimed. "Up-down-up-up-down! There's a planny-plan."

"Is it for us to die horribly?" Fidget wondered.

"Come on—hurry!" Ozzie urged the moto.

The smoke began to dissipate, revealing a new figure in the arena, standing directly between them and Ku.

It was Captain Cho.

"He's alive!" Ozzie cried, his heart singing at the sight of the mighty man. Cho was still dressed in his Zoone uniform, and though it was scuffed and smeared, he looked strong and determined. "Hurry!" Ozzie urged Scoot, tugging on his ropes.

"Ku T'en Nedra," Cho called in a loud voice. "You stole these people from beyond your territory. They are not yours to take. Set them free, at once."

Ku arched his head back and issued a guttural laugh. "*You* make demands, Cho Y'Orrick? Look about you, boy. You are surrounded. All I need do is flick my fingers and a hundred warriors will descend upon you. So here is *my* demand. Leave now, walk away. *Alone*. We will feast on these magics. You will live. Everyone wins."

"Except us," Ozzie heard Fidget grunt.

Cho dropped to one knee. "You cannot take them, Ku T'en Nedra," he said. He bowed his head and exposed his neck to the chieftain's sword. "But you can take me."

"What?" Ozzie cried. "Cho—no!"

"Y'Orrick scum!" Ku growled, spitting on the ground. "Your blood will do nothing to satiate our hunger. We need these outsiders' magic to save us."

Cho looked up. "They *can* save you, Ku T'en Nedra; just not in the way you think. They will stop the metal men. If you let them go."

Ku said nothing. He paced the sand in front of Cho like an impatient predator.

Cho's hand flitted up to rest on the pommel of his blade. "If you do not accept my offer, I shall defend my clan."

Clan? Ozzie thought.

Ku seemed to have the same thought. "Clan?" he scoffed, his eyes flashing wide and white. "CLAN?! You call these outsiders your clan?"

Ozzie saw Cho squeeze the hilt of his sword. "I do."

Scoot had finally succeeded in burning through Ozzie's ropes. As soon as he was free, he burst forward to join Cho's side—only to freeze after a few steps. One of the warriors had hammered his gong and the sound reverberated through the arena like a warning.

"So be it," Ku said, spitting again at Cho's feet. "Fight for your pitiful clan. After you lose, you can burn together in the fires of Ru-Kavell."

The chieftain raised his Valdune blade and Ozzie watched, entranced, as it transformed into a long, curved shape. It reminded Ozzie of a scimitar, except it had two half-circle notches near the bottom.

"Do you see the shape my sword has taken?" the chieftain taunted as Cho rose to his feet. "The steel knows you, boy. It has tasted your flesh once before. The notches are to remind you of that."

What? Ozzie thought, but a terrible suspicion began to nibble at him. He had always thought Cho had lost his two fingers fighting a Thrakean lizard—not from an attack by his own clan.

"Yes," Ku hissed, "my blade hungers for you again, Cho Y'Orrick."

Then, without warning, the chieftain charged. Cho unsheathed his sword, but it was not quite in his hands before Ku was upon him. A clang sounded through the arena as Cho's sword was ripped from his grasp. The blade twirled through the air and stabbed into the sand, where it quivered, far beyond Cho's reach.

It's his missing fingers! Ozzie thought as the clansmen whooped in jubilation. *He couldn't get a firm grip in time.*

Cho didn't even look to see where his blade had landed. As Ku swiped at him, the captain ducked, then turned, planted his feet, and faced the chieftain.

"You betray our customs," Cho accused him, circling with the chieftain. "You attacked before we could exchange bows."

"You are Y'Orrick," Ku jeered, stalking forward with his blade. "You are not worthy of that rite."

He lunged forward, swinging. Again, Cho dodged the assault—but just barely, and when Ozzie next caught a glimpse of the captain's front side, he could see the sleeve of his coat torn open in a mess of blood. Ku thrust once more; this time his blade nicked Cho's chin.

Ozzie couldn't stand by any longer. He scrambled to where Cho's blade was still standing in the dirt, gripped it by the hilt, and pulled it free. It was far heavier than he could have ever imagined, but he managed to lug it toward Cho.

Ku was still viciously slashing at Cho, but as soon as he noticed Ozzie approaching, the chieftain turned on him.

Ozzie instinctively tried to step out of the way, tripped on his own shoelace, and crashed to the dirt. Ku's sword stabbed into the ground next to him; Ozzie could feel the rush of air.

Ku lifted the blade for a killing blow, but Cho plowed into him from the side. Both men crashed into the sand and Ozzie heard the crunch of breaking bone. Cho got to his feet, turned, and helped Ozzie up. Ozzie had dropped Cho's sword, but he collected it again and passed it to the captain.

"Thank you, lad."

Ku was still on the ground, struggling like a beetle on its back. His breathing was sharp and ragged.

"Rise," Cho commanded, marching back over to Ku. "Find your feet, and we will complete our duel."

That's Cho for you, Ozzie thought. *He fights fairly. Even though Ku doesn't.*

Using his sword as a crutch, Ku pulled himself to his knees, his face contorting with agony and rage. "Clan of Nedra!" he shouted to the assembled throng. "Kill him! KILL THEM ALL!"

A war cry erupted from the Nedra, and then they spilled into the arena like a tidal wave of fury. Ozzie collapsed to the ground in panic.

But Cho didn't. He calmly turned in a circle, confronting the onslaught. When they were almost upon him, he thrust his sword high above his head as if announcing victory.

"What are you doing?!" Ozzie screamed. "Aren't you going to fight? Aren't you—"

Cho's blade began to change. A crackle of lightning flared up the steel, accompanied by a thunderous, reverberating boom. It was so loud that it caused the clansmen to skid to a halt, many of them dropping their weapons. Ozzie only allowed them a glance before returning his attention to Cho's sword. It was cycling through different forms. At first it was long and broad, next short and curved. It bared countless serrated teeth, then four sharp prongs, and still next it became an undulating blade that crackled with blue fire. It took the shape of a battle-ax, a triple-bladed katar, a quoit, a spiked mace . . . on and on in a dizzying blur.

Ozzie knew the blade could transform, but not like this. Not so quickly. Not so dramatically. And perhaps neither did the Nedra.

"It's . . . it's impossible," Ku stammered, his own sword sliding from his grip. "You, Cho Y'Orrick—you have never hunted magic."

"No, he hasn't," Ozzie said proudly.

Ku's eyes looked like they would roll into the back of his head. "Then . . . h-how?"

"Perhaps things aren't as you have always claimed they must be," Cho said.

Ku bowed his head in resignation. "Claim your right, Cho T'en Nedra."

"Cho T'en Nedra!" the audience of warriors chanted, all standing at attention. "Cho T'en Nedra! Cho T'en Nedra!"

"Cho *T'en Nedra*?" Aunt Temperance asked. Scoot had freed her, Fidget, and Tug, and now they crept forward to gather around Ozzie and Cho. "Why are they chanting that?"

"I think Cho's about to become chieftain of the Nedra," Fidget said. "But first, he has to . . . behead Ku."

"He can't do that," Aunt Temperance gasped. "Captain!" she shouted. "CAPTAIN!"

Her words were drowned out by the roar of the warriors. Cho remained where he was, unwavering, sword still poised in the air.

"I can't watch this," Aunt Temperance said. She grabbed Ozzie and Fidget and reeled them into her arms, burying their faces into her chest. "You must not see this."

Suddenly, the crowd went silent. Ozzie squirmed free of Aunt Temperance's grasp to see Ku still bowing in the sand, the same as before. But Cho's sword was back in its sheath.

"You must kill me!" Ku beseeched. "If you do not, you cannot lead the Nedra."

"I have no desire to serve as chieftain," Cho said, looming over him. "As I have said, I already have a clan."

Us, Ozzie thought, his heart bursting with pride.

"You must obey our customs!" Ku cried, scrambling forward on his knees, clasping his hands together in desperation. "Slay me! Else you leave us in chaos. This is the way of the Valdune. This is the way it has always been."

"You will have to find a new way," Cho declared solemnly. "As I once did." He turned from the groveling man. Blood dripped from his chin, and the sleeve of his jacket was soaked red.

"Captain," Aunt Temperance started.

"Mere scratches," Cho assured her as he stooped to inspect Tug's wing. "I'm afraid it's broken, cub. When we are free of this place, I will splint it for you. Can you walk?"

"Oh, sure, Cho," Tug said, licking the captain's cheek. "But, just to tell you, I'm starving."

Cho stroked the top of the skyger's head. "I know a cave not so far from here. I used to go there as a boy; it is a hidden place, a comfortable place. Once there we can rest, eat." He glanced at Scoot. "And repair." Then, gathering himself to his full height, he added, "Let's leave this wretched arena. Scoot, lead the way."

The moto gave him a salute, passed Aunt Temperance's bag to her, then escorted them to the entrance to the slot canyon. The pathway in front of them was as black as a ninja's gi, but Scoot pressed a button on the side of her metal cap and out came an accordion arm holding a small flashlight.

"Here we go!" the moto beckoned as she rolled into the crack.

The others followed, though Ozzie paused to cast a final look at the arena. Ku was still on his knees, staring dejectedly at the ground. The rest of the Nedra had erupted into animated arguments with one another.

"Do not linger, lad," Cho said, doubling back to grab his arm.

Ozzie gaped at the giant man. "Your sword, Cho. You stopped them. All of them."

"No, lad," Cho told him. "*We* stopped them. Together. I could not have done it without you."

Ozzie followed the hulking man into the throat of the long-dead dragon. Scoot was up ahead, leading the way with her light beam. Aunt Temperance knelt on the ground, scavenging through her bag.

"Everything's still here," she said, standing up and turning on her own flashlight. Then she looked at Cho with a worried expression. "Will they pursue us?"

"I do not think so," he replied.

"But, Cho . . . are you sure you're okay?" Ozzie persisted. "Did you really lose your fingers to the chieftain? I thought it was a fight with a Thrakean lizard."

"The lizard gave me this," Cho said, pointing to the scar on his face. "But the Nedra took my fingers."

"And the chieftain . . . that was . . . is he your dad?"

"I have no father. Not anymore. I am Y'Orrick. Alone."

"Not alone," Aunt Temperance said quickly. "As you said, Captain, you have a new clan."

Cho managed a melancholic smile. "You two go ahead. I'll take up the rear."

Ozzie hesitated, but Aunt Temperance put her hand to his back and steered him forward. "Leave him be," she whispered into his ear.

"I'm worried," Ozzie said. "He's bleeding."

"He's lost more than blood," Aunt Temperance said, half to herself.

"What do you mean?" Ozzie asked as they rounded a curve in the path.

Aunt Temperance sighed. "He does have a new clan, Ozzie. But it's a monumental task to leave your old one behind. And now he's had to do it twice."

She said no more after that, but Ozzie had an inkling that she knew something of what Cho was feeling.

A DOOR TO MANY PLACES

Cho let them rest the night in his hidden cave, only to press them on the very next morning. There was a lot of exhaustion and grouchiness to go around. Even Tug was more sedate than usual. It wasn't because of his injured wing, Ozzie knew. Cho and Aunt Temperance had worked together to splint and bandage it; what they couldn't do, however, was find a way to satisfy the skyger's bottomless appetite.

"I never thought I'd say this, but I'm getting a little tired of Arborellian nectar," Tug confided to Ozzie and Fidget as they trudged across the sand. "I sure miss the proper meals we get at Zoone."

"Me, too," Ozzie agreed. He noticed Scoot wobbling ahead of them, swinging her arms and humming a peculiar song, which prompted him to add, "Sometimes I wish I was a machine."

"Why would you like to be like *that*?" Fidget retorted, gesturing at the strange moto.

"She doesn't need food or sleep," Ozzie said. "Look how cheerful she is—she doesn't have to feel things the way we do."

"I wouldn't want to be some bucket of bolts," Fidget said. "Though I do envy her not having to go to the bathroom—I'm tired of squatting in the bushes every time I have to go. It's a real pain."

"Maybe you should choose places with less cactus," Tug suggested.

Fidget rolled her eyes. "That's not exactly what I . . . never mind."

Cho guided them across the foreboding desert of Ru-Valdune for a day and a half, until finally they arrived at a narrow passageway in the cliffside of a valley.

"We are about to leave the wild lands," the captain revealed. "On the other side of this tunnel is the Land of Thrak."

Ozzie exhaled in relief. Then he felt something swish past his ear. He instinctively swatted at the air and felt the sharp sting of metal.

"Moto probe!" Fidget shrieked.

She swung at the robotic flying death bug with her fist. She missed, but her attack caused it to veer out of the way—right into the path of Tug's unpredictable tail. The next instant, the probe was lying in a crumpled heap on the ground.

Ozzie knelt to examine the now-defunct machine. It looked exactly like the one he and Aunt Temperance had seen in The Depths. "Why is it here?"

"Part of the motos' expansion," Cho said grimly. "They're sending their probes into every corner of the 'verse. Preparing for . . ."

"Multiversal motonization," Fidget finished for him.

Ozzie exhaled. "We really need to get to Zoone. *Fast.*"

The cavern was dark, but they had Scoot's and Aunt Temperance's flashlights to guide them. Still, the trek was long and boring, and Ozzie was thankful when the monotony was finally disrupted by the roaring sound of water coming from up ahead.

"Is there a river down here?" he wondered.

"That," Cho answered, "is one of the fifty-seven wonders of the multiverse: the Thrakean Leaps."

"The Thrakean Leaps?" Aunt Temperance echoed dubiously. "What exactly is doing the leaping?"

"The water," Fidget replied for the captain. "Most

places in the multiverse, water *falls*. But in Thrak, it goes the opposite direction."

"Sorry—are you trying to tell me the waterfalls are going *up*?" Aunt Temperance questioned.

"Maybe it's best that you see it in person," Cho told her.

They continued on for several more minutes until a blurry light shone from up ahead. With every step, the sound of rushing water grew louder. Cho led them through the opening in the mountain and onto a shelf of rock. Ozzie gaped in awe. They were facing a concave wall of surging water, almost a complete circle of it, and, just as Fidget had explained, it was going straight up—not like a geyser, but like a waterfall simply going in reverse.

There were no railings on the ledge, but Ozzie mustered the courage to peer over. All he could see were clouds of cool steam billowing up from the source of the leaps, somewhere far below. They were standing about halfway up the falls; Ozzie had to crane his neck to see the water spilling away at the top.

It's almost like standing in a drain, Ozzie thought as he felt water spray against his cheeks. *Well, a reverse drain? What did you call that? Just a pipe?*

Aunt Temperance would have certainly known, but he couldn't ask the question out loud. The deafening rumble of the waterleaps obliterated all other sounds in the pit.

That included Cho's normally loud and authoritative voice. Ozzie could see the captain's lips moving, but he couldn't hear him. The captain must have realized this, because he began motioning for Ozzie and the others to follow him.

Into the pit? Ozzie wondered. But Cho was already on the move, so Ozzie took a deep breath and stepped forward.

As it turned out, the ledge was actually an all-too-narrow bridge of rock that jutted over the mind-boggling drop; it was just that it was obscured by the clouds of mist. As he walked, Ozzie decided to keep his gaze planted on the rocky path. It was damp and slippery, and the mist was writhing around his feet. One misstep and—well, he tried not to think about it.

Finally, Ozzie was at the opposite end of the leaps, next to Cho. The same circle of water was hurtling upward here but, somehow, it was quieter on this side.

"A bit of magic is at work here," Cho explained as everyone congregated. "Now we can hear each other."

"I think I prefer the tightrope," Aunt Temperance complained as she wiped her glasses. "Was this treacherous route necessary, Captain?"

"Aye," Cho said, pointing to the waterleap in front of them, "because this is our doorway."

"The door's hidden?" Fidget ventured. "Behind the waterleap?"

"No, the waterleap *is* the door."

Ozzie frowned. During his time at Zoone, he had encountered many types of doors—ones made of wood, of steel, even of stone. What he hadn't seen was a door made of water. But now, as he stood there, staring at the leaps, an image began to shimmer into view. At first it was bleary, but it eventually began to sharpen. What Ozzie saw was a long stretch of arid, cracked earth, fiery red in color.

"Is that it?" Ozzie wondered. "The world on the other side of this door?"

Cho nodded. "No handle, keyhole, or even hinges, but a portal nonetheless."

"Oh!" Tug exclaimed. "The image just changed. It's like watching TV. *Cool.*"

"Quoggswoggle!" Fidget gasped. "It's a ripple door! I thought they were a myth."

Cho chuckled. He had been sullen the past couple of days, ever since the duel, but now his eyes were shining with familiar warmth, as if leaving behind Ru-Valdune had lifted a weight from his heart. "It *is* a ripple door, lass," he said. "It's real, and it can lead us to any number of destinations, depending on where it's pointing to at any given moment. It's also free."

"What do you mean, 'free'?" Aunt Temperance questioned.

"It doesn't require a key," Fidget relayed in excitement. "There aren't many free doors left in the 'verse. The Council of Wizardry controls most of the tracks, and they added all the doors and locks and rules. But this one—anyone can take it."

"Will it lead us to Zoone?" Ozzie asked.

"With any luck," Cho answered. "We have to watch the worlds revealed in the doorway. When Zoone pops up, then we go through."

"But will it?" Ozzie pressed. The door was currently showing a dense jungle with rainbow-colored foliage.

"Ripple doors aren't known for their consistency," Cho conceded. "Sometimes a location shows, sometimes it doesn't. Even if a world does appear, it might only be for a brief moment. Or it will appear several times in one hour. Or once in a year. Or never."

"Doesn't seem like a very efficient system, if you ask me," Aunt Temperance decided. "Didn't you use this door previously?"

"Yes, but I didn't take it to Zoone," Cho said. "If the nexus doesn't appear as an option, we'll need to travel to another land first, one we know has a door that will lead us directly to the nexus."

"What if we make an oopsy?" Scoot beeped in alarm.

"That's not going to happen while I'm here," Fidget insisted, elbowing her way past the moto. "If there's one thing I'm pretty good at, it's multiversal geography."

She plopped down, put her chin on a hand, and gazed into the rapids. Ozzie leaned over her shoulder. The portal was still showing the jungle with multicolored leaves.

"That's definitely not Zoone," Ozzie said.

Fidget hushed him, so Ozzie settled for pacing behind her, glancing up every now and then to check if the scene had changed. Some of the worlds stayed for several minutes; others, as Cho had warned, appeared for only a few seconds. None of them came back.

"If we find a sure bet, we'd better take it," Cho advised.

The scene shifted to show a series of mountain peaks encircled by clouds—though for all Ozzie knew, they could have been islands floating in the sky. Then, weaving gracefully between those islands, he saw a greenish speck. One of the rocky mounds of land erupted in a wave of movement, and he suddenly comprehended that there was some sort of crowd assembled there. The spectators were cheering on the green specks—because now, there wasn't just one, but a whole line of them. And then they weren't even specks anymore; as they approached at what seemed like breakneck speed, Ozzie saw that they were dragons with long, diaphanous wings—and each one had a rider!

"Oh, this is Selvanas," Fidget said nonchalantly.

"They're known for racing."

"*Dragon* racing?!" Ozzie exclaimed.

"We don't want to go there, then," Aunt Temperance said. "What?" she added, when Ozzie fired a look in her direction. "It looks dangerous."

The door rippled again, and a world of water and waves appeared. Amid this gentle turquoise sea, tall limestone islands jutted toward the clouds, each capped with an ornate building.

"Quoxx!" Fidget cried out.

"Oh!" Tug purred. "Your home world."

"Yeah, but we can't go there," Fidget said with a sigh. "Not unless . . . unless I want to turn myself over and deal with the Quoggian crown prince."

With a wistful glint in her purple eyes, she sat back and crossed her arms. She stewed in this position until the image in the doorway changed to depict a vast desert landscape. Yellow sand stretched as far as the eye could see, dotted with enormous bell-shaped temples made of stone.

"The tombs of Dossandros," Fidget announced. "Another one of the fifty-seven multiversal wonders, by the way."

"I've been to Dossandros," Cho said. "We can definitely find a door there that will take us to Zoone."

"Let's just wait," Fidget argued.

"What if it's our best chance?" Ozzie worried. "We don't want to miss out."

"They've got spiders in Dossandros," Fidget warned him. "Big ones."

Ozzie grimaced. "It might be worth the risk if—"

"When I say big, I mean the size of houses," Fidget told him. "They hide their webs by burying them just beneath the surface of the sand. One minute, you're trudging across the desert, then—BAM—you're all entangled, and it's lunchtime."

"Just to tell you," Tug said, perking up, "that's my favorite time of day."

Fidget groaned. "Not lunchtime for *you*. For the spiders."

"Oh," Tug said, swishing his tail. "Well, I saw this one story on the TV where a house was infested with bugs and they used BuzzzzKill to get rid of them. By the way, have you ever noticed that 'Z' is really popular on the TV? 'X,' too, but mostly 'Z.'"

"Ooh!" Scoot chimed. "I want to be Scoot-ZX! Can I be Scoot-ZX, Creator?"

"You could try being quiet, Grease-Brain," Fidget retorted. "How about that?"

"Will you just stop it?" Ozzie said. "You don't have to be so . . ."

The scene in the waterfall had changed again, and this

time it showed something completely different. Something breathtaking. Something that had stolen the words right off Ozzie's tongue.

Before them was a palatial blue building with fanciful towers, raindrop spires, and gabled arches. In front of that, there were doors—hundreds upon hundreds of doors.

They were looking at Zoone.

21

ZOONE'S MOST UNWANTED

Ozzie wasn't about to waste another second. How many hours had he spent sitting on the cold cement floor in The Depths below Apartment 2B, staring at the broken door to the nexus? He had endured pirates, motos, magic hunters—even a flea-bitten Revellian monkey—and now, here at last, was Zoone, glimmering in front of him like a dragon's treasure hoard. He sped past Fidget and plunged through the ripple door.

The first thing that struck him was that he didn't get wet, even though he was stepping through a rush of water. The second thing that struck him was a wall—or, to be fair, he struck it. He had assumed there would be some sort of track beyond the ripple door, but there wasn't. There was just him, racing through the leaps and immediately face-planting into bricks.

"Careful!" he shouted over his shoulder, but Tug was already plowing into him, turning Ozzie into the central ingredient of a wall-and-skyger sandwich. By the time he extricated himself, everyone else had come through the door and was mumbling in surprise at their surroundings. Ozzie still couldn't see anything, but he could smell that the air was stale and close. He had this sense that they were deep underground.

"I thought we were supposed to end up in Zoone," Ozzie said, his heart sinking. "What happened? Where are the platforms? Did the ripple door change on us?"

"I hope not," Fidget said. "We could be any—OW! You just rolled over my foot, Bucket-Head!"

"Oopsy!" Scoot beeped apologetically.

Aunt Temperance clicked on her flashlight, offering some meager relief from the darkness. She waved the beam about, revealing a narrow passageway built of ancient, roughly hewn bricks. Murky alcoves leered at them from the shadows.

"Looks like a crypt of some sort," she said.

"I'm detecting motos!" Scoot reported. "Far uppy-up, but they're definitely here."

"We're back in Moton?!" Ozzie cried.

"No," Cho reassured them, brushing his hand along the nearest wall. "This *is* Zoone. We're in the original foundations of the station house, sunk beneath the ground after so many centuries. We call it the catacombs now."

"This isn't what the door showed," Ozzie said.

"No—I should have told you. The ripple door doesn't show you exactly what's on the other side of the door, it just shows you a picture of the world. A scene that depicts its overall . . ."

"Essence?" Aunt Temperance wondered. "Like a travel brochure?"

"Or a TV commercial?" Ozzie added, hearing an approving purr from Tug.

"I suppose," Cho answered. He swished his hand through the air where they'd come from. "No sign of the door; it must only go one way. Well, no point lingering. Let's find a more *modern* part of the station."

"I'll lead the way, Captain!" Scoot proclaimed. She wheeled ahead through one of the archways. "Everyone follow m—"

There was a deafening clang, like the sound of someone hitting a very large gong with an even larger mallet. Everyone raced after the moto, turning a corner to see Scoot wobbling at a standstill, her head twisting round and round like a top. It was going so quickly that it spun right off her neck and arced through the air. Ozzie reached out to catch it, only to have it fly through his open arms. The moto's head hit his foot; he gave a sort of awkward half kick and the head bounced upward, right into his hands.

"Good catch," Tug said, as if Ozzie had planned it that way.

Ozzie turned Scoot's head over in his hands to stare at her eyes. There was a flicker of light, a static buzz, and then they turned dark. Her now-headless body meandered aimlessly past Ozzie, and began bumping repeatedly against the nearest wall, like a stuck wind-up toy.

"How do you like them kettle o' snarfs?" came a voice from the shadows. "It looks different, but it sure sounds the same when you whacks it."

Aunt Temperance whirled her light toward the sound of the voice to reveal a humongous, blubbery creature emerging from the darkness.

"M-Miss Mongo?" Ozzie stammered.

"You're Miss Mongo?" Aunt Temperance gasped. "Zoone's cook? Ozzie told me about you, but I thought you would be less . . ."

"Less what, luv?" Miss Mongo entreated as she lurched forward.

"Everything?" Aunt Temperance hazarded.

Just between him and himself, Ozzie couldn't blame

Aunt Temperance for her reaction. If a mountainous blob of jelly could contract the mumps, then you would have Miss Mongo. She was a groll, which meant she didn't have feet—or possibly eyes, though rumor had it that they were just hidden somewhere within all the folds, knobs, and bumps that covered her body. The only things that made Miss Mongo seem a little less threatening were the apron tied around her waist—or what passed as her waist—and the rolling pin she held in one hand. Except, Ozzie realized, she had probably used the rolling pin to do the clobbering.

"Why did you do that?" he asked, cradling Scoot's head in his arms.

"Well, it's a moto, innit?" Miss Mongo said, brandishing her rolling pin. "That's what I do when I sees a moto. I whacks it."

"Just to tell you, she's a she," Tug told the groll. "Plus, she's on our side."

"Is that so?" Miss Mongo said. "Never heard of a moto that defected."

"How about one that's defective?" Fidget quipped, gesturing to Scoot's body.

The headless moto had managed to rotate away from the wall and was beetling down the corridor, as if intent on avoiding a second encounter with Miss Mongo's rolling pin.

"Stop!" Ozzie cried. Still holding Scoot's head, he stuck out a leg to try to block her progress, but she rolled right past him—though, in the process, her wheel snagged his shoelace. Suddenly, Ozzie was hopping along behind her just to keep up.

"Kitchen staff used to complain about me takin' their heads off," Miss Mongo prattled as Cho jumped to Ozzie's rescue by yanking out Scoot's battery. "Of course, that was for burnin' me soup. I never actually whacked them—don't believe 'em if they says I did. How'd you lot get down here, anyway? Cap'n, you been missin' for weeks. Thought you was a goner."

"So did I," Cho said with a chuckle. He steadied Scoot's body while Aunt Temperance came over to untangle Ozzie's shoelace. When everything was sorted, the captain and Aunt Temperance rolled the moto back to the group (Ozzie kept out of the way). "Truth is, I've been stuck in Moton," Cho told Miss Mongo. "But it wasn't all bad. It allowed me to meet up with our old friends and make our way across the wild lands. We discovered a ripple door in Thrak that led us here."

"Ripple door, eh?" Miss Mongo said. "Shows it to me then."

"It only goes one way," Fidget told her. "You can't even see it from this side."

"Too bad," Miss Mongo said, putting her hands on

her—well, Ozzie decided, "hips" wasn't quite the right word. "Could use an escape route, if it came to that."

"The motos," Ozzie said, comprehending. "Is that why you're down here? In the catacombs?" Miss Mongo was famously known for her dedication to her job. As head of the station's food service, she rarely left the bustling kitchens of Zoone.

"Anything good on the stove?" Tug asked, rubbing his head against the groll's amorphous body. "Snirf and snarf? Grumffles? Torgivian stew?"

"Nothin'," Miss Mongo said. "Not up in the proper kitchens, anyway. I've been made redundant. I don't fit the desired physical profile."

"What?!" Ozzie blurted. "This is Zoone. You can't be fired for how you look."

"Well, it wasn't for me Ippeian soufflé," the groll said. "Because if that was the case, I'd have a job for life. I'm too . . ." She gestured at Aunt Temperance. "It's like she said. Too everything. Too lumpy. Too fat. Not symmetrical enough, the way he likes his staff. An aberration. That's what he calls folks like me."

"Who's *he*?" Aunt Temperance asked.

"Klaxon," Miss Mongo replied bitterly. "Ruler of Zoone."

Aunt Temperance jolted like she had just been jabbed

by an electrified moto claw. "What do you mean 'ruler'? Zaria runs the nexus—"

"In name only," Miss Mongo interjected. "Klaxon's runnin' the show behind the scenes. Fired anyone he doesn't like the look of."

All the color drained from Aunt Temperance's face. "I don't understand," she murmured. "He's not Klaxon, he's—"

"Where we supposed to go, hmm?" Miss Mongo wondered. "Zoone's the only home I got, me. So now I'm bumblin' round down here, lookin' for slugs and snails to supplement our soup."

She paused, and Ozzie wondered if she was getting teary. Something was dripping off her chin—though, for all he knew, it might have been drool. Or maybe just her chin itself.

"Bunch of us aberrations hid away down here, standin' against Klaxon," Miss Mongo continued. "We're the Zoone Underground, that's what we are. Zoone's guardians."

"What about the rest of the 'verse?" Ozzie asked. "What about the Council of Wizardry?"

Miss Mongo snorted. "As far as them wizards know, Lady Zoone is still in charge and nothin's wrong. Station's still runnin', innit?"

"Send them a quirl," Fidget suggested. "Tell them—"

"You don't think we thought of that?" Miss Mongo grumbled. "Klaxon shut down the quirlery. All mail delivered 'technological' now, which means restricted. Sent me kitchen girls, Panya and Piper, to try and sniff out a wizard or two in person, but I don't know what happened to them. Maybe they made it. Maybe they didn't. It's been a week; could be in prison for all I know."

"Zoone doesn't have a prison," Ozzie said.

"It does now, luv," Miss Mongo told him. "And if them girls did make it? Well, you know wizards. Bunch of bureaucrats. Don't do anything quickly. Come along, then. I'll take you to our headquarters. It's not much, but at least I can brew a pot o' tea."

"What about Scoot?" Ozzie asked. "We have to fix her."

"Bring 'er along, luv." Miss Mongo beckoned as she began slithering into the shadows. "Mr. Whisk can fiddle with her. He's the best tinker in the 'verse, despite what *some* think."

"You carry her head, lad," Cho told Ozzie, passing him Scoot's battery. "I'll take the rest of her."

Ozzie pocketed the ring and began to follow before realizing that Aunt Temperance was still lingering in the shadows.

"Mercurio can't be the one in charge," she mumbled,

staring at the wall. "It's . . . it's . . . it's not in his nature. He's not capable . . ."

Fidget threw Ozzie a knowing glance, then snatched the flashlight from Aunt Temperance and gave her an encouraging nudge down the passageway. Miss Mongo was already up ahead; she didn't seem to have any problems navigating the darkness.

Their route through the catacombs involved ramps and a few stairs. In the scant light of Aunt Temperance's flashlight, Ozzie caught glimpses of ancient runes carved into the walls. He knew Lady Zoone's ancestor, Zephyrus Zoone, had built the first station house millennia ago. Maybe he had built these very passageways.

They reached a humble gray door, its wooden planks so old that they were worn smooth as river stones.

"Welcome to Underground HQ," she said before knocking on the door and announcing, "No one here 'cept us aberrations."

There was the sound of someone removing a crossbar from the other side, then Miss Mongo pushed the door open and led them through. A few guttering lanterns were perched about the space beyond, providing enough light for Ozzie to see a chamber with a low, vaulted ceiling and filled with crates, kegs, and bits of makeshift furniture. Ozzie was put in mind of the warehouse on Moton. That place at least had access to light; this one felt like a glorified dungeon.

"Look what I turned up on patrol," Miss Mongo announced—seemingly to no one. "More aberrations. Don't worry about the moto. She's on our side. I whacked her anyway, jus' to be sure."

A head poked out from behind the door. It was Mr. Whisk, who—until recently, at least—had managed the luggage repair shop located in the station's central hub. Ozzie knew why Klaxon considered Mr. Whisk an aberration, even though it angered him to even think about the tinker that way. Mr. Whisk had a tail, seven fingers on each hand, and a crop of facial hair that changed according to his mood. Based on the spiky bristles bursting from his chin, Ozzie guessed that Mr. Whisk was not feeling very cheerful at the moment.

"This is it?" Fidget asked. "Your resistance is you and Mr. Whisk?"

Ozzie silently agreed with her reaction. Mr. Whisk was a talented tinker, but he wasn't exactly young and spry. Or intimidating. Miss Mongo, at least, had her rolling pin and a reputation to go with it. Mr. Whisk's greatest asset was an unpredictable beard.

"Used to be more of us," Miss Mongo replied defensively as she closed the door behind them, "but we been gettin' picked off and thrown in prison, like what I said. But it's not just us two. We also got—"

"Ozzie, my boy? Is that you?"

A scruffy ball of fur scampered out of some nearby hidey-hole and launched itself at Ozzie's leg. Ozzie shifted Scoot's head in his arms and looked down. It was as if his leg had just snagged a very large burr with eyes, an arrow-like nose, and long fuzzy ears. "Fusselbone?!" Ozzie cried. "You're here, too?"

The mouse-man definitely wouldn't fit most people's parameters for "normal," but Ozzie felt a spike of anger to see him hiding down here. Fusselbone was Zoone's chief conductor—Ozzie couldn't even begin to imagine how the station would run without him.

"Seriously?" Fidget fumed, echoing Ozzie's sentiment. "Klaxon fired you, Fusselbone? *You?!*"

Fusselbone de-clamped from Ozzie's leg and hopped from foot to foot in front of the princess. "It's a preposasterous situation!" he squeaked. "Nothing's running on time. Luggage is being lost. People are missing connections! Preposasterous!"

His panicked outburst snapped Aunt Temperance out of her trance. "Preposasterous?" she echoed. "That's not a proper word."

"In Zoone, it is," Tug purred, giving the top of Fusselbone's head a friendly lick.

Fusselbone wiped away Tug's slobber with a large checkered handkerchief before turning on Aunt Temperance.

"Who are you, anyway?" he demanded, jabbing her leg with a furry finger. "I haven't seen you before! Are you a spy? You look like a spy." Fusselbone pivoted toward Cho. "I'm grateful to see you, Captain—I can see you've had some preposasterous adventures and I can't wait to hear about all the ways you nearly died during them—but the very core of our secret base has been penetrated by this intruder. Quick! Apprehend this diabolical damsel so we can begin interrogating her."

"Ah, Ferbis," Cho said with a warm smile. "I've missed your enthusiasm during my exile. There is nothing to fear; let me introduce you to Ozzie's very own aunt: Temperance Sparks."

Fusselbone dropped his handkerchief. His mouth fell open and he audibly gasped. Mr. Whisk took a noticeable step backward. Miss Mongo seemed to pale.

Aunt Temperance's brow furled. "What is it?"

"It's you," Fusselbone answered. "You're the one . . ."

"The one?" Aunt Temperance balked. "The one *what*?"

"The one that all of this is about," Fusselbone replied. "You're the reason the nexus is falling apart! The reason we're all in this absolutely preposasterous situation."

22

A MISFIT MIND

Ozzie stared at the fidgety mouse-man. "Fusselbone, what are you talking about?"

"It's her!" Fusselbone insisted. "The one Klaxon—"

"Mercurio," Aunt Temperance interrupted.

Fusselbone blinked at her.

"His name is Mercurio," Aunt Temperance stated firmly. "And the thing that none of you seem to understand is that *he's* the victim. The motos are controlling him. Torturing him. I've seen it with my own eyes."

"The motos aren't controlling him," Miss Mongo grunted. "He's the king. He's controlling *them*."

Aunt Temperance turned and kicked the nearest crate.

If it hurt—and it must have, Ozzie thought—she didn't show it. "I believe there was a promise of tea," she snarled between clenched teeth.

Miss Mongo made a motion that might have been a nod, then burbled over to a hot plate in the corner of the room. She began puttering with the kettle while Fusselbone and Mr. Whisk seemed to suddenly discover a keen interest in their feet, then the corners of the ceiling— basically anywhere that allowed them to avoid eye contact with Aunt Temperance.

Ozzie turned in bewilderment to Fidget. "What's going on here?" he whispered.

"I'm not sure," Fidget whispered back. "But your aunt sure has them freaked out. Don't you think?"

Ozzie wasn't sure *what* to think anymore. Aunt Temperance wasn't a threatening person. She let Ozzie's parents boss her around all the time. But now, as he stared at Aunt Temperance, he suddenly became conscious of just how wild, unkempt, and possibly deranged she appeared. Her glasses were askew and—uncharacteristically—there wasn't a braid, bun, or knot to keep her hair pinned in place, leaving it to stick out in every direction. Of course, they all looked pretty rough, but it was the emotion boiling inside of Aunt Temperance that set her apart. Her entire body had turned rigid, her hands were balled into a pair of trembling fists, and there was heat rising in her cheeks that could make a teakettle jealous.

That was when it occurred to Ozzie. Yes, he had braved pirates, motos, and magic hunters to get here—and a flea-bitten Revellian monkey, too—but so had Aunt Temperance. Ozzie had endured these things in order to escape boarding school and return to Zoone, but she had done it to find Mercurio. To save him. Now everyone was telling her that he was a villain.

"Hey, Quoxx to Ozzie," Fidget prodded. "Where did you go?"

"Everything's backward," he murmured. It was like the first time he had picked up a manga and realized it read right to left. All this time, he had been reading Aunt Temperance incorrectly, too.

"Okay, luv," Miss Mongo announced, bustling over to thrust a cup into Aunt Temperance's hands. "That'll fix you. Anyone else for a spot?"

No one replied, except for Tug, who gave an eager purr, prompting Miss Mongo to set a bowl down for him and fill it to the brim.

Aunt Temperance sat down, took a long sip from her cup, then closed her eyes and released a luxuriant sigh. "Okay," she said. "That's better." Then she narrowed her gaze at the members of the Underground crew and said, "So, tell me. How am *I* responsible for what's occurring here?"

Fusselbone began wringing his paws.

"I believe the word you used was 'preposasterous,'" Aunt Temperance said. "It must be a dire situation if we must concoct words that otherwise don't exist." She took a purposeful sip of tea.

"Everything's changed—for the worse, my dear lady, the worse!" Fusselbone burst out. "The motos have taken over and Kla—Mer—well, we think—hold on!"

He fumbled through a nearby crate and pulled out an old photo. The frame was chipped and the glass a spider web of cracks. The photo itself showed a much younger Aunt Temperance, entwined in Mercurio's arms.

Aunt Temperance gasped. "Where did you get that?"

"That's Lady Zoone's photo," Captain Cho said. "I've seen it in her study."

"Me kitchen girl Piper ended up with it," Miss Mongo explained. "Happened after you went missin', Cap'n. After Klaxon took over the station. I sent Piper up to Lady Zoone's tower with some soup, but Klaxon wouldn't let her deliver it. He was sittin' there like he owned the place, broodin' and mutterin' over that photo."

"Piper tried to get through—she did, she did!" Fusselbone jabbered. "But Klaxon chased her away!"

"But not before hurling the photo at her," Mr. Whisk added. "Piper hid it her apron and passed it on to us."

"Somethin' about that photo that Klaxon found

upsettin',", Miss Mongo said. "Look at the inscription." She snatched the photo out of Fusselbone's hand and flipped the frame over.

Ozzie leaned forward to read in flowery handwriting: *Tempie & Mercurio.*

"Didn't recognize you at first," Miss Mongo said to Aunt Temperance with an accusatory tone. "But that's you, innit . . . '*Tempie*'? With *him*."

"That's right!" Fusselbone added, hopping excitedly, as if dancing on coals. "Piper thinks you were in love. That you broke his heart, sent him into a downward spiral, made him—"

"Piper's a gossip queen," Ozzie interrupted, feeling the need to jump to Aunt Temperance's defense.

"Been starin' a lot at this photo, doin' some speculatin'," Miss Mongo said, ignoring Ozzie's outburst. "Take away the machine parts and that's Klaxon, ain't that right?" She thrust a fat finger at Aunt Temperance. "You two got history. What is it? What did you do to him? Whose side you on, anyway?"

Ozzie didn't need to defend Aunt Temperance this time. "What is this?" she demanded, flying to her feet. "An interrogation? Zaria knows the truth. She knows Mercurio. She sent me a message, you know—she told me Mercurio was in trouble. She told me to save him."

"That was before," Miss Mongo said.

"Before what?" Ozzie asked.

"Before she realized what Klaxon was capable of."

Aunt Temperance turned and hurled her teacup against the nearest wall. It shattered into pieces, leaving tea trickling down the bricks. "Not Klaxon. *Mercurio*," she insisted vehemently. "That's the thing no one seems to understand. They're not one and the same."

"No, they're not," Miss Mongo agreed after an uncomfortable moment of silence. "He's all funny in the head—that's what I think, me. Thinks like a machine. Wants everything pure and simple. *Clean.* He finds us lot upsettin' because we don't . . ."

"Fit in?" Fidget guessed.

"That's right," Miss Mongo said. "That's why we're out of work while Klaxon sits up there, puttin' everything in order."

"It's not in order at all!" Fusselbone squeaked. "It's absolute—"

"His version of order," Miss Mongo corrected him morosely. "That's what I meant."

Ozzie contemplated the crew. He knew they had been misfits in their own worlds, but at one time or another each of them had found a way to the station, where Lady Zoone had taken them in, given them jobs, and made them feel like they were a part of something important.

She did the exact same thing with me, Ozzie thought. *And now she's gone.*

Aunt Temperance was so focused on Mercurio, he realized, that she had forgotten about Lady Zoone. The most important person in the nexus. Maybe in the entire multiverse. "Aunt T," he said, "what we have to do is—"

"You want to know whose side I'm on?" Aunt Temperance said. "I'm on the side of *right*. I can put an end to all of this. Take me to him. Take me to Mercurio. I'll talk to him. I'll—"

"You can't go up there!" Fusselbone sputtered. "It would be preposas—well, it would be bad!"

"Mercurio isn't who you think he is," Miss Mongo informed Aunt Temperance. "Not anymore. You think you'll jus' march up there and it'll be all slugs and slurps?"

"I think they do romance a little differently where Miss Mongo comes from," Fidget whispered to Ozzie.

"I've seen him in his . . . his current state," Aunt Temperance said in a fluster. "If I can just talk to him, see him, I can . . . I can . . ." She took a deep breath. "You know what? It doesn't matter. I'm done trying to convince you people."

She stomped to the door, threw it open—and came to an abrupt halt as she was confronted by the darkness of the corridor. Then, turning on a heel, she marched back into the room and snatched up her bag of essentials.

"Aunt T—" Ozzie began.

She silenced him with a glare. Fishing out her flashlight, she stormed into the passageway, but not before emphatically slamming the door behind her.

Ozzie moved to follow her. "We can't let her just go up there all alone!"

"Leave her be, luv," Miss Mongo advised. "She'll never find her way outta the catacombs. Worst case, she'll fall in some hole."

"Fusselbone and I will retrieve her," Cho assured Ozzie.

He rose to his feet, only to freeze an instant later when Aunt Temperance screamed, "NO ONE FOLLOW ME!"

Cho sat back down and offered Ozzie a faint smile. "Perhaps we'll give her a minute or two to calm down first."

Ozzie, Fidget, and Tug hovered around Mr. Whisk in his makeshift workshop, watching the old man tinker with Scoot. Ozzie could hear Miss Mongo in the next chamber, cleaning up the shattered teacup. Cho and Fusselbone, as promised, had gone to find Aunt Temperance.

Ozzie looked about the small alcove. He had seen Mr. Whisk's actual workshop in the station above, and this place was a sort of replica—albeit a much smaller one. Bins of scavenged tools and spare parts were scattered and stacked around an improvised workbench. Many of the spare parts, Ozzie realized, came from disassembled motos; he spotted legs, arms, and even a few heads.

"Where did all these come from?" Ozzie asked, picking up one of the moto arms.

Mr. Whisk peered over his glasses at Ozzie, eyes smiling. "This is the work of the Underground. Whenever someone 'eliminates' a moto, they pass on the bits and pieces to me so that I can fiddle with them, figure out how they work."

Suddenly, something small and furry dropped onto the workbench from the shadows above, making Ozzie jump. Then he realized what it was.

"A quirl!" he exclaimed, gaping at the tiny rodent. "What's she doing all the way down here? Miss Mongo said that Klaxon closed the quirlery."

The quirl scurried over and under the various moto parts littered about the workbench until she reached Mr. Whisk. She offered him a pitiful squeak, prompting the old man to smile and produce a crumb from his pocket. The quirl quickly devoured it.

"Quirls are native to Zoone," Fidget reminded Ozzie.

Mr. Whisk nodded. "Most of them are hiding in the depths of the Infinite Wood, but this little soul seems to have decided to join the Underground."

The quirl twitched her nose and stared at Ozzie with bright eyes. He noticed she had one slightly bent ear, as if she had experienced her share of adventures. She scuttled up Ozzie's sleeve and began to root around in his hair. Ozzie couldn't really get mad at her for that; Aunt Temperance often compared his hair to a squirrel's nest.

Mr. Whisk turned his attention back to Scoot's head. "Quite ingenious inventions, these motos, I will admit. You say this one is on our side?"

Ozzie nodded. "Her name is Scoot."

Mr. Whisk turned the moto's head over in his seven-fingered hands. "She's been around awhile, this one. She doesn't look like the rest of them."

"No kidding," Fidget piped up. "All the other motos are symmetrical. Glitch-Brain here has one eye bigger than the other. And crooked teeth."

"They're not crooked," Ozzie huffed, which made the quirl in his hair give a squeak.

Fidget shrugged. "She'd never survive in TV Land. That's all I'm saying."

"Where's TV Land?" Mr. Whisk wondered, as he began rooting through a box of tools.

"Just this place that Tug thinks is great," Fidget said. "But it's not real."

"It's not *that* great," Tug said with a pensive twitch of

his tail. The space was so cramped that he knocked over a bin of scrap moto parts—though the skyger himself didn't notice. "I've been thinking, and it's kind of strange that no one on the TV has crooked teeth or seven fingers or even purple eyebrows."

"Because everything there is perfect and happy," Ozzie said sarcastically.

Mr. Whisk began prodding Scoot's head with an awl. "Perfect and happy. Two different things, if you ask me."

At that moment, his tool found a release lever, there was a click, and Scoot's hat popped open on a hinge to reveal a network of gears, cogs, and what looked like miniature bicycle chains.

Ozzie hadn't even known Scoot's hat could open. "That looks complicated," he said as he examined the mechanical brain. "Can you fix her?"

"There's a broken belt here," Mr. Whisk said, pointing with his awl. "I can take one from one of the other moto's heads."

"Wait," Fidget said. "I just remembered—Scoot and the other motos can detect each other. So, if we switch her back on, Klaxon's motos might pick up her signal. They might find this hideout."

Ozzie grimaced, and it wasn't because of the quirl bedding down in his hair. He knew Fidget didn't like Scoot, so she was probably glad for the excuse to leave her switched off. But even he had to admit that she had a point.

"Ah," Mr. Whisk said, holding up one of his long fingers. "Not a problem. See this cable right here? I'll just unplug it. From what I've gleaned from the other motos, this is what connects her to the motos' overall communication system. They have a sort of hive mind. Don't worry—she'll work mostly the same. She just won't be able to detect the other motos. Good news is, they won't know about her, either."

He replaced the broken belt and closed her lid hat. "Nothing else seems out of order," Mr. Whisk said. "Time to pop her head back on and see what happens."

Ozzie and Fidget braced Scoot's body while Mr. Whisk slid her head onto her rodlike neck. After it clicked into place, Ozzie reinserted Aunt Temperance's ring and gave it a twist. Scoot's eyes instantly began to flicker, and her body lurched forward. It was exactly like back on Moton, when they had first switched her on.

"Up-down-up-up-down," Scoot announced, her head spinning slowly. "Oh . . . I had the most strange dreamy-dream."

"Motos can dream?" Fidget asked skeptically.

"I was playing bash-the-ball," Scoot said.

"I'm not sure you were playing exactly," Fidget informed her. "*Participating*, maybe, but I don't think you can call it playing when your head is the ba—"

"It's okay," Ozzie interrupted, scowling at the princess. "You're fine now, Scoot."

The moto wheeled out into the main room and everyone else followed. Miss Mongo had finished cleaning up the mess and was now shifting around various crates, as if attempting to make the place seem a bit homier.

"Oh, hello," Scoot greeted her, rolling up to shake her hand. "You seem familiar."

"Huh," Miss Mongo grunted as her arm was jostled up and down by Scoot. "It *is* an aberration, innit?"

"No sign of Aunt Temperance yet?" Ozzie asked.

"Don't worry, luv. I'm sure the Cap'n and Fussel—"

She was interrupted by a loud thump on the wooden door. Everyone turned toward it.

"Open up, aberrations," ordered a monotonous voice.

Ozzie looked at Fidget in surprise. The quirl burrowed deep into his hair.

"Motos," she mouthed, her periwinkle eyes wide with alarm. "They found us."

23

A MISSION TO SAVE LADY ZOONE

Ozzie felt like a robotic flying death bug was scuttling down the back of his neck. How had the motos found them? He glanced over at Scoot, wearing her usual unintelligible expression. She was disconnected from the moto network *now*, Ozzie realized, but she hadn't been when they had first stepped through the ripple door. Had that been all the motos needed to detect her signal?

"Outta me way," Miss Mongo grunted. She slid over to the door and yanked it open—to reveal not motos but a scrawny teenaged boy holding a box that seemed much too heavy for him. The quirl in Ozzie's hair squeaked in relief.

"You didn't say the correct passphrase!" Fusselbone panicked, scurrying out of the darkness behind the boy. "It's: *No one here except us aberrations!* Get it right, my boy, get it right! We might think you're a moto! Or worse!"

"What's worse than a moto?" the boy said in a deadpan tone as he lugged in the box and set it down on the nearest crate. The box was filled with limp-looking vegetables and some dusty jars of canned food.

Fusselbone followed the boy into the room, jabbing at the back of his leg. "You weren't followed by any probes, were you? Did you hear any buzzing on the way down?"

"I followed protocol," the boy promised as Cho and Aunt Temperance wandered in, too.

She doesn't look any happier than when she left, Ozzie thought.

"Meet one of our upside operatives," Miss Mongo said, nodding at the teenaged boy. "He's the last person I hired before I lost me own job in the kitchens. We calls him Minus. Though, sometimes, he's a real zero."

Minus released a melancholy sigh, collapsed onto the nearest seat, and removed his cap to reveal a nearly bald head, with only a hint of lime-colored fuzz showing through his scalp.

"Hmm," Aunt Temperance grunted in disapproval. "Your hair is inappropriately green."

"That means it's almost time to shave again, my boy," Fusselbone told Minus, leaping onto his shoulder and inspecting his head. "Best do it before you get in trouble!"

"Why would you get in trouble for not shaving?" Ozzie wondered.

"Oh, you know," Minus answered slowly, grimacing as Fusselbone continued to inspect him. "Klaxon doesn't like hair. Too messy. Too unpredictable. Doesn't like fancy colors, either. Like mine. So, if you want to keep your job, you have to shave. Even your eyebrows. Unless you dye them an acceptable color."

"Acceptable?" Aunt Temperance snapped. "Mercurio's hair was wild. *Circus-wild*; black and red and . . ."

"This is ridiculous," Fidget huffed. "Everyone who works at the station has to shave their heads?"

Minus nodded.

Ozzie ran his fingers through his own thick hair, causing the quirl to give him a playful nip. His hair grew so fast that he had to get it cut every three weeks. Trying to keep it flat was futile; no amount of spray, gel, or wax could keep it from springing up. He wasn't sure shaving would work, either—not for long, anyway. But at least being bald would discourage quirls from nesting.

"Truth of it is there aren't many flesh-and-bone folks workin' up there anymore," Miss Mongo said. "Most of 'em have disappeared or been thrown in the clink."

"Minus will probably be next," Fusselbone fretted. "The motos will catch him doing something illicit, then that will be it! Right into prison! Then who will bring us food? We'll starve."

"And, well, I'll be in prison," Minus added.

"*This place* might as well be a prison," Aunt Temperance complained, gesturing to the dingy walls. "I couldn't find my way out of it. This is not what I expected of Zoone."

No kidding, Ozzie thought. *Me, either.* "Look," he announced. "Aunt T is right about one thing. We need to do something. We can't just wait around."

"Yes, listen to Ozzie," Aunt Temperance insisted. "Zaria said to save Mercurio."

"Actually, Aunt T," Ozzie countered, "her message said: '*We* can save him.' That means you *and* Lady Zoone. Together."

"But Zaria's not here," Aunt Temperance said slowly. "She's . . ."

"In trouble, too," Ozzie said emphatically.

Aunt Temperance brushed the locks of silver hair out of her face and slumped onto a crate. "That's not the way I'm used to thinking about Zaria," she confessed. "As someone in trouble."

"Well, she is," Fidget said. "And we have to help her."

"Then we can all face Mercurio together," Cho added.

"It's not something you have to do alone."

"Not face him," Aunt Temperance said. "*Save* him. But . . ." She exhaled, then turned her gaze to Ozzie.

"We start with Lady Zoone," he said.

Aunt Temperance slowly nodded.

"We need a plan," Cho declared. "The first step is to find out where Lady Zoone is exactly. Is she under house arrest in her personal tower? Is she in the prison with the others?"

"We don't know," Miss Mongo said. "Sent out some of our Underground to do some searchin', but they never came back."

"The station is enormous, Captain, simply enormous!" Fusselbone said. "And old. There are towers and sections that not even I know about!"

"Me, either," Cho admitted. "Lady Zoone could be anywhere. Which means we need to do our own reconnaissance. We need a scout."

"Ooh! That's me," Scoot volunteered, waving her hand exuberantly in the air.

Cho chuckled. "I'm afraid it has to be someone a bit more inconspicuous. Which counts out most of us in this room."

"It won't make a difference," Mr. Whisk said. "The upper levels of the station are restricted, locked down and patrolled by motos. It's impossible to get up there."

"Not if you have this," Fidget said, pulling Lady Zoone's multiversal key from beneath her shawl. She spun one of the many gears that were clustered on its bow. "With this, I can open any door in the station."

"Are you sure you know how to use it?" Ozzie asked, ogling the key.

Fidget rolled her eyes. "I've seen Lady Zoone use it enough times. You set the gears to the right combination, and you can go to any destination in the station. I just need a keyhole to get started."

"None of those down here, luv," Miss Mongo said. "You'll need to go upside. But you better not go alone."

"I can help," Tug offered, ears twitching.

"We can't disguise a skyger," Fidget said.

"I'm a Zoonian skyger," Tug protested. "I can change color."

"Oh, sure, because a purple skyger doesn't draw any attention. Not at all like a blue one."

Tug swished his tail, which happened to bowl over Minus and send him toppling to the floor. The poor guy obviously didn't have much experience dealing with skyger tails.

"Listen, cub, I need you down here," Cho said, scratching Tug's chin. "You can help us . . . *plan*. Fidget, you should take Ozzie with you; he's perfect for this sort of mission."

Aunt Temperance jumped to her feet. "Captain!" she cried, even as Ozzie's chest was swelling with pride. "You can't send the children to face danger."

"What in Quoggswoggle have we been doing up till now?" Fidget demanded.

Ozzie ignored his aunt. "We can do it, Cho," he declared.

"Are you sure?" Fusselbone asked, tugging on Ozzie's leg. "What do you know about espionage? Have you ever cracked an Ormese cipher? Read *The Spy Who Came through the Red Door*? Administered the antidote for a Simmean spider dart? You've got to watch your heels, my boy, watch your heels!"

"Er . . . ," Ozzie mumbled.

"I'm coming with you," Aunt Temperance announced.

"You don't know the station," Ozzie argued. "Fidget and I do."

"They have a better chance of success than any of us," Cho assured Aunt Temperance.

"You came all the way here to save your boyfriend," Fidget told her. "Well, I came here to save Zoone. And that's what I plan to do."

"Me, too," Ozzie said, leveling a look of determination at Aunt Temperance.

She finally sighed in capitulation. "What if they get in

trouble?" she challenged Cho. "How will we know?"

"I'll take the quirl," Ozzie suggested. "If something happens, I'll send her down." As if to agree with this idea, the tiny rodent leaped from his hair to his shoulder and began chirping.

Aunt Temperance blinked in surprise. "That's a quirl? I thought they would be . . . *bigger*. Where did it come from?"

"She's part o' the Underground," Miss Mongo answered. "Clever rodent knows what side to take. The one with the best cook."

"So, we're agreed?" Cho asked Aunt Temperance.

She didn't reply; instead, she paced into the nearest alcove and stared into the bricks.

Ozzie followed her. "Cho trusts me. Why don't you?"

Aunt Temperance turned and wrapped her arms around him, which was a bit embarrassing, especially in front of Fidget and the rest of the Zoone crew. "Oh, Ozzie. I trust you. It's just . . ."

"What?"

"You told me so many things about this world. *These* worlds. And now I'm seeing them firsthand, and . . . now I see it."

"See what?"

"It's not just me anymore. It's not just you."

"Huh?"

"It's not just us." She sighed and hugged him tighter. "Be careful, Ozzie. Really careful."

Ozzie and Fidget knew the station, but they didn't know the catacombs, which meant Minus was assigned to lead them through the labyrinthine network while the rest of the crew prepared for a rescue operation. Just before leaving the headquarters, Ozzie took one last look at the ragtag crew: Cho had attached a homemade blueprint of the station to the wall and was conferring with Fusselbone, Miss Mongo was polishing her rolling pin, Scoot was cleaning her blender gun, and Tug was curled up in the corner, taking a nap. Then there was Aunt Temperance. Mostly, she was pacing.

"If this doesn't end soon, I think she'll explode," Ozzie confided to Fidget as they plodded after Minus. The quirl, perched on his shoulder, offered a sympathetic chirp.

"Yeah, well, 'soon' may never happen," the princess whispered. "Minus is as slow as a Hibian sloth."

Minus glanced over his shoulder. "I heard that."

"What kind of name is Minus anyway?" Fidget wondered.

"Just a nickname," the soft-spoken boy replied, stuffing his hands into his pockets. "It's because of my age.

Basically, I'm a walking cadaver."

"But you're still alive," Ozzie said to Minus, before quickly adding, "aren't you?" Maybe he was some sort of zombie. In a place like Zoone, anything was possible.

"I'm alive," Minus replied sullenly. "But I shouldn't be. I'm technically minus-ten years old."

"That doesn't make any sense," Ozzie said.

"I'm from Numerria," Minus responded, as if this was all the explanation required.

"Oh," Fidget said as they rounded a corner. "*Numerria*. When you're born, they calculate your life expectancy with statistics and stuff, which means you start life with a final estimated age. Then you count down by one each year." She looked at Minus. "Right?"

Minus nodded. "I started at age eight and reached zero ten years ago. But I didn't die."

"Isn't that a relief?" Fidget prompted.

"Not really," Minus said. "How would you feel if you were supposed to die a decade ago?"

"Happy?" Ozzie suggested.

"I'm a walking time bomb," Minus moaned. "It could happen any day now. I mean, I *am* minus-ten. Well. Here we are."

They had arrived at the foot of a spiraling set of stone steps. "These lead into the station's kitchens," Minus revealed as he began a laboring ascent. "Unless the motos discovered the entrance. Maybe they blocked the stairs. Which is likely."

"Why?" Fidget asked.

"Because," Minus answered, "bad things always seem to happen to me."

"Well, you've outlived your due date," Fidget reminded the morose boy. "Don't you think that's a positive, um . . . Minus?"

The only reply she received was a sigh, so up they continued, without further words. The corkscrew staircase ended at a cast-iron hatch. It was only once they had popped it open and climbed out that Ozzie realized that they had come through the belly of an enormous cauldron. It was sitting dormant in a fireplace in a forgotten nook of the kitchens. It was a perfectly hidden doorway.

Ozzie took a deep breath. He didn't detect any of the delicious smells that usually wafted through the kitchen. But at least he was here, in Zoone. Proper Zoone.

"I suppose I better stick around," Minus told them. "You know, do some work. I'm technically on shift. Only managed to sneak away because 33-487B assigned me to clean the storage room."

"33-487B?" Ozzie repeated.

"The new head cook," Minus answered. "There's a door at the end of the hall, a shortcut to the west platform."

"All we need is the keyhole," Fidget told Ozzie as they hurried down the corridor.

"Right," Ozzie said, grabbing the handle. "But, first, I want to take a peek outside."

"That's not our mission!"

Ozzie stared her down. "Do you know how long I've been waiting to get back here?"

"Do you know how dangerous it is?" she snapped.

"Fine," he said. But before she could react, he twisted the handle and stepped through the door, and onto the platform.

A NEXUS TURNED NAVY

Ozzie took his first few steps across the cobblestones of the west platform, drinking in the sights and sounds of the station. *I'm here*, he thought. *Actually here.* He was looking at Zoone—not through a daydream, a memory marble, or a TV screen, but at the actual, real-life nexus. He could see the countless doors radiating out before him in concentric circles, doors made of wood and metal and stone. Doors of every shape and color. Doors that led to different corners of the multiverse. He took a few more steps, only to come to a sudden stop.

"We have to go back inside," Fidget hissed, coming up behind him.

"Something's wrong," Ozzie told her.

"No kidding. The station has been taken over by motos."

"Yeah, but that's not it," Ozzie murmured as the quirl leaped from his shoulder back into his hair. He slowly turned, pondering the scene around him. The nexus was busy, just as he remembered it. Travelers were coming and going out of doors, headed this way and that, from one end of the multiverse to the other. On the surface, everything was running smoothly.

And that was exactly the thing that was needling Ozzie. It was *too* efficient.

There was no hustle or bustle on the platform, no energy, no . . . *life*. Where were the travelers with their misplaced tickets? Where were the lost toddlers who had wandered away from their parents? Where were the Sir Pomposities and their runaway pets? Now, as Ozzie ambled in bewilderment around the platform, it looked like the most thrilling thing that might happen would be a sticky door handle. Travelers were walking not quickly, not slowly—just methodically, eyes planted on the platform below their feet, as if eager not to draw attention to themselves.

Ozzie shifted his focus to the motos. The mechanical men were systematically patrolling the platform, stopping various travelers to examine their tickets and to interrogate them about their destinations.

"It's gotten so much worse since I was last here," Fidget said.

"Worse than what we saw on the monitors," Ozzie added as he slowly turned around to contemplate the station house. Something was wrong with it, too. There was scaffolding set up in one section, and a half-dozen motos were at work on the walls. It took a moment for Ozzie to work out what they were doing. The station was supposed to be a vibrant turquoise blue, but it was being repainted.

"Navy?!" Ozzie cried. "They're painting it *navy*?!"

"The weakest of colors," Fidget murmured. "Isn't that what Aunt T said?"

"It's . . . it's . . . an abomination," Ozzie seethed. "How can they do this?"

"Halt," came a voice.

They turned to see a moto security officer confronting them with its blank, expressionless eyes. "Please state your destination."

"Hello to you, too," Fidget retorted. "Why, welcome to the nexus, the magical center of the multiverse."

The moto thrust out a metal claw. "Friends, please present your tickets."

The quirl gave a worried squeak; Ozzie felt her tunnel deeper into his hair.

"Hey, 33-589D," someone called from across the platform. "I need your assistance here."

Ozzie turned to see a non-moto worker waving from the foot of the stairs that led to the station's west gate. It took a moment for Ozzie to recognize her; it was Keeva, his fellow porter, but her hair had been shaved to the scalp to meet Klaxon's regulations. Keeva gave Ozzie a knowing wink as she distracted the moto security officer. Fidget quickly pulled Ozzie away and they ducked behind one of the countless doors.

"We shouldn't have come out here," the princess complained. "There are a lot of motos—way more than the last time I was here."

"Heyff! You guyth can't thand there."

Ozzie and Fidget exchanged a look of surprise. The voice was coming from the front side of the door, but it was definitely not a moto. They peeked out to see that it was Door 457 to Jeongo. Its wood was painted bright orange with yellow trim and it had an ornament in the middle that seemed part sun, part dragon. It looked fierce, but the door knocker in its teeth caused it to lisp.

"If you're going thoo hang out, ath leafth thalk to me," the knocker implored. "No one haff time for pleathantrieth anymore."

"No kidding," Fidget said. "Well, keep your hinges on, Sunshine. Ozzie, we have to get out of here."

They circled the station, away from the moto that had interrogated them, then climbed the stairs to the south gate.

"Quoggswoggle," Fidget uttered, coming to a stop once they were inside and gazing at the station hub.

Before them was another picture of despair. In his time at Zoone, Ozzie had known the hub to be the heart of the station—and possibly the multiverse. But now it was as if that heart had been yanked out and replaced with a cold and emotionless stone. There was a fountain in the center, featuring a statue of Zephyrus Zoone, but it wasn't even running. Lining the circumference of the cavernous space were many shops and services, but Ozzie noticed that many of them were closed. One of these was the quirlery, as Miss Mongo had mentioned, but the one that really surprised Ozzie was The Squeaky Hinge. He had never been inside the tavern (he was too young), but he had passed it many times while working as a porter. It was usually a lively place, full of boisterous patrons and lively chatter that you could sometimes hear from halfway across the hub. Now? It was boarded up with crooked pieces of wood. Above the shops, lining the upper walls, were schedule boards describing the status of different doors and tracks. Line after line read "canceled" or "closed until further notice."

"No one wants to hang around here anymore," Fidget

guessed. "They just want to get to where they're going."

She clutched Ozzie by the arm and led him to the nearest doorway, which led to the crew's tower in the southeast section of the station. The door was locked, but that didn't matter; all they needed was the keyhole.

"Just going to find the right setting," Fidget murmured as she began spinning the gears on the key. "I'll take us directly to Lady Zoone's chambers."

"Halt," sounded another moto voice.

Ozzie looked over his shoulder to see two of the mechanical men marching toward them.

"Friends, that area is restricted. We will help you find the right place to go."

"You can go to Quogg!" Fidget growled.

"Hurry!" Ozzie urged. "I thought you knew how to use that thing!"

"Just hold on!" She plunged the key into the lock and they scrambled through the door.

Ozzie blinked. "Um, Fidget? This is *not* Lady Zoone's study."

They were standing on one of Zoone's many terraces. This one, it appeared, overlooked the south platform.

"You rushed me," Fidget grumbled.

"No, that was the motos," Ozzie retorted as he wandered over to the railing to take in the view.

It was now nearing the end of the day, the fingers of

the sun retracting across the grounds, but they still had a good vantage point to observe the south platform and the Infinite Wood that lay beyond—or at least what was left of it. Giant swaths of the forest were missing.

"It's being wiped clean," Ozzie said, his voice cracking as he stared at the expanse of stumps. "Like Untaar." He could picture the gauge in the control hub on Moton. *What does it say now?* he wondered. *Ten percent? Fifteen? Twenty?*

"We're not going to let the same thing happen here," Fidget told him. "We're *not*." She tugged him back to the door they had just stepped through. "I'll get it right this time," she promised, twisting the gears on the key again.

When she was done, she led them through the door and they arrived directly into Lady Zoone's study.

The place had been ransacked. Chairs and shelves had been tipped over. Books littered the floor. There was an assortment of strange relics in the study, but Ozzie noticed that many were smashed against the floor.

"Klaxon did this!" Fidget growled.

Ozzie nodded, but the worst thing, he decided, was how deathly quiet it was. The last time he had visited this room, it had been alive with the sounds of the birds and rodents that lived with Lady Zoone. Now it felt like an abandoned museum.

"Lady Zoone obviously hasn't been here for a long

time," Fidget said, using her toe to nudge at the remnants of a broken hourglass.

"Where to now?" Ozzie wondered.

Fidget frowned. "I'm not sure." She ambled over to a statue situated in a nearby alcove. It depicted a man with wide, crazed eyes and a sneering lip. In one fist he was clutching a set of shackles. Behind him, on the wall, was a stone-relief carving of a door.

Ozzie studied the plaque at the base of the statue. "Dreyuss Atroxi," he read before looking to Fidget. "Who's that?"

"A former steward of Zoone," Fidget answered. "There hasn't been a prison in the station, at least not during Lady Zoone's tenure. But there used to be, when Atroxi was in command. It's said he became so mad with power, so paranoid, that he started imprisoning staff. When he was finally removed as steward, they boarded up his tower."

"Why would Lady Zoone keep a statue of him?" Ozzie wondered.

"She told me it was to remind her of the responsibilities of being a steward. I wonder . . ."

Fidget squeezed behind the statue and touched the keyhole in the stone-relief door with her finger. There was the grinding of stone, and the door creaked inward.

Ozzie gaped at her. "How did you know?"

"I didn't," the princess replied. "But I grew up in a

palace. Finding secret passageways is kind of my thing. Come on."

They stepped through the door and found themselves transported to another alcove, opening onto a dimly lit corridor.

Ozzie glanced up and down the passage. The walls were lined with empty cells. "Your hunch was right," he whispered to Fidget. "This must be the abandoned prison tower."

"Maybe not abandoned anymore," Fidget said. "Let's explore."

Ozzie followed her into the corridor, only for the quirl to scamper out of his hair, down his body, and onto the floor, where she began chittering loudly.

"Shh!" Fidget hissed. "You're going to get us caught."

But the tiny rodent didn't stop—and now she began darting around their feet.

Fidget scowled. "What's going on with this thing?"

"I think she wants us to go back and report to Cho," Ozzie guessed.

"We haven't found out anything yet," Fidget argued. She turned to go farther down the hall, but the quirl nipped at her ankle. "OW!" she yelped, kicking the rodent away.

"Hey—careful!" Ozzie said. The quirl squealed, then disappeared back through the keyhole in the wall behind them. "Great," Ozzie complained to Fidget. "Now she's gone. You didn't have to kick her."

"She didn't have to bite me!" Fidget retorted. "*Scaredy quirl*. Look, Lady Zoone might be here. We have to find out for sure."

She was already halfway down the passage, so Ozzie hurried after her. Every cell they passed was empty, but then they turned a corner and suddenly saw multiple faces staring at them.

Zoonian faces.

Ozzie's mouth dropped open. These were the people he had come to know during his time at Zoone. He had worked side by side with them, eaten meals with them in the mess hall, traded stories with them. And now they barely looked like themselves; their heads were shaved and their faces were pale and gaunt.

"Ozzie? Fidget? Is that you?" called a girl from the nearest cell.

They rushed over to her. She only had a hint of hair, which meant Ozzie didn't recognize her at first.

"Piper?" he gasped.

The teenaged girl self-consciously touched her head, as if suddenly remembering that her blue-and-green hair had been shaved off. At least her eyebrows were still there. It looked like they had been previously dyed, but now the natural color was showing through; the left one was green and the right one was blue.

"I guess you never made it out of here to find any wizards," Fidget said.

"Got captured trying to sneak out of Zoone," declared a second girl, emerging out of the shadows. It was Panya, Piper's older sister. She was slightly taller than Piper, and all her hair had been shaved off, too.

"But *you're* here, Ozzie," Piper said excitedly. "You made it! Do you know what I found before I ended up here? This photo of—"

"Yeah, yeah, I know," Ozzie cut her off.

"Your aunt and Klaxon were in love—weren't they?" Piper pressed.

Ozzie snorted. Being thrown into prison had clearly not blunted Piper's personality.

"How come they didn't end up together?" she asked.

"I don't know," Ozzie snapped. Which was the truth.

"Sounds like a tragic love story," Piper continued dreamily. "It's so romantic, so—"

"Look," Panya interrupted, "you guys have to break us out of here! Scuffy Will's here, and he's really sick."

Ozzie squinted into the darkness and could just make out a figure curled against the back wall.

"There's no keyhole on this cell door," Fidget said. She glanced around, then frowned and pointed to a panel on a nearby wall. "Great. Just like Moton. Lady Zoone's key won't work here."

A series of groans came from the cells. Different crew members began calling out suggestions. Ozzie began flicking switches on the panel, but it was to no avail. "It's going to take forever to solve this," he said.

"That's more time than we have," Fidget said. "Look, guys," she said, turning to Panya and Piper, "we're going to bust you out somehow. But Cho told us—"

"Captain Cho's here?" Panya asked, craning her neck to peer down the hall. "Where? What about Miss Mongo? And Keeva! What about Keeva?"

"She's *soooo* in love with Keeva," Piper informed them. "And now they're separated by bars. They're separated by—"

"Look, they're safe," Fidget said. "*For now.* But we need to find Lady Zoone. Is she here?"

Piper and Panya exchanged a glance. "She's through that door at the end of the hallway," Piper said. "But . . ."

"But what?" Ozzie pressed.

"Something's not right about her," Panya said.

Fidget turned away and began hurrying down the corridor, toward the door. Ozzie chased her.

"Hey, what about us?" Piper called.

"We'll be back," Ozzie promised over his shoulder.

There were no more cells in this direction; Panya and Piper's had been the last in the row. The door at the end of the passageway was old and wooden. It wasn't locked, so they pushed through to find still more corridor. They followed it until they arrived at a large chamber. There was no cell here, no iron bars—just a tall, angular figure leaning against the wall.

"Lady Zoone?" Ozzie called. "Is that you?"

There was no response. Ozzie and Fidget tentatively stepped farther into the chamber—and the figure's eyes lit up. It began lurching toward them. Lady Zoone had never been graceful at walking—Ozzie had always been under the impression that it was something that didn't come naturally to her—but this was different. It was as if something terrible had happened to her, like she had broken some of her limbs and now they were in stiff casts. It was like . . .

Ozzie jumped backward.

"Quoggswoggle!" Fidget cried.

It wasn't Lady Zoone teetering toward them, even though it looked almost exactly like her.

It was a moto.

25

THE UNDERGROUND RISES UP

"She's a fake," Ozzie murmured in shock. "A replica."

"I told you something wasn't right!" Fidget exclaimed. "If you see her from far away, you might almost believe it's her."

"Where's the real Lady Zoone?!" Ozzie panicked.

"She is on Moton."

Ozzie and Fidget whirled around. There was a passageway leading off to the side; it was just so dark that they hadn't noticed it at first, and standing at its entrance was the last person in the multiverse they wanted to see.

Klaxon looked the same as when they had encountered him on Moton, still mostly metal from his chest to his head, with switches, dials, and hoses protruding from every surface. Though, Ozzie noticed, there *was* something different about him. Klaxon seemed stronger, more confident. Maybe it was because he had just come out of surgery when they had last seen him. *Or maybe*, Ozzie thought, *he's even more machine now.*

Klaxon focused his goggles on the moto Lady Zoone. "My masterpiece," he announced. "I have built many mechanical creatures in my life, but nothing so marvelous as her." As he spoke, Ozzie caught flashes of silver between his lips. Even Klaxon's teeth were metal.

"Lady Zoone isn't on Moton," Ozzie said. "She . . . she can't be."

"She did it to herself," Klaxon continued impassively. "She would not accept my plan to save the multiverse."

"What in the name of Quoxx are you talking about?" Fidget growled.

"The Destiny Machine," Klaxon said. "My invention to save the multiverse from pain. Unfortunately, when I showed Zaria what I was building, she conveyed only dismay. It is unfortunate that she did not possess the wisdom to comprehend my gift. She left me with no choice but to abandon her on Moton and activate her moto replacement. Now I can complete my work without dissension."

Fidget gasped. "You left her to wander that wasteland? That was weeks ago! She wouldn't still be . . ."

Fidget was right, Ozzie knew. Cho had survived Moton, but he was a lot stronger than Lady Zoone. And younger.

Klaxon pressed a button on his chest and the moto Lady Zoone lumbered back to the chamber wall. "She refused to embrace my plan. Now she knows pain," he said. "Slow, agonizing pain. It is not my fault."

"What did you do?" Ozzie demanded.

"Zaria is an Arborellian," Klaxon replied. "When in extreme danger, they revert to their natural state."

Ozzie looked to Fidget. "What's he talking about?"

"I don't know," she admitted.

"The poison will leach into her," Klaxon continued emotionlessly. "She will wither. She will die. But not for a very long time."

"Wither?" Ozzie murmured. It was a strange way to describe a person wasting away. "Wait a minute . . ." Something had just occurred to him, something that made him queasy.

"What is it?" Fidget asked.

"The tree," Ozzie told her quietly. "We were standing right in front of her. In that garden of rust. And we left her there."

Fidget's eyes fluttered wide. "We have to save her," she whispered, pulling Ozzie close. "We have to go back. We—"

"You will get your wish," Klaxon decreed.

Ozzie shivered. It didn't matter how quietly they had tried to speak. Klaxon must have heard every word with his motonic hearing.

Two moto guards scuttled out of the shadows behind Klaxon and gripped them with metal claws. Ozzie tried to twist free, but there was no way to escape. Not unless he wanted to leave a chunk of his shoulder behind.

They were herded down the passageway Klaxon had come from and through a series of doors and turns, until they suddenly popped outside, beneath the night sky.

They had been brought up to the terrace at the very top of the station house. It was like a giant open-air court-yard; Ozzie could feel the breeze against his skin and see the stars and many moons of Zoone in the sky above. The terrace itself was lit by lampposts, but they were all that remained of the place Ozzie had known from his last time at Zoone. Everything else had been removed—the benches, the gables, even the beautiful potted trees that had once lined the circumference of the vast space. In the very center of the terrace, situated on a large, circular dais, was a doorway, constructed of thick iron girders. There was no door hanging on the frame, just the sheet of electrical static. Several motos patrolled the perimeter.

"We've seen that door," Ozzie said, with a horrified glance at Fidget. "It leads to Moton."

"Where it leads," Klaxon corrected him, "is to the Destiny Machine." He climbed onto the dais and stood beside the iron arch. "The device is now complete. At last, I can begin saving the multiverse."

"We don't need saving, Metal-Head," Fidget jeered.

Klaxon's eyes telescoped out, then back in, like he was frowning or furling his brow. "Of course you do. You are flesh. You can feel pain. But soon you will not."

The motos began forcing them toward the door, but before they were even halfway there, a triumphant blare erupted across the night.

"That's Cho's horn!" Ozzie cried excitedly.

Suddenly, several of the doors that led to the terrace banged open.

"It's not just Cho!" Fidget exclaimed. "It's the entire Zoone Underground!"

Cho charged onto the terrace, swinging his hunting horn with such force that it decapitated the first moto he encountered. Miss Mongo came from the opposite direction, clobbering motos with her rolling pin. Then there was Scoot, who wheeled onto the impromptu battlefield and began firing her blender gun in every direction. "Doo-do-do-doo!" she trumpeted.

"The quirl got them!" Ozzie said, spotting the tiny rodent as she darted onto the terrace.

Even the Zoonians that Ozzie would have never

expected to fight—Mr. Whisk, Minus, and Fusselbone—had come to do their part. Then Tug burst onto the scene, bounding across the platform with Aunt Temperance clinging to his back like a knight on a steed. Tug couldn't fly because of his broken wing, but plowing across the terrace caused plenty of disruption. Mostly, he took out robots accidentally—but that, Ozzie decided, still counted. And Aunt Temperance might not have had a lance, but she did have her flashlight—and she was using it to smash every moto in sight. In fact, as Tug whipped past, she took out both of the motos holding Ozzie and Fidget captive.

"Come on!" Fidget yelled. "Let's kick some moto butt!"

There was a dismembered moto arm lying near Ozzie's feet. He snatched it up and tried to slash the nearest moto, but it pivoted unexpectedly at the elbow. He might have cuffed himself in the back of his *own* head, except for the moto attacking from behind. The arm struck that moto instead, felling it instantly.

This thing is kind of like a pair of nunchucks, Ozzie thought with a grin.

He gave the moto limb a couple of test swings, then charged farther into the fray, still swinging. Out of the corner of his eye, he spotted Klaxon standing impassively next to his doorway. He wasn't joining the fight, just watching. Then the moto-man flicked some switches on the door's control panel and it shimmered open. Ozzie could see the Moton command center beyond—but only for a second before motos began spilling through and onto the terrace. There were too many to count—and they kept coming.

We have to close that door! Ozzie thought. "Scoot!" he cried. "We need your blender!" He whirled around to search for her in the fracas, only to have his moto-arm-club smash right into her—or more specifically, right into her blender gun. The glass jar exploded, and the canteen clattered to the ground.

"Oopsy!" Scoot warbled.

"Great, Oz," Fidget told him. "Gear-Guts was actually being useful. And now we're done for."

She was right, Ozzie knew. An endless supply of moto reinforcements was flowing through the door—and without the blender gun, the crew was in trouble. Dread swept over Ozzie as he saw Minus get zapped by one of the electrical prongs of the attacking motos. The boy dropped to the ground, quickly followed by Fusselbone.

Then, suddenly, all of the motos stopped and the terrace fell silent. Ozzie glanced around at the Zoone Underground. Cho had a black eye. Aunt Temperance had a gash on one cheek. Mr. Whisk had been felled and Miss Mongo was leaning over him, clucking pitifully. The old man's beard had shriveled up to his chin and the quirl was there, sniffing him.

"I do not want death," Klaxon announced. "If you die, I cannot save you. It is time to enter the Destiny Machine."

"O'er my empty belly!" Miss Mongo roared.

She lunged forward with her rolling pin, only to be immediately zapped by a moto. That didn't stop her—but six more zaps from the surrounding motos did. At last, the giant blob that was Miss Mongo burbled to the ground. Ozzie stared at her in awe and despair; she looked like a heap of warts.

The motos closed in on them like a noose. Fidget wrenched the moto-arm-club out of Ozzie's hands and hurled it at the nearest robot. It clanked harmlessly off its body.

So much for that, Ozzie thought. The canteen of Arborellian nectar was still lying on the ground, leaking fluid. Ozzie quickly snatched it up and passed it to Scoot. "Here," he whispered. "Cap this and hide it in one of your compartments. For later."

"You betcha!" she said.

She had barely finished hiding the canteen when Klaxon marched through his circle of motos and stopped a few steps in front of Aunt Temperance. He flicked a button on his chest and the moto army came to a halt, though with their weaponized hands still pointing at the group.

Ozzie's gaze flew from his aunt to Klaxon, then back again. The two of them were staring at each other, not saying a word. In fact, no one was saying anything, not even Fidget, who always seemed to have a comment. The terrace was fraught with tension, but it wasn't just between Aunt Temperance and Klaxon, Ozzie realized. *Everyone's been wondering about them,* he thought, sucking in a deep breath. *And now, here we are . . .*

"Mercurio," Aunt Temperance said, finally breaking the silence. "What . . . what happened to you?" The confusion and devastation were clear in her voice. She tucked away a strand of disheveled hair and took a deliberate step toward the machine-man. He stood stiffly before her, unresponsive except for the flickering of his helmet lights.

Does he even recognize her? Ozzie wondered. Were those flashing lights an indication that he was trying to remember? Or were they like warning bells? Because Klaxon wasn't moving. At all.

Aunt Temperance slowly lifted a hand toward Klaxon. "Your limbs," she said quietly, gently touching his robotic arm. "Your face," she said, caressing his metal cheek. "You've been injured."

Ozzie shuddered—because he wasn't so sure anymore

that's what had happened. Klaxon was clearly in charge of the motos. If they had hurt him, it was because he had *let* them . . .

But that was something Aunt Temperance didn't seem like she wanted to admit. "We can help you," she told Klaxon. "It's not too late."

Yes, it is! Ozzie screamed in his thoughts. *He's a robot. How can you love him?*

Aunt Temperance lifted her locket from around her neck and clicked it open to reveal the picture of her and Mercurio. "Don't you remember *us*? We had something *real*. We can go back to this."

Klaxon reached out with his metal fingers and grasped the locket. His goggles telescoped toward the picture. A sound sputtered from his lips and Ozzie realized that something had changed in his demeanor. Was it seeing the locket? Or Aunt Temperance in person? Ozzie had this sense that he was losing control of his emotions, like he was a pot on the stove, trying to contain what was simmering under his lid. Eventually, he was going to boil over. Ozzie was sure of it—it was just a matter of when. But what exactly was beneath that lid?

"We can help you," Aunt Temperance repeated. "*I* can help you."

Klaxon snapped the locket shut and lifted his chin to Aunt Temperance. "You," he said, a hint of humanness in his voice. "You . . . you cannot trick me. Oh, I remember. I remember *everything*." Then he squeezed the locket in his metal fingers, crushing it like a car in a junkyard.

"Hey!" Fidget shouted.

Ozzie's own voice died in his throat. That locket had meant so much to Aunt Temperance. She had kept it all these years. She had carried it across the multiverse. And in an instant, Klaxon had destroyed it.

"Mercurio—no!" Aunt Temperance cried.

She snatched at the chain of the locket, dangling from Klaxon's fingers, but he merely lifted his hand and pitched the crumpled metal. Ozzie watched it sail right over the edge of the terrace.

Tears streamed down Aunt Temperance's cheeks. Ozzie instinctively went to her side, glaring at Klaxon as he did so. Now he understood what was simmering inside the moto-man: rage and torment.

"You are right to say that I was injured," Klaxon told Aunt Temperance. "But it is not my flesh that felt the pain. It was my soul."

"Wh-what?" Aunt Temperance stammered. She slipped an arm around Ozzie, pulling him close. Usually, that was the sort of thing he resisted. But not this time.

Klaxon's lenses began to spin, round and round, as if he couldn't quite focus on what he was seeing. "I was alone. A-lone-a-lone-a-lone."

"No one's alone at Zoone," Fidget told him, stepping forward. From behind her, Tug purred in support.

"Alone-alone-alone," Klaxon repeated in monotone. "I must not feel alone."

"I . . . I understand," Aunt Temperance told him. "I've felt that way, too. But what if pain is important? What if—"

"I am left alone," Klaxon insisted. "Alone-alone-alone." It was as if he had a glitch. The antennae on his helmet were shooting up and down—it was just what Scoot did when she was trying to process information, Ozzie remembered. "You found someone," Klaxon declared with a hint of anguish. "Someone else to love. And I am left alone-alone-alone."

Aunt Temperance shook her head in bewilderment. "What are you talking about?"

Yeah, Ozzie added silently as he clung to her. *What are you talking about?* He remembered Captain Traxx accusing Aunt Temperance of giving up her life for someone, someone who wasn't Mercurio. *Had* there been someone else? Another boyfriend?

"It is because of you," Klaxon announced. He raised a long, mechanical finger to emit a red beam, like a laser pointer.

Fidget audibly gasped. Ozzie turned to stare at her,

only to realize she was already staring back.

"What is it?" he asked. Then he slowly turned his gaze downward, to his own chest, where a pinprick of red was flickering.

Klaxon was pointing at *him*.

DOORWAY TO DESTINY

Ozzie felt like he had just been clobbered by one of Moton's giant mechanical hammers. *None of this makes sense*, he thought, his mind swirling. *None of this . . .*

"Ozzie," Aunt Temperance said. She was still clutching him, but now even more tightly, with both arms.

"Yes," Klaxon said, the despair clear in his voice. "There he is. The symbol of your true love."

"I don't think you understand," Aunt Temperance told him.

Klaxon clasped his two mismatched hands, one flesh and one metal, behind his back. Then he began pacing back and forth in front of them in a straight line, taking sharp, measured turns. "There I was, years ago. Waiting for you. Waiting for my fiancée. My love. But you did not come."

"I went to find you, I went to be with—"

"NO!" he roared, a mechanically enhanced cry so loud that it reverberated off the walls of the terrace, twisted with pain.

And maybe menace, Ozzie thought as Scoot whistled in surprise. Tug mewled and tried to thrust his massive head into Fidget's armpit, like an oversized kitten hiding from thunder.

"After you abandoned me, I wandered the multiverse," Klaxon continued. "I sought relief from my pain. But true succor does not exist for a broken heart. Finally, in my despair, I returned to Eridea, to seek you."

"I wasn't with the circus anymore," Aunt Temperance explained, "but if you had looked harder, you would have found—"

"I did find you," Klaxon stated. "I can see you now. Pushing your carriage down the street. Pushing him." He was pointing his red beam at Ozzie again. "Who is the father?" Klaxon asked. "Not-me-not-me-not-me."

"This is Ozzie," Aunt Temperance announced, now standing behind him with both hands on his shoulders. "He is my *nephew*. His father is my *brother*. You misunderstood everything. After Ozzie was born, his mother

received a once-in-a-lifetime career opportunity over-
seas. And my brother was sent to open a new regional
office in South America. There was pressure to stay, to
help the family."

Ozzie started. He hadn't known *any* of this. Aunt
Temperance had stayed to *"help"*? If anything, it was
more like his parents did the helping, just showing up
whenever it was convenient for their careers.

Klaxon's antennae were gyrating again. "You chose
him. Over me. Over-me-over-me-over-me."

Aunt Temperance bristled. "Not *over* you. But I chose
to stay with him. Yes."

Ozzie felt an unfamiliar shiver down the back of his
neck. He had never thought of himself as chosen. Ignored?
Yes. Abandoned? *Yes.* But chosen?

He slowly turned and stared at Aunt Temperance. He
knew her better now than ever before. Knew she could
do so much more than he had ever given her credit for.
But for most of his life he had taken her for granted. He
had latched on to her, depended on her, but it had never
occurred to him to wonder what she had given up. It
hadn't even occurred to him that there had been anything
to give up.

But she had given up something—many things. Mercurio. The circus. Her whole life.

For me, Ozzie realized.

Aunt Temperance's gaze was fixed on Klaxon. "And what about what *you* chose? You could have chosen to stay. To talk to me. To find out what was going on. What I was going through! You could have chosen to stick with us . . . you could have been a *part* of 'us.'" She squeezed Ozzie's shoulder again. "You *chose* to be alone."

"I chose to end pain," Klaxon declared. "That is why I returned to my home world. To the machines. People, with all their emotions, are unpredictable. Fallible. But machines are not-not-not."

"You can't simply decide to think like a machine," Aunt Temperance said.

"I am not worried about thinking," Klaxon said. "It is feeling that I mean to end."

"That's why you're going to unleash your motos on the multiverse," Ozzie said. "You're going to . . . eradicate everyone."

"I do not want to end the people of the multiverse," Klaxon insisted. "I want to end-end-end their suffering. I want to save them. Just like I am being saved."

"Mercurio, what are you talking about?" Aunt Temperance implored. There was a quaver in her voice, but also—*finally*, Ozzie thought—a hint of suspicion. "How are you being saved? These mechanical monstrosities have broken you! They've—"

"You have it backward," he declared. "The motos did

not break me. They are rebuilding me. Saving me. I do not live in despair anymore. I chose motonization."

He undid a latch at the side of his torso and pressed a button, and the entire front panel of his chest creaked open.

A gasp caught in Ozzie's throat.

Lights flashed from within a metal cavity. Gears whirred and pistons pumped. Some sort of bag was inflating and deflating, slowly, rhythmically. There was no flesh there—no organs, no heart. Everything *inside* Klaxon had been replaced with machinery.

Aunt Temperance emitted a painful, animal-sounding moan and collapsed to her knees. Ozzie clung to her, desperate to do something to help her. But he had no idea what that might be.

"Now you see," Klaxon declared. He shut his chest, swiveled, and marched back to the dais to stand next to the archway. "Take the fallen ones to the prison," he directed his motos. "They will be saved later."

"The deviation must be destroyed," the robots responded. They were pointing at Scoot, prompting Klaxon to turn toward her.

"My long-lost moto," he said. "I regret creating you."

Ozzie's jaw dropped. "*You're* the one who built her?!"

"Her?" Klaxon said. "It is not a her. It is an it."

Scoot began spinning around in an anxious circle,

wringing her hands. "But . . . but . . . ," she sputtered, pivoting toward Ozzie. "I *am* a her. I want to be a her. Creator, you said I can be a her."

"Do not look at the human boy," Klaxon commanded. "I am your creator."

"No, you're not!" Scoot warbled, rotating to him. "I remember Creator! He wasn't like you."

Klaxon's lips curled upward—almost in frustration, Ozzie decided—his metal teeth glinting in the light. "Moto, I cobbled you together from the bits and pieces of other machines when I was nothing more than a naive boy in the last days of Creon."

"You told me you were born in Europe," Aunt Temperance murmured. "You . . . you lied."

Klaxon inclined his head slightly toward her, robotically, without emotion. "That was before I was machine. When I was imperfect." He considered Scoot again. "My family could not take you during our hurried evacuation of Creon. At the time, it caused me great sorrow. Now it saddens me that you exist. You will be terminated."

Scoot released a mournful whistle and clung to Ozzie's sleeve.

"You won't touch her," Ozzie said, glaring at Klaxon.

"She's fine just the way she is," Fidget added.

"She's an aberration, you know," Tug supplied.

"It comes to Moton," Klaxon decreed. "After I am

done saving the rest of you, I will melt it down. I will create something new. Something better."

Scoot wailed. Ozzie caught sight of the quirl darting into the shadows. *There's no one else she can call for help,* he thought sadly as the moto army closed in on them.

They had no choice but to go through the door to Moton.

Ozzie grimaced as the motos forced him and the others into the command center. Even more terminals and panels had been installed since the last time he had been there. He craned his neck toward the gauges, but he was surrounded by motos and couldn't quite get close enough to read them. It didn't matter, he decided; he didn't need to read the meters to know they were in trouble.

"Welcome to the completed Destiny Machine," Klaxon announced as he stepped through the Zoone door and sealed it behind him with the flick of a switch.

Ozzie turned to the moto-man. "This whole complex is the machine?"

"You are correct," Klaxon said, seeming pleased that he had asked. "The simulations require extensive computing power and an amelthium reactor of a scale never before built." He pointed to the door labeled *Simulations,* the one they had seen their first time in the command center.

"You will all enter the simulation chamber, and you will comprehend that no matter which path you choose, it will lead to the same destiny: agony. Once that is made plain to you, you will decide to be moto."

"And if we don't?" Cho demanded.

"Why would you refuse to end torment?" Klaxon asked, seeming genuinely confused.

Ozzie pressed closer to Aunt Temperance, his mind working furiously. *Is that what happened to Lady Zoone?* he thought. *Did he try to make her choose?* "You want us to make the decision," he said to Klaxon. "So that means if we don't choose motoniza—"

"You will."

"Yes," Ozzie persisted, "but if we don't? What then?"

Klaxon stared at him, lenses slowly spinning. "If you do not choose motonization, then I will release you," he said at last. "But it will not happen. You will see."

Aunt Temperance finally seemed to collect herself. Pulling away from Ozzie, she stepped in front of Klaxon and held out a hand. "You don't have to do this," she told him. "You . . . you are still Mercurio. I know you are. I still see you in there, that inventive and slightly sad young man. Let's go back to Zoone. We can talk, just you and I—"

"You do not understand that I am trying to save you," Klaxon interrupted. "I ask you to imagine a multiverse without strife or agony. But your limited mind cannot conceive of it. Instead, you insist on cradling your humanity. You clutch it to you like a wounded limb. You will see, in the Machine."

"I will face your contraption," Cho declared, stepping forward.

"Stand down, Captain," Aunt Temperance said. "I will go first. This is my responsibility."

"It's my duty to take the lead," Cho insisted.

"Why? Because you're used to being the hero?"

"That's not Cho," Ozzie argued. "He—"

"Because I'm the Captain of Zoone," Cho announced. "The *rightful* captain"—he cast a glare in Klaxon's direction—"and it's my job to protect the nexus. I'll find a way to defeat the Machine."

"So will I," Aunt Temperance declared. "I know him better than you. How he thinks. How his machine will think."

The silvery locks of her hair were hanging loose and wild, but she let them dangle. She lifted her head high and marched forward. Ozzie felt a swirl of pride—and worry. He tried to step toward her, only to be confronted by the electrified fingers of a moto soldier.

Klaxon gave Aunt Temperance an approving nod, then strode to the nearby terminal and began tapping buttons.

The door to the simulation chamber slid open, revealing a dark cavity beyond.

"Aunt Temperance?" Ozzie called out. It sounded weaker, needier, than he intended.

She turned around and flashed him a smile—it seemed forced. "I'll be back, Ozzie. Before you know it."

She stepped through, and the door slammed shut, leaving Ozzie to stare at the blank wall of metal. Then he noticed the screens on Klaxon's terminal flickering with images, hundreds per second, so many that Ozzie couldn't absorb any meaning from them. Klaxon seemed to, though. He had plugged a wire from the control panel directly into his helmet and was completely engrossed by the activity on the screens.

He's interacting with the Machine, Ozzie guessed. *Maybe he's actually communicating with Aunt Temperance while she's in there.*

"It's like TV Land," Tug said, staring up at the screens. "Is that where we're going?"

Ozzie shook his head. After a few minutes, a red light began to whirl and blare.

"Decision made," Klaxon announced, turning to the group.

"What?!" Ozzie cried. "So quickly?"

"That's how TV Land works," Tug said knowingly.

"Except I don't understand. Our stories are real. TV Land is fake."

"The simulations are very realistic," Klaxon declared proudly. "And it only seems quick to you. Time does not work the same way inside the Machine as it does here. She has chosen wisely. She has chosen motonization."

Cho was radiating fury, the scar on his cheek hot and red. "Let me in there. NOW."

"Your enthusiasm is admirable," Klaxon commended him.

"Cho, wait—" Fidget tried to say, but the captain was already standing at the door.

The metal panel slid open and the captain stepped through. Now the adults were gone—unless you counted Klaxon, which Ozzie didn't. After the door closed behind Cho, the machine-man turned to contemplate the screens at his console. Once again, images began to flicker and flash.

"I'm going through next," Ozzie announced to his friends.

"We need to work *together*," Fidget said. "There's no way I'm ending up as some machine."

"Me, neither," Tug concurred.

"At least you wouldn't have the munchies all the time," Scoot told the skyger.

"But I *like* having the munchies."

Ozzie frowned. "If we beat the Machine, he releases us. That's what he said. I'm going next."

"Listen to me!" Fidget implored. "We need to go through all at once. That's how we'll win."

"As a team!" Tug purred in agreement.

Ozzie shook his head. "He's not going to let us."

"We can do it," Fidget insisted. "We'll barge through the door the moment it opens."

"Ooh!" Tug said. "Just to tell you, I'm good at barging. And Scoot can, well, she can scoot."

"Definitely!" Scoot beeped.

Ozzie peeked over his shoulder. Klaxon was still pre-occupied with his control panel; he hadn't even flinched. But that didn't mean he wasn't using his motonic hearing to eavesdrop on their every word.

Ozzie exhaled in frustration. If they tried to force their way into the Destiny Machine, Klaxon might just send them directly to the operating room. Then they'd have no chance at all.

"I can beat him," Ozzie said. "I know I can. I beat the glibber king, didn't I?"

Fidget snorted. "Is that what you think? That it was just—"

"I've been overruled enough," he cut her off. He had been told to go to boarding school. He had been told to go to Moton in the first place, way back when they had been aboard the *Empyrean Thunder*. Enough was enough. Now it was time for everyone to listen to *him*.

But thinking of the pirate ship reminded him of something else: Captain Traxx's beacon. He fished it out and passed it to Fidget.

"What's this?" she asked.

"Backup. I'm going through next. But if I don't come back, activate it."

"What? We should do it now!" She clicked open the small orb, revealing a stubby switch. She flicked it and a tiny light began to blink.

Klaxon was suddenly looming over them. His goggled lenses spun; Ozzie could see angry red laser lights flickering from within those deep and otherwise dark wells. Then Ozzie realized the alarm in the ceiling was wailing again.

Cho had failed.

Somehow, incomprehensibly, he had chosen motonization.

Klaxon snatched the beacon from Fidget's hands, betraying a temper that should have been impossible for a machine. "Where did you get this?" he demanded.

Fidget crossed her arms.

"It does not matter," Klaxon said. He lifted the beacon in his metal claw and squeezed. Ozzie watched in despair as the orb crumpled in his fingers, the same as Aunt

Temperance's locket. When Klaxon opened his claw, all that was left of the beacon was a mangled lump of metal. A tiny wisp of smoke curled from its remains.

Klaxon cast away the beacon, then grabbed Ozzie by the scruff of the neck and lifted him completely off his feet, seemingly without the slightest physical exertion. He activated a switch on his chest plate and his moto-men clattered forward to surround Tug, Fidget, and Scoot.

Ozzie fixed his eyes on his friends as he was carried across the command center, toward the door. He had finally gotten his way; it would be up to him, just like he wanted. But as he saw Fidget's periwinkle eyes stare back at him in panic, he suddenly felt a wave of doubt and dread. Aunt Temperance had failed, and so had Captain Cho.

Maybe we should have gone with Fidget's plan, he thought. *Maybe we should have stuck together.*

But it was too late.

"Time to confront your destiny," Klaxon announced— then he heaved Ozzie through the doorway.

A MANGLED MULTIVERSE

Ozzie tumbled into darkness, the door sliding shut behind him with a menacing bang. He pulled himself to his feet and looked around. A solitary chair sat in the very center of the room. It reminded him of a dentist's chair, but far more threatening, with tubes, wires, and cords pouring out of the sides. A row of cylindrical glass tanks lined the far wall, containing some sort of viscous and slightly green liquid. Except for the two tubes at the very end. They also contained *people*: Aunt Temperance and Captain Cho.

Ozzie stumbled forward and pressed his face to the glass of his aunt's tank. She was suspended in the liquid, her mouth and nose enclosed by some sort of breathing apparatus. Her eyes were open, but completely vacant, as if she were in stasis. Her glasses floated forlornly next to her head.

Ozzie banged on the tank. "Aunt Temperance!"

"Do not despair at their state," Klaxon's voice boomed over some speaker hidden in the shadows. "The surgeons will come for them soon. They will be motonized and their pain will be no more."

Ozzie desperately ran his hands across the surface of Aunt Temperance's tank, hoping to find a clasp, a lever—anything to release them. Then he pulled out Aunt Temperance's key from the cord around his neck. Maybe he could use it to stab through the glass.

Suddenly, a robotic arm extended from the ceiling, plucked him off his feet, and transported him to the chair. Ozzie quickly tucked the key back inside his shirt in an effort to hide it.

"You may keep the key," Klaxon's voice said. "It will not be with you in the simulation."

As soon as Ozzie was in the chair, shackles shot up from below, clamping his wrists and ankles down. Then a helmet descended and another metal arm fitted it onto his head. Out of the corners of his eyes, Ozzie could glimpse wires trailing from the sides of the device.

The helmet began to vibrate, and Ozzie heard Klaxon

say, "Calculating. Calculating. Calculating."

"Calculating what?" Ozzie demanded.

"Your current trajectory," came the reply.

There was a static buzz, the kind Ozzie was used to hearing when he turned on the ancient TV in Apartment 2B. The next thing he knew, he was no longer in the chair. Or perhaps he was, but it didn't feel like it. He was standing among the platforms of Zoone—except they were nothing like he knew them.

Ozzie slowly turned around. Many of the doors were broken, hanging off their frames by mutilated hinges. Some of the doorframes were empty, while others had been reduced to stumps. Beyond the platforms, where the Infinite Wood should be, was nothing more than an empty expanse, an endless field without a tree in sight. Ozzie kept turning until his eyes found the station. It was now entirely navy in color. Even the trim of the windows and doors was navy. The only color at all came from the rust and grime.

But the worst thing was that the grounds were completely deserted. Not a soul was in sight—that was, until a tiny quirl came limping across the crumbling platform. The rodent paused in front of Ozzie, and he knelt to pick her up. It was the same one that had gone on the mission with him and Fidget. He could tell from her one bent ear. But now she was scrawny and missing patches of fur.

Ozzie wished he had some morsel of food to give her, but the only thing he could do was cradle the piteous creature against his chest.

He stood and slowly turned, taking everything in. The nexus was dying. Its magic was fading. The multiverse was fragmenting, which meant worlds would lose their connection to one another.

"What have you done?!" he yelled.

"The Machine has estimated the course of events based on their current trajectory," Klaxon's voice called, seemingly from the heavens. "The nexus is one hundred percent motonized. And you feel alone."

Ozzie swallowed and peered down at the quirl, only to realize that she had died in his hands. Trying to hold back tears, he set the rodent's body gently on the cracked cobblestones.

"This causes you pain?"

"You know it does!" Ozzie screamed. "You did this! You and your motos."

"This simulation is not about assigning blame. It is about choice. Do you wish to proceed on this path? Or do you wish to choose another? Of course, you will soon discover that pain and suffering are inevitable. I must remind you that if you become moto, none of this will matter. Join us, human boy, and you will be relieved of your despair."

"I don't want to be a moto," Ozzie hissed through his teeth.

"You will change your mind," Klaxon said calmly—and ominously. "We can go backward, forward—sideways even. Such is the power of the Destiny Machine's simulations. You can pick any alternate path you desire. Is that what you wish?"

"Yes," Ozzie said immediately, mustering his resolve. *Because*, he added to himself, *I'm going to beat you.*

There was another static flash and Ozzie was dropped onto a different platform. Instead of the cobblestones of Zoone, there was just a flat black surface beneath his feet. He was surrounded by countless doors, all slowly spinning around him, floating in an abysmal darkness.

"Where am I?" Ozzie wondered.

"You are still in the simulation," Klaxon's voice explained. "You can think of it as a nexus of its own sort. These doors do not lead to places, but to points in your timeline. Ask a question and the answer will be calculated."

The doors were all different shapes and sizes. Ozzie could see that some were made of old and weathered wood, while others were sparkling with polished metal. They were different colors, and each was covered with a series of symbols. There were so many of them. How could he possibly decide?

"What do you mean 'a question'?" Ozzie asked Klaxon. "What kind of question?"

"A what-if question," the moto-man replied over the speaker. "What if I did better in school? What if I had never gone to Zoone? That sort of question."

Ozzie frowned. *What I need is to defeat this contraption. The question's the key. Ask the right question. Find the right door. The right path.*

He exhaled.

How could he defeat the Machine? Aunt Temperance and Cho had both failed.

Maybe the simulation wears you down, Ozzie pondered. So what if I had never gone to Zoone? That doesn't change Klaxon's inhumanity. Or Aunt T's sadness. Or . . .

Then it occurred to him.

"I have my question," he announced.

"Yes?"

"I want to know what would happen if you and Aunt Temperance *did* get married."

A terrible noise exploded over the speaker, like the sound of a car with worn brakes screeching to a halt. It took a moment for Ozzie to realize that it had come from Klaxon.

"That is unacceptable!" the moto-man thundered. "You must ask a question about your own life."

"How is that *not* a question about my life?" Ozzie

argued. "If you and Aunt T had gotten married, it would have completely changed mine."

"I demand a different question."

"What does it matter?" Ozzie asked. "If all paths lead to pain, what does it matter if I go down this one?"

At first, only silence greeted Ozzie. He turned slowly in the darkness, staring at the swirling doors.

"You think you are clever," Klaxon eventually replied. "But your human brain is imperfect. You will see. Very well. I accept your question. Calculating . . . calculating . . . here is your-your-your door."

One of the portals approached Ozzie; the others grew small, then faded away. The door before Ozzie was plain and wooden. It was the dullest of doors, without trim, ornamentation, or even a scuff mark.

Ozzie stepped forward and gripped the simple metal handle.

"You asked for it," Klaxon's voice grated. "And so you have it."

Ozzie woke up in his bedroom. At least he thought it was his bedroom. It had all his things in it, though something about it didn't feel quite right. He climbed out of bed and made his way to the window. He looked out and saw a familiar street below. Yes, this was the building he lived in, the Ulysses Apartments, but something felt slightly off about the view. Actually, it wasn't exactly the view. It was the perspective . . .

He turned around and considered his room again: the clean white walls, the shiny hardwood floor, and the fashionable furniture. *This is my room all right*, he thought. His father owned the entire building, and that included the stylish penthouse apartment on the top floor. His parents were gone most of the time, but this was still their "official residence," as they liked to call it.

Ozzie shook his head. He knew all this, but he had the vague idea that he had been somewhere else in his dreams, somewhere special. He couldn't quite put his finger on it. Whatever it was, it was quickly slipping away, so he wandered down the hallway to the kitchen.

"Thought you would sleep all day," Miss Blunt grumbled, because she was the sort of person who thought kindness was a rare commodity and shouldn't be spent frivolously.

"Had a weird dream," Ozzie said as he took a seat at the breakfast bar. Miss Blunt had conveniently set the pamphlet for Dreerdum's Boarding School for Boys there. Ozzie frowned and pushed it away.

Miss Blunt set a plate of toast in front of him. "You're going to have to face it sooner or later."

"Later," Ozzie said. "That place looks awful."

Miss Blunt grunted. "Wish I'd had rich parents to

waste all that money on my education."

"I'd rather have parents who were *here*," Ozzie protested. "They're always traveling. I'm stuck here."

"Not anymore, you're not," Miss Blunt reminded him. "Soon, you're off to Dreerdum's. Looks like I'll be seeking new employment. And a new home."

There was annoyance in her tone, which kind of confused Ozzie. She continually griped about her job as a live-in nanny. He wondered why she didn't just find a different job. *If I had the power to switch my life, I'd do it in a heartbeat*, he thought as he stared glumly at the pamphlet. There was still something niggling at his brain, but he wasn't sure what. "I'd rather go to Zoone!" he blurted out.

"What's that?" Miss Blunt said. "Another one of them worlds in those video games you play?"

"I'm not sure," Ozzie admitted. He suddenly realized he was groping at the collar of his shirt, like he expected something to be dangling there.

"Don't forget, your aunt and uncle are coming tonight," Miss Blunt announced.

"My aunt and uncle?"

"Yes, long-lost crazy Aunt Temperance," she huffed impatiently. "Don't you remember? You're spending Saturday with her, so don't be making any plans with friends. Oh, right. We don't have to worry about that, do we, 'Mr. Popular'?"

Ozzie sank into his chair, her sarcasm cutting him to the bone. No friends, no plans. But he was slightly excited about the prospect of meeting his aunt. She had never visited—that he could remember, anyway—but he somehow had this feeling that he would like her.

"How come she's never visited before?"

Miss Blunt leaned over the breakfast bar and shrugged. "Traveling around the world with the circus and that weirdo husband of hers. *Mercurio*. What kind of name is that, anyway?"

Ozzie tugged at his shirt collar again. "Aunt Temperance is still in the circus?"

"What do you mean 'still'?"

"I don't know," Ozzie admitted. "I just had this idea that she had an office job."

Miss Blunt nearly spat out her mouthful of coffee. "Your aunt? I think that sounds just a little too tied-down and responsible for the likes of her. Airy-fairy hippie. That's what your parents always say, anyway."

School that day was atrocious. Or, to put it another way, the usual. Ozzie hurried home, rushed to the door, meaning to barge through excitedly to see if his aunt had already arrived.

But the door was locked.

Which was strange. Miss Blunt was supposed to be

home. He jiggled the handle, only to look up and see the number on the door.

2B. He was at completely the wrong apartment.

What am I doing down here? he thought.

Ozzie frowned, turned away, and stared at the door on the opposite side of the hallway, just a bit farther down. It had no number on it, which meant it didn't belong to an apartment. Curious, Ozzie wandered over, tried the door, and found himself gazing down a spiraling set of stairs.

What's down there? he asked himself. *Definitely not a parking garage. This basement looks like it was built before the invention of the car. Maybe even the wheel.*

The bottom of the staircase was lost in shadow, causing a slight shiver to meander down Ozzie's neck. Then he heard the knock; it was loud and hollow and floated up the steps like a moan. Ozzie instinctively jumped back and slammed the door shut.

"Yikes!" he muttered to himself before racing up the stairs to the penthouse (the building was so incredibly ancient that it had no elevator—a constant source of complaint by Miss Blunt).

"What's gotten into you?" Miss Blunt demanded as he barged into the penthouse.

"Um . . . nothing. Is Aunt T here yet?"

"Aunt T?"

"Yeah. Aunt Temperance, I mean."

Miss Blunt sighed. "She called. Got delayed; won't arrive till late."

That was a disappointment, but Ozzie decided to wait up. He stayed in his room, blasting his way through rounds of *Zombie Killer II* on his gaming console. At some point, he must have dozed off because the next thing he knew, he was jerking awake to the sound of the apartment buzzer. He raced out of his room to see Miss Blunt greeting Aunt Temperance at the door.

As soon as he saw her, Ozzie froze, suddenly feeling shy. For some reason, he had imagined her to look a certain way, and what he saw in front of him didn't match. He had expected her to have glasses, but she didn't. Then there was her hair, which had a stylish pixie cut. She was wearing capri pants, a vibrant green blouse, and a long, patterned scarf. She looked, for lack of a better word, cool.

"You must be Oswald," Aunt Temperance greeted him. She moved to hug him, but he stepped away. He was a little old for hugging.

"Most people call me Ozzie," he said, which made Miss Blunt snort, because it was a complete and utter lie.

Aunt Temperance nodded. "*Ozzie.* The last time I laid eyes on you—well, let's just say you were probably too young to remember. But *I* remember. And I've been filled with excitement to see you again."

Something tingled inside of Ozzie. Excitement wasn't

exactly the word that occurred to most people when they thought about him. Disappointment—sure. Punching bag—yes. But not excitement. He felt his inhibitions slinking away and when Aunt Temperance tried for another hug, he gave in.

It was only now that he noticed the man standing out in the hallway, clutching a suitcase. He was tall and handsome and after stepping confidently through the door, he leaned in and smiled at Ozzie with glinting white teeth.

"Hello, son," he greeted him. "I'm your uncle. Uncle Mercurio."

28

KLAXON CLOSES THE DOOR

Ozzie gawked at the peculiar man. He had never seen anyone like Uncle Mercurio, not in real life anyway. His hair was a tangle of whimsical black curls, tipped with bright scarlet, while his blue eyes twinkled with a hint of mystery. He had an easy, friendly smile and his clothes were a wild combination of flared cuffs and ornate patterns. He looked like a magician or a movie star. It was no wonder he worked in the circus.

Ozzie instantly liked him.

"Nice to meet you, Ozzie," Uncle Mercurio said, extending his hand.

Ozzie shook it enthusiastically. "You, too!" He turned

back to Aunt Temperance. "Do you have a key?" he blurted out, though he wasn't sure where the question had come from.

"A key?" Aunt Temperance wondered, glancing hesitantly at Miss Blunt. "A key for what?"

"I don't know," Ozzie confessed. "A key with a 'Z' on it."

"Oh!" Aunt Temperance exclaimed. "My grandfather gave me that key—that's your great-grandfather, Ozzie: Augustus Sparks." She tilted her head inquisitively. "How do *you* know about it?"

Ozzie frowned. The truth was, he wasn't sure.

"It's not the sort of thing I wanted to take on the road with me," Aunt Temperance explained. "I think it's packed away in storage."

"Don't worry about an old heirloom like that," Uncle Mercurio told Ozzie. "We've brought you gifts."

"I was going to give them to him in the morning," Aunt Temperance said with a hint of disapproval.

Uncle Mercurio put his arm around her. "Come on, Tempie. Let's give them now."

"Oh, all right." She rustled through a bag and produced a set of comic books and a chunky robot figure. "The books are manga," Aunt Temperance said. "I got them when we were on tour in Japan."

"I mostly like video games," Ozzie told her, which he

realized a moment later was a bit rude, so he tucked the manga under his arm and took the robot. It was heavy, made with actual metal.

"It's an automaton," Aunt Temperance explained. "Mercurio builds them himself. He has his own sideshow at our circus: Mercurio's Menagerie of Mechanized Marvels!"

Ozzie turned the figure around in his hands to see a tiny wind-up key protruding from its side. He was too old for toys, especially ones that looked like they had come from an antique shop, but he decided to crank the key.

"Up-down-up-up-down," the automaton chimed.

"Huh?" Ozzie muttered.

Uncle Mercurio leaned over to examine the automaton in Ozzie's hands. "Hmm. It's not supposed to say *that*! Not to worry. Merely a malfunction. I'll tinker with it tomorrow."

"This is the part where he tells you he can fix anything," Aunt Temperance said lightheartedly. "Or he'll tell you about the time he once built a machine to save the environment."

"Oh?" Miss Blunt wondered. "You'd think something like that would have made the news."

"It's still in development," Uncle Mercurio admitted, blushing. "Maybe one day I'll sort it out."

"Come on then," Miss Blunt said, ushering them farther into the apartment. "I'll show you the spare room.

It's getting late, Oswald. Off to bed with you."

"We'll see you in the morning," Aunt Temperance assured him, giving him another hug.

Ozzie meandered down the hall and set the automaton on his bedside table. It was a peculiar thing, with giant, protruding teeth and round, vacant eyes.

If there are nerd robots, then this one's the queen of them, he thought—though he wasn't quite sure why he had decided it was a girl.

Miss Blunt didn't need to rouse Ozzie, even though it was Saturday morning. Ozzie usually liked to stay cocooned in bed on weekends (well, admittedly, school days, too), but today was different. He had company! The dull routine of the penthouse had been disrupted for once.

Ozzie quickly got dressed. He could hear voices coming from the kitchen; Aunt Temperance and Uncle Mercurio were already up. He hurried down the hall.

"Miss Blunt took the day off," Aunt Temperance explained when she saw Ozzie glancing around. "We're going to spend the day together, remember?"

Ozzie nodded. He got himself a bowl of cereal and climbed up to the stool next to her at the kitchen bar.

"What is that?" Aunt Temperance wondered, staring disapprovingly at his bowl.

"Um . . . cereal?"

"Looks like a cauldron of sugar."

Mercurio chuckled. "Well, I think I'll leave you two to it. Let you get to know each other better."

He vacated the penthouse, leaving Ozzie and Aunt Temperance to sit there, side by side.

"Well," Aunt Temperance said, "what do you want to do today?"

"I don't know," Ozzie answered. "We could go to the mall."

"That sounds a bit uninspired," Aunt Temperance said. "How about the art gallery?"

Ozzie scowled.

"Have you ever been?"

"Well, once. For school." Which was kind of a lie. His class *had* taken a field trip there, but he had ducked out that day and gone to the arcade instead.

"Come on," Aunt Temperance encouraged him. "It'll be fun."

That was the exact opposite of the word Ozzie had been thinking of. But, as he stared into her smiling eyes, he decided she was the sort of person who was worth the risk of gazing at agonizingly boring artwork all day.

"How do you like that old building of ours?" Aunt Temperance asked as they sat on the bus, heading for the gallery. "It's been in our family for generations. I grew up there, too, you know."

"Really?" Ozzie asked. "Have you seen the basement?"

"Ah," Aunt Temperance said with a smile. "You mean 'The Depths.'"

"The Depths?"

"That's what I used to call it when I was your age. It's mostly storage for the tenants. But Grandpa always said there was a hint of magic down there."

Ozzie snorted. "Like what? Unicorns and fairies?"

Aunt Temperance laughed. "I think he meant something a bit more . . . spiritual. He was one of a kind, Grandpa. I wish he was still around; then you could have met him, too."

"My dad never talks about him," Ozzie said.

Now it was Aunt Temperance's turn to snort. "They were very different people. One believed in magic and the other in . . ."

She trailed off.

"What?"

Aunt Temperance frowned. "Maybe we should change the subject."

Ozzie nodded. "What's it like being in the circus?"

"And now we're right back to talking about magic," Aunt Temperance said. "You know, we're going to be performing in the city all this week. I wanted you to come to one of our shows, but your parents . . . well . . . they don't really approve."

"Of what?" Ozzie asked.

Aunt Temperance didn't reply. She just tapped her fingers on her knee and stared out the bus window.

Ozzie stood on the curb with Uncle Mercurio and Aunt Temperance, waiting for their taxi to arrive. The art gallery had been better than Ozzie had expected. To be fair, he hadn't expected much, but gazing at the paintings—an exhibit of French Impressionism—with Aunt Temperance serving as his personal tour guide had been its own type of magic.

"When am I going to see you again?" Ozzie asked her as the taxi pulled up.

"I'm not sure," she replied. "Hopefully soon. It depends on when we're back in this part of the world. But we'll stay in touch, right? I'll send you postcards."

Inwardly, Ozzie groaned. He already got enough of those from his parents. But he didn't say this to Aunt Temperance as she wrapped him in a hug and clutched him tightly.

"We have to go," Uncle Mercurio said.

Aunt Temperance nodded, kissed Ozzie on the forehead, and followed him into the cab. Ozzie watched wistfully as they pulled away, then went inside and trudged up the stairs to the penthouse. Miss Blunt was heating up some instant noodles.

"They left?"

Ozzie nodded, wandered off to his room, and threw himself on his bed. He wasn't sure what he had hoped would happen when he met Aunt Temperance, but he had this feeling that an opportunity had slipped through his fingers. A familiar sensation burbled inside of him.

Loneliness.

There was nothing unusual about that but now it seemed . . . worse. Accentuated, somehow.

He thought of the trip to the art gallery.

"There's something about painting that I've always found enchanting," Aunt Temperance had told him. "It's like life. You start with a blank canvas and get to create anything you want."

Not for me, Ozzie grumbled to himself as he languished on his bed and thought of boarding school. To him, it felt like someone had already done the painting for him. He couldn't add to or smear the colors because they had already dried. They were hard: fixed, permanent, and black. No, that wasn't quite the right color. Dark blue, or navy. Miss Blunt's favorite color. She said it was comforting. Ozzie had always thought of it as boring. But now it felt like it was the only color on the canvas.

"I don't want to go on like this," he murmured.

Miss Blunt stuck her head through his door. "Didn't you hear me calling you? Come get your noodles."

Ozzie didn't even look at her. "Not hungry," he said. He gazed at the ceiling until he eventually drifted to sleep.

Ozzie awoke to find himself shackled to a chair by his wrists and ankles. There was even some sort of helmet on his head.

"What the . . . ?" he mumbled, tugging at his restraints. "Where am I?" He felt vaguely ill, like he had just awoken in a different time zone. The *wrong* time zone. But if this was a dream, it was the most realistic one he had ever experienced. He could actually feel the metal cuffs digging into his skin and a tingle in his scalp from the helmet. He tried looking around, but it was hard to move.

A monitor lowered from the ceiling on a long mechanical arm and stopped at eye level. The screen was buzzing with static, but a moment later it tuned in to reveal the leering face of some strange half-robot man.

Ozzie screamed.

"Give it a moment," the man on the screen advised. "It will come back to you."

And it did come back, like a dam bursting open and

flooding his memory. Zoone. Klaxon. Aunt Temperance and Captain Cho in the stasis tubes. The Destiny Machine.

This isn't a dream, Ozzie realized with a shiver. *This is real.* He reached to rub his forehead, but his hand only made it as far as his chest because of the shackles.

"Now you see what lies before you," Klaxon said from the screen. "Misery. Despair. No matter which path you choose, you end up the same. Without Zoone. And—"

"Alone," Ozzie murmured.

"Yes," Klaxon agreed, his voice rich and heavy with satisfaction. "Alone."

Ozzie's stomach ached with hollowness. Everything in the simulation had felt so real. In that artificial existence, he had never visited Zoone. Never met his friends. Never gotten to know, truly know, Aunt Temperance. These were terrifying possibilities to consider. But . . .

What was worse? Was it knowing that Zoone *did* exist but that it was going to be destroyed by motos and he was helpless to stop it? Or was it never knowing about the nexus to begin with? *Ignorance is bliss*, he recalled one of his teachers saying (though had that been in reality or in the simulation?), but Ozzie wasn't ignorant in *this* moment, strapped to Klaxon's chair.

"I can see that you are in torment," Klaxon said. "Do you not want to end this agony?"

Yes, Ozzie thought instantly.

"You have seen different paths and how they end. It does not matter. Motonization is the only way to prevent pain."

"No," Ozzie moaned. He strained against his bindings, only to slump against the chair, feeling exhausted and heavy. It was like the tubes connected to his helmet were siphoning away his will, his resistance.

"Suffering, despair, misery: These things are inevitable. The constants of the multiverse. You have experienced this firsthand. Everyone feels pain, no matter what the path."

Ozzie shook his head, felt the tug of wires and cords. And that was when another answer occurred to him. "Actually," he told Klaxon, "not everyone."

The rims of Klaxon's goggles spun. "What?"

"Not everyone was unhappy in the simulation," Ozzie said.

The lights on Klaxon's helmets began to flash red, rapidly, as if an alarm had been activated. "You were unhappy."

"It wasn't miserable for Aunt T. It wasn't miserable for *you*."

Klaxon showed his metal teeth. "It was miserable for YOU, human boy. You cannot go back there. You will be in pain. Terrible pain."

Ozzie suddenly remembered something Aunt Temperance had said, not in the simulation, but here, in reality, not long before entering the machine herself.

What if pain is important?

Ozzie stared at the image of Klaxon on the screen. How many times had Ozzie himself wondered what it would be like to have a switch for his emotions, to be able to turn them on and off with the flick of a finger? To ignore his feelings? To not be—as his mom put it—too sensitive?

It had just been a grumbling, unconsidered idea . . . but Klaxon *had* considered it. And he'd done it. He had tried to extract his humanity, replace it with gears and cogs. Villains always liked to strut around in comic books and taunt heroes with lines like "We're not so different, you and me. We're the same." But, in this case, Ozzie realized with a sinking feeling, it was true. He *was* like Klaxon.

But he didn't have to be.

"What if . . . what if I want to feel my pain?" he murmured.

The lights on Klaxon's helmet began to blink more rapidly. "Why would you want that?"

This is the way through, Ozzie realized. *The way to beat him. . . .*

"Send me back," Ozzie announced.

"NO!" Klaxon roared in his mechanically enhanced

voice. "It will be terrible for you. Do you need me to tell you what happens to you on that path? Do you need me to show you more? Because—"

He abruptly stopped, as if suddenly becoming conscious of his outburst. "Oh," he said in a more level tone. "I see. You think you have defeated me. That you have chosen the alternative to motonization."

"I didn't make the choice you wanted me to," Ozzie declared proudly. "You need to release me."

"Yes," Klaxon agreed. "You will be released. Back to your chosen life."

"Good—wait! What?!" Ozzie cried. "What do you mean 'back'? You said if I didn't choose motonization, you'd let us go."

Klaxon reached up with his metal hand to flick a switch on his helmet. The red lights stopped flashing. "No," he said. "I said I would *release* you. And I am going to release you. Into the simulation."

Ozzie wrenched in vain at his shackles. "You rigged everything. I never had a chance of winning, no matter what."

"You could have chosen motonization," Klaxon said impassively. "Instead, you will experience a lifetime of being unloved and alone. You will know only pain."

"But that's just a simulation," Ozzie said in confusion. "What about me here? In reality?"

"You will live out your life in this chair, confined to a coma-like state as you experience the simulation," Klaxon explained emotionlessly. "My motos will feed you intravenously, and you will grow old, and you will die. But do not worry. Not for a very long and agonizing time."

"No!" Ozzie shrieked, thrashing in his chair. "You can't do this! You cheated!"

Klaxon leaned forward, and his face became bigger, more menacing on the screen. "I believe you are crying, human boy."

He was right, Ozzie realized. Hot tears were streaming down his cheeks. He couldn't even wipe them away. Instead, he fell limply against his chair. He felt so heavy again.

"Tug!" he moaned. "Fidget! Scoot . . ."

"They cannot hear you," Klaxon said. "No one will ever know what happened to you here. Your friends will become motos. Everyone you know will become motos. The entire multiverse will eventually become motonized. You will be the last human alive. In a way."

Klaxon clicked a series of buttons and Ozzie felt his helmet begin to buzz. Then he felt a prick in his arm, and everything started to fade away.

"You could have chosen motonization," Klaxon said, though now his voice sounded faint and distant. "But now it is too-too-too late. I am afraid that door has closed."

29

DOWN IN THE DEPTHS

"Hey, spaz!"

"We're talking to *you*, Oddball Sparks."

Ozzie turned around in the school hallway and sighed as the infamous Twin Tormentors, Billy and John, swaggered toward him. They weren't literally twins, but they dressed more or less the same and had the same haircuts. Ozzie prided himself on being immune to their insults, but even he wasn't immune to their fists. After they circled him like a pair of sharks, John shoved him into Billy, who expertly shoulder-checked him into the nearest row of lockers. Ozzie slammed into the wall of metal, face-first. With a groan, he crumpled to the floor and listened to the symphony of laughter coming from the horde of onlookers.

"Maybe one day, you'll get your shirt on right, Oddball," John heckled.

"No wonder you're an orphan," Billy added.

"I'm not an orphan! I've got parents!" Ozzie retorted. *Somewhere*, he added to himself.

The bell rang; everyone bustled off, except for Ozzie, who just remained on the floor, leaning against the lockers. "At least they didn't pick on Aunt T," he murmured, though he instantly wondered why they would. The Twin Tormentors didn't even know her. It was just that Ozzie had this distinct memory of being teased about his "hysterical" aunt.

Must have been a dream, he thought.

Weeks had passed since Aunt Temperance and Uncle Mercurio had come to visit. For just the briefest of moments Ozzie had felt like his life had brushed up against something different. Something unusual. Maybe even magical.

But now it was back to reality. And, in a way, it was almost worse. He couldn't explain why exactly. Maybe it was because he *had* glimpsed something, had seen it dangled in front of him—and then it had been abruptly yanked away.

Ozzie sighed. "I really hate my life," he announced to no one.

A teacher thrust her head out of the nearest doorway. "OSWALD SPARKS! Stop goofing off and get to class!"

Miss Blunt's going to freak, Ozzie thought as he trudged home after school. The cheek below his left eye had started to swell. It hadn't turned purple yet, but it was definitely yellow and tender to the touch. There was no way he'd be able to hide it from Miss Blunt, which would mean she'd insist on telling his parents, which would mean they'd contact the school, which would mean Ozzie getting hauled to the office to explain the situation, which would mean an agonizingly fake apology from the Twin Tormentors in front of the principal. Then it would just be more of the same.

Wash, rinse, repeat.

The washing machine of life sucked.

He took the long way home, trying to delay the start of the inevitable cycle, which took him past the swanky apartment building on Portage Avenue. The building was old, but not outdated like the one Ozzie lived in. For starters, it had elevators. It even had a doorman, though, as Ozzie passed by the front entrance, he noticed that he was new. He couldn't quite remember what the usual doorman looked like, but this one was tall, with broad shoulders and a chest as wide as a tree. It looked like he might burst right out of his snappy turquoise uniform.

Ozzie slowed down to stare. The doorman seemed to have a bruise under one eye, just like Ozzie. He tipped his hat at Ozzie, then turned to open the palatial doors of the apartment. A kid bounded out, giggling and full of mirth—which really annoyed Ozzie, prompting him to stick his foot out and send him tumbling across the pavement. His backpack burst open to disgorge a pile of books, snacks, and toys.

The kid slowly rolled over and stared at Ozzie, his bottom lip quivering.

Ozzie snorted. Tripping the kid had made him feel better. *Look*, he wanted to say, *it's a bully-eat-bully world, and I need to get fed as much as the next guy.* But instead, he just spat at the kid's feet and kicked the nearest of his books. It skidded into the street.

The doorman wandered over. Ozzie expected to get lectured, but instead the man patted the kid on the shoulder, fetched his book, and wiped it dry on his coat. He calmly helped him repack his bag, then tipped his hat again at Ozzie.

What a weirdo, Ozzie thought.

He continued home, fuming, and the next thing he

knew, he was standing in front of the door to Apartment 2B.

Again.

It was the third time this week.

Why do I keep coming here? he wondered in frustration. As far as he knew, the apartment was vacant—no one, at least according to Miss Blunt, wanted to live there.

His eyes landed on the opposite door, the one he had heard the knock come from before. And now he heard it again.

This is ridiculous. If someone's knocking, that means someone's down here. Whatever trepidation he was feeling was overruled by an overwhelming sense of curiosity, so he began the descent. Down he went, turning and twisting into the darkness.

He reached the bottom, expecting to find an apartment door, but instead found a narrow passageway. He continued along, following the sound of the knocking. He eventually reached a T-junction and turned right. There was a door at the end of the corridor, but it definitely wasn't the kind that would lead to an apartment. It had wide wooden slats, ornate metal hinges, and a strange metal "Z" hanging lopsided halfway up it. The knocking was coming from the door all right—*from the other side*, as if someone was trying to get out. Which was more than just a little eerie, but he had come this far, so Ozzie approached the door. Once he was right up next to it, he could see just how old it was. The hinges were streaked with rust, and bits of turquoise paint were peeling from the gray wood.

"Hello?" Ozzie called. "Who's there?"

No one replied, but the knocking continued. Ozzie frowned, tried the handle, and found that the door wasn't locked. Tentatively, he pulled it open.

There was nothing there; just a wall of bricks.

"What the . . . ," Ozzie muttered. He could still hear the knocking. "Hello!" he called, more loudly now. He put an ear to the bricks. He could feel them vibrating from the force of the thumping.

It was a door to nowhere, a door he couldn't answer—and now his mind started to run frantic laps. What was behind those bricks? Maybe it was a group of convicts who had dug a tunnel from the local penitentiary, and they had ended up here. Maybe it was some giant anaconda that had been set free in the sewer system and was now trying to bust through the wall. Maybe it was a ghost!

Ozzie dashed back up the long set of spiraling stairs, then up the four flights to the penthouse. He didn't stop running until he was in his bedroom, with the door shut and the blankets thrown over his head. His legs burned and his chest heaved from his escape from near-death-by-anaconda.

"Up-down-up-up-down."

Ozzie peered out from the covers. It was the automaton Uncle Mercurio had built for him. She was still sitting on his bedside table, eyes slightly flickering. "Up-down-up-up-down," she repeated. Which was strange because Ozzie hadn't wound her up.

Still glitched, Ozzie thought. *Uncle Mercurio said he was going to fix her. But I guess he forgot.*

The next day, on the way to school, Ozzie avoided the fancy apartment building on Portage Avenue and went past the park instead. There was a street performer near the main entrance. She was young—barely a teenager—and she had awful hair. It was as if she had tried to dye it purple, but it hadn't really worked and instead ended up a dirty pink. Her costume was equally atrocious, with striped sleeves and leggings, and she was juggling, of all things, three umbrellas.

Weirdo, Ozzie thought as he stopped to stare at her.

He passed by this park all the time and had never seen a street performer at this corner before, at least not one who looked like this. Though, just between him and himself, it wasn't just her appearance that annoyed him. She reminded him of something, something he couldn't quite figure out.

The girl winked at him, causing Ozzie to blush. He turned to leave, but not before giving her collection hat a swift kick, sending her coins flying.

Serves her right, he thought.

Once he made it around the corner, he peered back to see her reaction, but she hadn't even paused to gather her money. She just kept juggling, which frustrated Ozzie even more. He stormed back, glared at her, and shouted, "Don't you care about all your stupid money? And why don't you juggle normal things?"

She ignored him, so all Ozzie really managed to do was be late for school.

Miss Blunt *had* discovered his black eye the night before but hadn't succeeded in getting hold of either of his parents, so the agonizing bully-and-principal exchanges were avoided, at least for the day. What he couldn't avoid was an end-of-day detention (for being late too many times).

By the time he was released from the torture chamber otherwise known as school, it was later than usual, which meant he had to head straight home. He was just about there when, suddenly, a giant cat flew down from the tree in front of him and landed at his feet. Ozzie was so surprised, he leaped backward and tripped on his untied shoelace. He ended up on the ground, flat on his back; the cat strolled over to him, crawling onto his chest and licking his face.

"Ugh!" Ozzie grumbled.

He wriggled free of the cat and tried to kick it, but it expertly dodged his foot, then flopped to the sidewalk and stretched out luxuriously in front of him. It was a huge creature, light gray in color, almost blue. It was also purring like a lawn mower, which only served to increase Ozzie's irritation.

"Just stay out of my way," he warned, only to have the cat leap to its feet and begin butting its massive head against his leg.

"Leave me alone!"

He kicked at it again, but the cat only purred louder. Then it sat on the sidewalk in front of him and gazed at him with giant sapphire eyes. Ozzie had this sense that the cat was trying to smile at him. Which was nonsense, of course.

He navigated around the feline and hurried toward home. The cat chased him, purring the entire way. It didn't even stop when Ozzie reached his building; it just trotted up the steps, as if expecting to go inside.

"You can't come in here," Ozzie told the cat as he inserted his key in the apartment building's front door.

The cat was so persistent that he had to kick it again—forcibly—then quickly squeeze through.

The cat sat down on the other side of the glass door, looking like a massive triangle of blue fur. Ozzie was sure it was frowning. But if a cat couldn't smile, he decided, then it couldn't frown, either.

OPPORTUNITY KNOCKS

The next day was Saturday and Ozzie was feeling bored and empty. He didn't even feel like blasting zombies. He decided to go sit in the park and try out some of the manga Aunt Temperance had given him. He stuffed the books into his bag and at the last moment decided to take Uncle Mercurio's automaton.

Maybe I can tinker with her myself and figure out what's wrong with her, he thought.

The giant blue cat was waiting for him on the front steps. In fact, it looked like it hadn't moved since yesterday and as soon as it saw Ozzie approaching the door, it rose to all fours and began pacing back and forth, tail twitching like a whip. When Ozzie opened the door, the cat tried to bolt through.

"There's nothing in here for you!" Ozzie insisted, blocking the cat with his leg. "And I'm going out."

The cat looked dismayed. Ozzie wandered down the sidewalk, the cat trailing behind him, its fluffy tail still twitching.

Weirdo cat thinks it's a dog, Ozzie thought.

He reached the corner of the park to see that the street performer was there again. She must have made another attempt at dyeing her hair, because now it was a brighter color, almost purple.

Inappropriately purple, Ozzie decided, though he wasn't sure where that idea had come from.

The girl was juggling umbrellas again. Ozzie paused to watch, and the cat sat down beside him.

The girl threw a cryptic glance at Ozzie and winked again. That deserved another kick of the collection hat, but he decided against it and headed into the park, toward his favorite bench, which was in a quiet, secluded corner. It was his thinking place. His calm place. Except, today, there was someone there.

A very strange someone.

Everything about her was . . . elongated. Her neck was stretched out, her arms were thin and spindly, and she even wore a very tall hat, which made Ozzie wonder about the shape of her head. She was standing very still, with her arms spread wide, and she was completely swarmed by pigeons. Some were even perched on *her*. She didn't so much as flinch when Ozzie approached.

He wasn't about to give up his favorite spot, so he slipped quietly onto his bench, casting surreptitious glances at the statuesque woman. The cat trotted over to her and began brushing up against her long skirt, which was when Ozzie realized how old-fashioned her outfit was, all buttons, clasps, and intricate floral patterns. Her costume only added to her strangeness but, at the same time, she felt familiar to Ozzie.

Then she turned, ever so slowly, and smiled at him. Her eyes were intensely green, causing a shiver to dance down the back of his neck.

Weirdo, he thought, inching down the bench, just to put a little bit more distance between them. He opened one of the manga and tried to distract himself in its pages. The cat jumped up beside him, curled into an enormous ball of fur, and was soon purring. Ozzie tried to nudge it out of the way, but it was heavy. It was so firmly ensconced it would take a bulldozer to shift it, so he sighed, resigned himself to the unwanted company, and continued to read. The next time he looked up, it was to see that the girl with inappropriately purple hair had moved into the corner, close to Pigeon Lady. Except now, instead of juggling umbrellas, she was juggling blenders!

Where did she get those from? Ozzie wondered.

The blenders looked way too heavy to lift, let alone juggle, but the girl didn't miss a beat, didn't drop any of them. Then, right in the middle of her act, the girl waved at Ozzie.

Ozzie gaped at her, wide-eyed. It took a moment for him to realize something was vibrating at his side; it was coming from his knapsack. He opened it up, peered inside, and saw the automaton's head spinning round and round.

"Up-down-up-up-down!" she warbled.

"Quite the assortment of friends you have."

Ozzie looked up, startled. It was Pigeon Lady. She was still covered in the birds, but had somehow maneuvered to stand in front of him. Ozzie hadn't heard her move; in fact, he had a hard time imagining her possessing the ability to walk. But here she was, and now she leaned down—way down—to stroke the bluish cat. It meowed happily in response.

"Does he have a name?" Pigeon Lady asked.

Her voice was slow and sweet, like syrup, but Ozzie found himself shrinking away from the peculiar woman. Now that she was so close, he could see her almond-colored skin was as rough and wrinkled as bark. She was far older than he had first realized.

"Well?" Pigeon Lady coaxed, returning to full height.

"It's not my cat," Ozzie managed at last.

The lady gave him a skeptical look. "He certainly *seems* like your cat."

"Yeah, well, are those your birds?"

The woman responded with a flowery laugh, which sent many of the pigeons fluttering away—only to alight on her hat and shoulders again a moment later. "No, I suppose not. Birds only belong to birds, that's what I always say."

Ozzie tilted his head at her. "Then why do they come to you? Did you bespell them?"

Pigeon Lady's eyebrows arched in curiosity. Ozzie couldn't help noticing they were a greenish color. "That's a fancy word. You're an intelligent boy, aren't you? A dreamer."

"No, I'm not!"

Pigeon Lady put her hands on her hips. Her arms were so long that they reminded Ozzie of branches.

"Well, so what if I am?" Ozzie demanded. "What's wrong with dreaming?"

"Nip me in the bud—I meant no offense. I meant it as a compliment. Seems to me that you could use one."

"What does that mean?" Ozzie retorted. "You don't even know me."

"Don't I?" Pigeon Lady wondered. The pigeons cooed,

as if in support. "I believe I know your type."

Ozzie let his manga drop to the bench and crossed his arms. "Yeah? And what type is that? Sensitive? *Too* sensitive?"

"Frost and fungus!" Pigeon Lady laughed. "Being sensitive means you understand. That you're in tune. How can you be *too* good at that? All around us, the worlds hum and—"

"World*s*?"

"There are more worlds than this one. Or didn't you know that? Sensitive boy like you. The type who *knows* things, deep down inside. That's sensitivity—that's what I think. If you ask me, a lot of people aren't sensitive *enough*. They don't listen. To themselves. To the hum of the worlds. To the opportunity knocking."

Ozzie stared at her in bewilderment—and slight frustration. The blue cat was licking one of his elbows, but Ozzie kept his arms crossed and his eyes locked on Pigeon Lady.

She returned his gaze from atop her impossibly long neck. "Tell me. Are *you* listening?"

"Yeah. Sure. I think so . . ." She was staring at him expectantly, so he quickly added with as much decisiveness as he could muster: "Yes."

Pigeon Lady smiled, causing her wrinkles to twist.

Ozzie could almost hear them creak. "Well, then," she said, "you'd better answer."

Ozzie narrowed his eyes at her. "Answer *what* exactly?"

"I told you. The knock of opportunity."

Is she talking about the door in The Depths? he wondered. *How could she know about that?*

"What if . . . what if the door is blocked?" Ozzie asked quietly.

"Oh. That." The lady thrust out her arms in what Ozzie perceived to be a shrug. "You just need to find the right key."

Then, with a final cryptic smile, she made a ponderous turn and wandered slowly away, a halo of pigeons circling her hat.

"Weir . . . do," Ozzie muttered, though even he could hear the lack of conviction in his voice.

The lady eventually disappeared from sight. The cat purred. The girl with inappropriate hair juggled. "Up-down-up-up-down!" the automaton chimed.

Ozzie sighed. He gathered his things and headed back to the apartment building, the pesky blue cat weaving happily along in front of him. As soon as he opened the front door—just a crack—the cat curved around it like a letter "S" and bolted down the hallway.

"Hey, wait!" Ozzie called, racing after it.

The cat seemed like it was on some sort of mission. It scampered past Apartment 2B and pawed at the door to the cellar.

Ozzie could hear the thumping from below. The cat butted its head against the door, as if overcome with a sense of urgency. Ozzie frowned, opened the door, and the cat soared down the stairs like a streak of blue. Its paws didn't even seem to touch the steps on the way down.

Ozzie followed the strange creature. He expected it to scamper right to the door to nowhere, but instead he found it scratching at a different door, one in the opposite corner of the cellar. Ozzie obliged the cat, swinging the door inward with a lazy creak, and the cat whisked through. Ozzie fumbled along the wall until he discovered a light switch. It was a small room—a glorified closet, really— crammed with cardboard boxes, crates, and chests.

"Just storage," Ozzie said, waving away the clouds of dust that had been stirred up by the blue cat as it leaped from box to box.

The air was stale and thick; Ozzie guessed no one had been down here in years. The cat continued exploring the stacks, as if it was hunting for something. *Probably mice,* Ozzie hazarded. *Bet there's hordes of them down here.*

At last, the cat settled on a large steamer trunk. It was

very old, tattered at the corners, and papered with stickers that had the names of different cities and countries on them. The cat leaned over the edge and batted at the clasps.

"It's probably locked," Ozzie warned, but he decided to humor the cat, so he dropped to his knees. That's when he noticed a tag dangling from the handle. He flipped it over to read: *Augustus Sparks.* "This used to belong to my great-grandfather," Ozzie told the cat, and it purred happily in response.

Ozzie tried the clasps; they were sticky, and he had to jiggle them, but at last they clicked open. The cat hopped down and Ozzie lifted the lid. He was immediately assaulted by the smell of must and mildew.

"Books," Ozzie announced. "Old ones."

The cat jumped right inside the chest and began scratching at the book right on top.

"Hey!" Ozzie scolded. "You're going to rip it even more."

He shooed the cat away and picked up the book. As soon it was in his hands, he felt it *rattle.*

Ozzie looked at the cat in surprise. "There's something inside!"

The cat meowed in agreement, its tail swishing so excitedly that it thumped against Ozzie's arm like a baton.

Ozzie slowly opened the book to see that someone had cut a deep, square compartment into the pages. Resting in the hollow was a key. Ozzie plucked it free and held it up in the faint light. It was ancient and tarnished, with a "Z" for its bow.

"Aunt T's key," Ozzie murmured. "Isn't it?"

There was a cord attached to the key, which the cat snatched in its teeth and began earnestly pulling.

"Tug, tug, tug," Ozzie said. "What do you think this opens . . ."

He trailed off.

He knew what it opened.

Of course he did.

He leaped to his feet; the cat was already bolting out of the room, down the dark corridor toward the door to nowhere. By the time Ozzie caught up, the cat was sitting in front of the door staring intently at the lopsided letter "Z" like it was a canary in a cage. Ozzie plunged the key into the waiting hole and turned it with a satisfying click. Then he clutched the handle, yanked open the door to see . . .

No bricks.

Not any longer.

Just blackness.

"Come on, Ozzie."

With a start, Ozzie looked down at the cat. "Was that you? Did you . . . speak?"

The cat gave a knowing twitch of its tail.

"All right then," Ozzie said.

And he stepped through the door.

SCOOT AND THE SHUTDOWN SEQUENCE

Ozzie was back in the command center. Everything was the same as when he had left; his friends were still huddled in the center of the room, surrounded by a ring of motos, and Klaxon was still at his control panels, hands on the levers. The only difference was that everyone—everyone who wasn't a moto anyway—was gaping at Ozzie in utter confusion.

"This is im-im-impossible," Klaxon sputtered. "How did you escape the chair? The Machine?"

Ozzie suddenly realized he was clutching the key to Zoone in his hand. He stared down at it, triggering a blurry memory of wrenching it free from his neck, straining to jam it into the console of the chair to release his shackles, then marching across the room and through the door. It was like he had been sleepwalking.

But he was awake now.

Fully awake.

He slowly raised his gaze back to Klaxon. The moto-man's face was twitching, his helmet lights flashing like alarm bells. Whatever thoughts—whatever *program*—was running inside of Klaxon was glitching hard. Ozzie had no desire to explain anything to him. As Klaxon fever-ishly began pushing buttons and tapping dials, Ozzie squeezed through the ring of motos to reach his friends.

"What was it like in TV Land?" Tug asked, looking at Ozzie earnestly.

"Terrible," Ozzie replied.

"No purple hair?" Tug wondered.

Ozzie laughed. "Not purple enough."

"Oz," Fidget murmured, "how did you . . ."

"You saved me," Ozzie said. "All of you."

"Wh-what do you mean?" she stammered.

"I heard you."

"We didn't . . . we weren't even talking."

"But you were calling to me," Ozzie insisted. "You must have been. I . . . *sensed* you or something."

"I called you, Creator," Scoot told him with a happy beep. "In my mindy-mind, that is. In my heart."

"Oh! So did I," Tug added with a happy twitch of his tail. "Just to tell you, I think it mostly came out as purrs."

Fidget grabbed Ozzie's hand, drew him close, and hugged him. "Yes," she whispered into his ear. "What they said."

Ozzie hugged her back. He didn't really understand what had happened, or how he had escaped. Maybe it was simply the power of having people on your side. Princess people. Skyger people. Even moto people. It didn't matter what type of people exactly. As long as you had them, and they had you.

Because everyone needs a crew. That's what Captain Traxx had said. *And you have to stick with them*, Ozzie thought.

Klaxon pivoted from his console. "I must run more diagnostics. The Machine must have a flaw."

"There *is* a flaw," Ozzie agreed. "Your idea's demented— that's the flaw."

Klaxon glared at Ozzie with his goggle eyes. "No. The simulations are sound. I should have predicted that children would be more difficult. The results of the experiment are acceptable. My plan for the multiverse shall proceed."

"Not if I have anything to say about it," Ozzie promised.

"That is the arrogance of humanity," Klaxon claimed.

"You will not be able to prevent the plan. In fact, you will assist in it. Because you will be moto."

He pressed a button on his chest plate, and the ring of moto soldiers began to methodically close in, brandishing their saw blades and scalpels.

"So much for choice," Fidget muttered.

"Give me the nectar," Ozzie said to Scoot.

She handed over the canteen, but as Ozzie went to raise it, Fidget held his arm. "I don't think fighting's going to work this time."

"Really?! You want to fight everyone. Always. And now you want to give up?"

"I didn't say I wanted to give up," Fidget retorted as the motos continued to inch closer. "But we need a better plan! You must have learned something about tin-can man when you were in that infernal machine. Something we can use against him."

Ozzie scavenged his memory. "I learned that he used to be kind."

"Kind?"

"Yeah. Gentle. Thoughtful. He even invented a machine to save the environment . . ."

He trailed off. He suddenly understood.

"What is it?" Fidget urged.

"Not the environment of *my* world," Ozzie said. "Klaxon's world. This one. Creon."

Even over the buzz of the moto weapons, Klaxon heard him. The lights and antennae on his helmet began going berserk, flashing and twitching. He surged forward, thrust his way into the circle by hurling two motos out of the way, then paused, as if he had suddenly remembered he should be a machine, that he should control himself. He lingered there in the gap between his motos, his goggle eyes whirling round and round.

Ozzie ignored him. "Take this," he murmured to Fidget, thrusting the canteen into her hands. Then he slipped around to the backside of Scoot.

"NO!" Klaxon screamed.

Ozzie looked at the bank of switches on Scoot's back. Five of them. They were all pointed in random directions. But they shouldn't be, Ozzie understood. They needed to be in a specific order. *Up-down-up-up-down.*

"Scoot's the device," Ozzie said. "That's why he built her!"

Klaxon tore forward, even as Ozzie began flicking the switches on the misfit moto's back. Fidget opened the canteen and hurled it at the moto-man, whacking him right in the chest. The canteen didn't break, but nectar spurted over him, leaking into the cracks and crevices of his metal body. Klaxon ground to a halt. One of the tubes on the side of his body burst away and began gushing smoke.

"Get them!" he yelled at his moto soldiers, sparks flying from his metal teeth. "Destroy them!"

The motos kept closing in—in fact, they had never stopped. But they didn't speed up, either. Ozzie flicked the last switch on Scoot's back to the down position and as soon as he did, the moto jerked. Her head began spinning, and her eyes lit up, so bright that Ozzie had to turn away.

Scoot curled up one of her chunky hands, put it to her mouth, and began to bugle. "Shutdown sequence requested!" she announced triumphantly.

She sped forward, past Klaxon, toward one of the control panels. The moto-man clutched at her with his metal claw as she zoomed past, but the artificial limb wasn't working properly, and he missed.

"Stop!" he commanded. "I am your creator! You must be loyal. TO ME!"

"I am loyal," Scoot warbled. "This is what Creator invented me to do!"

The moto guards were almost upon Ozzie, Tug, and Fidget. It was hard to see beyond them, but Ozzie could just glimpse Scoot reaching the console. She plugged her chunky fingers into a port, and her head began spinning like a top.

"Shutdown sequence initiated!"

Ozzie tried to press closer to Tug and Fidget; he could

feel the rush of air on his neck from the nearest moto saw blade.

"Ouch!" he heard Fidget screech.

Ozzie squeezed his eyes shut, then—

Nothing.

Ozzie opened his eyes. The motos had stopped dead in their tracks. Fidget shoved the one nearest to her and it toppled with a clang. They navigated past the deactivated robots, to where Klaxon was on his knees, clutching his chest, desperately trying to smear away the nectar. Fidget picked up the canteen and put the lid back on.

"In case we need it again," she said.

Ozzie wasn't really paying attention; he was looking at Scoot and the control panel. All the monitors had turned to static snow and the lights were flickering, as if in distress. Scoot's head began to spin faster.

"She's in trouble," Tug mewled anxiously.

Ozzie hurried toward her, but the entire room suddenly lurched, as if struck by an earthquake.

"No!" Klaxon gasped.

An entire section of wall peeled away, revealing a panoramic view of Moton—and what it was becoming.

The world was imploding. In one direction was the scrapyard, but in the other direction the factories were situated closer, and Ozzie could see the machines gyrating out of control. The conveyor belts were going backward, disgorging their payloads into the wrong end of the system. Grinders were spitting out rocks like bullets, peppering the control panels and obliterating them. Plumes of smoke billowed into the sky.

"What's happening?" Fidget cried.

"She's shutting down the machines," Ozzie realized. "I think she injected a virus into the system. To shut down the factories. And it's causing a cataclysm."

The base quaked again, causing the floor to tilt, and Klaxon suddenly began to slide. Then, with a mechanical screech, he tumbled right through the exposed opening of the building and over the edge.

"Ozzie!" Tug cried. "I think Scoot's stuck!"

Ozzie stumbled across the uneven floor toward the moto. Her hand was still plugged into the console, but her head was spinning so fast that it was just a blur. Before Ozzie could reach her, there was a thunderous boom. Scoot flew backward, across the room, and smashed into the opposite wall in an explosion of bright light and black fumes. Ozzie waved away the smoke to find the moto lying in a mangled heap. Her body had been split asunder, with gears and sprockets scattered in every direction. One arm was twitching on her body; the other was completely severed and lying on the floor. Her wheel had come loose and was rolling lazily in a circle.

"Where's her head?!" Ozzie screamed, only to spot it

rattling across the floor—toward the gaping hole in the wall.

He dove for it and missed, but Tug quickly leaped over him and snatched the moto's head by an antenna.

"Her—her battery," Fidget said, her voice catching. "It must have exploded."

"Ozzie?"

Dumbstruck, he slowly turned to see Aunt Temperance and Cho staggering through the door that led to the simulation chamber. Aunt Temperance pulled Ozzie into her arms, hugging him tightly against her body. She was still sticky with the goo from the stasis tank, but Ozzie didn't care.

"What happened?" he mumbled.

"We could ask you the same thing," Cho said as the floor beneath them continued to tremble. "Our tanks ruptured—what's going on?"

"Scoot shut down the Machine—and all the factories," Ozzie explained, pulling away from his aunt to look mournfully at the smoldering wreckage that only moments ago had been his moto friend.

"Oh . . . ," Aunt Temperance moaned. "Scoot. Poor Scoot."

"And Klaxon?" Cho pressed.

Ozzie numbly shook his head. "Gone."

"We have to get out of here," the captain declared. He

crossed the floor and braced himself against a girder to stare at the collapsing world. "The question is, how?"

"The door to Zoone," Aunt Temperance said. Ozzie turned to it, only to see that its arches were twisted and mangled. There was no more static; through it, he could see the factory city beyond.

"We didn't have the code anyway," Cho said. "We need to return to the station house."

"We don't have Scoot to lead us," Ozzie said, taking the moto's head from Tug and cradling it in his arms. "We have to fix her first."

"We will try," Cho assured him. "But we can't do that now."

He took off his coat and turned it into a makeshift sack. Then he began collecting bits of Scoot; her loose arm, her wheel, and the central mechanical core that lay exposed. He had to yank hard to pull it free. He put these bits in his coat, then slung it over his shoulder.

Ozzie hovered around him, watching. "What are you doing?! We have to take all of her."

"I can't, Ozzie," Cho said. "She's too heavy. This will be enough. And we have to leave." Even as he spoke, another explosion rocked the factory, causing the building to violently shudder.

"I'm not leaving without her," Ozzie said. "All of her." He held Scoot's head tight to his side and used a free hand to tug at the arm that was still attached to her body. But even though Cho had taken her corc, even though most of her body was now a hollow, ruptured shell, he could barely move her. Jagged pieces of metal, the edges of where her body had burst open, threatened to cut him.

Cho placed a heavy hand on his shoulder. "Lad, we have to go. Give me her head."

"No!" Ozzie retorted.

"We'll get her fixed," Fidget promised him.

"Oh, sure!" Ozzie spat. "This is exactly what you wanted all along."

Fidget grabbed him by both shoulders and looked him intensely in the eyes. "Oz, listen to me. There's nothing we can do for her, not right now. But there's someone we *can* save."

Ozzie stared at her. "Huh?"

"Lady Zoone."

"Fidget, what do you mean?" Aunt Temperance asked. "Do you know where she is?"

"She's the tree," Ozzie said, still clutching Scoot's head. "In the garden of rust."

Cho's eyes flew wide open with understanding. "I'll get us there. Come on."

They dashed down the corridors and ramps of the imploding base, and into the scrapyard beyond. Fires were blazing, the air was clogged with toxic smoke, and chemicals spewed from busted pipes. More than once, Ozzie was sure they were lost, but Cho had spent weeks in this wasteland. He knew the way. When they reached the river of sludge, they found that the crane had fallen across it, which meant they didn't have to swing. They simply scrambled across the long mechanical arm to reach the other side.

At last, they arrived at the edge of the scrapyard, where the remnants of the garden were located—and the lonely tree that was somehow Lady Zoone. She looked worse than before, leaning at a perilous angle with her branches drooping, some even snapped.

Aunt Temperance gaped desperately at Ozzie and the others. "How do we help her?"

"The nectar," Ozzie said. "Fidget, didn't you say it was the lifeblood of the Arborellia?"

"Yes; that's it!" The princess had carried the canteen all the way from the base and now she rushed to the trunk and began sloshing the never-ending flow of syrup around its roots.

Ozzie watched in despair as the dead soil swallowed up the syrup, almost as quickly as Fidget poured it.

"Zaria!" Aunt Temperance pleaded, wrapping her arms around the trunk. "We're here! Come back to us!"

"Listen!" Tug purred, his ears twitching intently.

A groan emerged from somewhere within the deepest

core of the tree. Ozzie looked up at its network of dry, brittle branches and was sure they twitched. Maybe it was the nectar, maybe it was Aunt Temperance's embrace—the tree began to quiver, to morph, until, suddenly, there was Lady Zoone, collapsing into Aunt Temperance's waiting arms. Her skin, normally so brown and warm, was leached of color and covered in angry blotches. Her arms were thin as twigs and her hair, usually alive with birds and rodents, was flat and empty.

"Tempie?" she moaned, reaching up with a trembling hand to touch her cheek.

"I'm here, Zaria."

"Oh. My dear, dear child," she murmured. Then her eyes, so pale and gray, fluttered shut.

Fidget gasped. "Is she . . ."

"Just exhausted," Aunt Temperance said, lifting her. "Oh! She's so light."

"Keep that canteen close by," Cho told Fidget, shifting the sack of Scoot's parts on his back. "Come on—time to leave Moton again."

But before he could even turn, another thunderous convulsion rippled through the world. One of the garden walls toppled completely; luckily it fell away from them, revealing a view of the factory streets beyond. There was a new sound now, but it wasn't mechanical.

"Water!" Tug cried, his fur turning an optimistic purple.

"The only water in Moton is toxic," Cho said as the rumbling sound intensified. "The sludge river is overflowing. Some holding tank—maybe even a dam—has ruptured. We need higher ground—now!"

Ozzie helped Aunt Temperance drape the limp body of Lady Zoone over Tug's back and everyone began scrambling up the nearest mound of rusted metal. By the time they made it to the top, the entire garden was flooding with a roar of reeking toxic sludge.

"We're trapped," Cho said grimly.

The poisonous water continued to rise, sloshing through the heap of metal beneath them. The garbage hissed and steamed as it was slowly devoured by the caustic flow, causing their mound to constantly shift and sink. Tug began to retch in the smoke, and his fur turned to a green almost as ugly as the slew that was licking at their feet.

"I wish my wing wasn't broken," the skyger said. "I could have flown us out of here."

Still clutching Scoot's head against his side, Ozzie wrapped his free arm around the skyger's massive neck. "At least we're together."

"That's true," Tug said, licking him with a pale tongue.

The fumes became overwhelming. Ozzie wondered what would get them first: the air or the sludge. Then he noticed that the clouds were growing darker, heavier; it was like a giant black monstrosity was looming over them, ready to finish them off once and for all.

Wait a minute, he thought, squinting into the smog. *Is that . . .*

"Well, well, well," a voice called from the sky, "if it isn't the guardians of Zoone."

32

BACK TO BLUE

The *Empyrean Thunder* resolved through the fumes, hovering above them in all its squid-like glory. Captain Traxx was leaning over the railing, eyes blazing.

"You took my words to heart, boy," she shouted at Ozzie. "Your situation couldn't be more desperate! Hold on. We're throwing down ropes."

It took some work to hoist everyone up, especially Tug, but eventually they were all aboard and the ship began to plow through the smog, above the fracturing factory world. Cho carried Lady Zoone below deck, and Fidget and Tug went with him to escape the noxious fumes. Aunt Temperance disappeared to the bow of the ship.

As for Ozzie, he felt too exhausted to do anything other than lean against one of the masts, cradling Scoot's head as Captain Traxx strutted in front of him. Her monkey pounced from her shoulder and landed in Ozzie's nest of hair, but he didn't even protest.

"You came," he said to the pirate queen.

"I keep my word," she touted. "The signal flashed for only a moment, so I figured it really *was* an emergency. Hmm. Looks like your crew has expanded."

Ozzie stared down at Scoot's lifeless head. "Yeah. Sort of."

A frantic scream came from across the deck, causing Meep to scamper away. Ozzie rounded the mast to see Aunt Temperance, silvery hair whipping in the wind, gesturing wildly overboard. Ozzie and Captain Traxx bolted to her.

"He's alive!" Aunt Temperance said, pointing at the river of poison below.

It was Klaxon. The would-be moto was all alone on a makeshift raft, a collapsed portion of some wall. His mechanical arm hung limply by his side and smoke was still sputtering from his chest and helmet.

"Mercurio!" Aunt Temperance screamed, clenching the railing so tightly that her knuckles were white.

Klaxon slowly, mechanically, lifted his head. One of his goggles telescoped outward; the other stayed put, as if malfunctioning. Ozzie could just make out his face, but it betrayed nothing: not sadness, not relief, not even anger.

"MERCURIO!" Aunt Temperance shouted again. The plea in her voice was sharp and painful.

Captain Traxx hurled a rope over the side. It unspooled alongside Klaxon. He contemplated the rope for a moment, then his eye telescoped back. He lowered his head and turned away from the ship to stare at the river of sludge before him.

"Take the rope!" Aunt Temperance beseeched him.

"He's repudiated us," Traxx replied solemnly. "He's repudiated *you*. We must leave this place, before the entire crew is endangered."

She turned to leave the bow, but Aunt Temperance clutched her arm. "We *must* save him."

"Must?" Traxx snarled, twisting out of Aunt Temperance's grasp. "Only he can save himself." She began marching across the deck.

"Heartless pirate!" Aunt Temperance jeered. "It's that easy for you, isn't it?"

Captain Traxx pivoted on a heel, freckles flaring. She looked like she was about to erupt—possibly into tears, Ozzie realized. The pirate queen crossed her arms and stared Aunt Temperance down.

"It's not easy for me at all. And it's not the first time in my life that I've tried to save that man." She drew a deep breath. "He was my brother."

Ozzie nearly dropped Scoot's head. Aunt Temperance gasped and fell back against the railing. "What? How . . . if—how can you leave him?"

Ozzie was thinking the same thing. The ship had already changed course, was already churning away through the smog. Traxx stormed back to the railing and stared at Klaxon, floating on the sludge and scum. Ozzie did the same, but the moto-man was quickly becoming a blurry dot in the haze.

"He *was* my brother," Captain Traxx repeated. "But I do not think he has been for a long, long time. I had to . . ." She paused, her fiery eyes flitting to Aunt Temperance. "Let him go," she said softly.

Then she clasped her hands behind her back, stalked slowly across the deck, and disappeared into her cabin below.

Ozzie already knew how difficult it was to track time in interstitial space. Feeling exhausted didn't help. He spent most of his second journey aboard the *Empyrean Thunder* sleeping. Sometimes his dreams danced with visions of his alternate life in the simulation, but whenever he awoke, the memories were faint and blurry. He had a feeling that he would eventually forget that life completely.

Lady Zoone was given a private cabin to share with

Aunt Temperance, who fed her sips of Arborellian nectar, tended to her like a nurse, and guarded her like a treasure. She wouldn't let the others come to see her—though they tried. There was only one exception; as soon as Lady Zoone was well enough, she beckoned Captain Traxx to her bedside.

The pirate queen stayed in the cabin for almost an hour while Ozzie lingered at the door, wondering what they could be talking about. When Traxx reappeared, she looked worn and sheepish.

"What did she say?" Ozzie dared to ask, following the pirate to the top deck. They had now left Moton far behind; their view was once again of colorful nebulae and swirling stars.

"It was a private conversation," Traxx retorted. "But, if you must know . . . she wanted to thank me for the rescue. Hah! I wouldn't have picked her up if I had known she was the steward of the nexus." Her freckles flashed hot. "She wants me to consider giving up pirating. And the first order of business? Help a couple of wizards infiltrate the slave markets of Kardoome so they can shut them down."

"What do you think?" Ozzie asked.

"I've been a pirate a long time."

"Is that what you told Lady Zoone?"

Captain Traxx grunted. "Yes. And she said she cared

a lot less about who I am and more about who I want to be."

Ozzie nodded, contemplating the starscape. "That sounds like Lady Zoone."

The *Empyrean Thunder* dropped them off right where it had first captured Ozzie and his friends: on the track between Eridea and Zoone. The tunnel was mending itself, but there was still a hole large enough for them to slip through. Ozzie was glad to see that the track itself was slowly trundling along; the way to Zoone would still be open.

They put Lady Zoone atop Tug and only had to wait for Fidget; the princess had been delayed by Captain Traxx and was the last to join them on the track.

"What did she want?" Ozzie asked her as they headed toward the faded blue door at the end of the tunnel.

Fidget gave him a cryptic look. "I'll tell you another time."

He would have pestered her about it, but then they were through the door, and instantly greeted by the warm and familiar buzz of Zoone. Ozzie was relieved to see that the station was in full and vibrant operation. Doors were opening and closing, travelers were darting across the platforms, and porters were collecting their bags and checking tickets. There wasn't a moto in sight.

Fidget nudged Ozzie. "Look, they're repainting the station."

"Turquoise again," he said with relief as they began plodding toward the magnificent building.

"Just to tell you," Tug added, "I think blue is my favorite color."

"Hey, guyth!" came a nearby voice.

Ozzie turned to see that they were passing by Door 457 to Jeongo. The door knocker that looked part dragon and part sun was grinning jamb to jamb.

"I'm tho glad to thee you guyth again!" the door knocker lisped. "Welcome thome!"

The nexus wasn't completely back to normal. Ozzie learned that the motos in Zoone had all suddenly collapsed due to Scoot's shutdown sequence, allowing Miss Mongo and the rest of the Zoone Underground to regain control of the station. Now came the hard work of getting everything back in working order. At lot of this seemed to involve Fusselbone running around, issuing orders, and compiling complicated new schedules.

"It's a preposasterous time," Fusselbone confided to Ozzie. "Wonderfully preposasterous!"

Mr. Whisk was back in his tinker's shop, Miss Mongo was back in her kitchen with Panya and Piper, and Minus was back to moaning.

"Though who knows for how long?" the glum green-haired boy wondered when Ozzie saw him again. "I could drop dead at any minute."

Ozzie happily threw himself into his old job of porting luggage for the multiversal travelers—anything to help the station get back on its feet. In his free time, he hung out with Fidget and Tug, and Scoot—sort of. Even though there wasn't the slightest spark of life in the moto, Ozzie carried around her head whenever he could. He just felt like she should be with him. Mr. Whisk was diligently working on a new body for her, trying to figure out how to resurrect her. He had the spare moto parts, the spare amelthium crystals; it was just a matter of time, or so he promised Ozzie.

Weeks passed, and life fell into a routine. One day, after a long shift porting luggage on the platforms, Ozzie was sitting on one of the terraces of the crew tower, watching the Zoone sunset. Fidget was still at work in the inn, and Tug was still finishing dessert (according to the skyger, he needed extra to help his wing heal). For the moment, it was just Ozzie and Scoot's head.

"Another beautiful evening sky in the nexus," came a voice from behind him. "It's left many a traveler mesmerized."

Ozzie peered over his shoulder to see Lady Zoone standing behind him. She still looked thin and pale; she was like the station, slowly returning to full health. She tottered over, stood beside Ozzie, and gazed ahead at the vista of the damaged turquoise forest.

"It will regrow eventually," Lady Zoone remarked. The birds and rodents had returned to nest in her hair; they chirped and chittered in agreement. "Why don't you tell me about your friend?" she asked.

"Huh?" It took him a moment to realize she was referring to Scoot. Well, her head at least. "Oh. She saved us, you know. She shut down Moton."

"So I've heard."

"She's not like the other motos," Ozzie assured her. "She's different."

"Then she'll fit right in here."

"She has to get fixed first," Ozzie continued. "And I'm not sure if . . ." He couldn't bring himself to finish the sentence.

Lady Zoone released a long, creaky sigh. "The truth is, Ozzie, that some things in life simply can't be fixed. Or they take a long time. But some of those are things you can't afford *not* to fix."

"You're talking about Mercurio," Ozzie gleaned. "But he *did* try to fix himself. He tried to fix everything. Just . . ."

"In the wrong way," Lady Zoone said. "When he first showed up at the station, I didn't comprehend how far his heart and mind had spiraled. I tried to nurture him, tried to help him. My dear old friend . . ." One of the birds in her hair issued a mournful tweet. "He pulled the moss right over my eyes. I thought your aunt could help him. I thought *we* could help him. But once he showed me that terrible Destiny Machine, I knew he was lost. Mercurio turned his back on emotion: love, hate, and everything in between. He tried to shut down. And the consequences were terrible."

It was like Aunt Temperance had said, Ozzie thought: *What if pain is important?* He traced a finger along one of the crooked seams on the side of Scoot's head. "You think I should go back to Eridea."

"Is that what *you* think?"

Ozzie shrugged.

"And your other option?"

"Stay here. Forget about Eridea. Forget about boarding school."

"And your parents," Lady Zoone added.

"They seem to forget about me," Ozzie replied.

It was a long time before Lady Zoone replied. "The door is open," she said cryptically. Then she turned to rustle away.

Ozzie lingered at the doorway to Eridea, Tug and Fidget huddled around him, Scoot's head cradled in his arms.

Aunt Temperance was off to the side, quietly conversing with Lady Zoone. Many other members of the crew had assembled: Cho, Miss Mongo, Fusselbone, and Mr. Whisk. Even the quirl was there, preening her one bent ear.

"Do you really have to go, Ozzie?" Tug asked, butting his massive head against his arm.

"The door's working now," Ozzie consoled the skyger. "I can come back anytime. But meanwhile . . . yeah, I have to go. There's things I need to deal with."

"We understand," Fidget told him. "But you're not going to take Scoot's head, are you?"

Ozzie shrugged. "I don't just want to leave her lying around in some dusty corner of Mr. Whisk's shop. I know it's stupid, but what if she gets lonely?"

"I'll look after her," Fidget said.

"Really?" Ozzie said. "But you hate her."

"I don't *hate* her," Fidget argued. "She's just extremely annoying. But still, she's one of us. You know, a . . ."

"Member of our crew," Tug finished for her.

"Yeah," Fidget said. "Something like that."

Ozzie nodded and passed Scoot's head to her.

"Don't worry," Fidget assured him. "Before we know it, Mr. Whisk will fix her and she'll be rolling around, irritating me again." She was smiling as she said it.

"You know, there's one thing you still haven't told

me," Ozzie said. "What happened on the pirate ship? What did Traxx say to you?"

"She tried to convince me to be her first mate again," Fidget replied. "She said that I'm good in a sticky situation."

"And a fight," Tug supplied.

Fidget grimaced. "I don't want to fight my way through the worlds. I want to be something else."

"Like what?" Ozzie wondered. "A princess?"

"I'm no princess." She gave him a hesitant look. "Promise not to laugh?"

"Why would I do that?"

"I don't want to solve problems with my fists all the time," Fidget said. "That's just how I've survived so far. What I really want to do is help the 'verse. Places like Untaar. Ru-Valdune. Even Quoxx has its problems; big ones. I want to be an advocate. An ambassador. Maybe a diplomat."

"That's cool," Tug said.

"You don't know what any of those things are, do you?" Ozzie asked the skyger.

Tug twitched his tail, nearly knocking Ozzie down. "Sure. It's helping people be weird."

"Huh?" Ozzie said.

"You know, even if they don't seem like they fit in with everyone else, like the type of people you see in TV

Land," Tug explained. "It's making sure they still have a place."

"Your brain's a Quoggsmire," Fidget told the skyger. "But you're kind of right."

Aunt Temperance came over and put a hand on Ozzie's shoulder. "Well? Shall we get going?"

Ozzie nodded, but Fidget pulled at his sleeve. "You never said what you thought of my plan," she whispered. "What do you think?"

Ozzie contemplated her, part of him wondering why his opinion even mattered to her. Usually, she was more like a big sister—she did the telling, not the asking. But she was staring at him intently, her eyes radiating a deep purple fire. He finally said, "I think anyone who is capable of juggling three deluxe household blenders can do anything she puts her mind to."

"Where in the worlds did you get that idea from?" Fidget asked.

Ozzie stood on the threshold of the doorway and laughed. "Actually," he admitted, "I'm not entirely sure."

FAIR WARNING

Apartment 2B hadn't skipped a beat; it looked exactly the same as when they had left it. The potted fern Tug had knocked over with his tail was still sprawled across the hardwood floor. Aunt Temperance's circus poster was still hanging on the wall, though one corner had become unfastened and was dangling. The mechanical cricket was perched on the coffee table.

Aunt Temperance crossed the floor and opened the curtains to let in the afternoon sun. Then she turned, leaned against the sill, and seemed to examine the room as if for the first time. Her hair had been braided into an extravagant nest of buns and braids, the silver strands intertwining with the brown. It was a style that had seemed so natural in Zoone, but it didn't feel out of place in Apartment 2B, either, Ozzie thought.

The truth was that he hadn't seen much of Aunt Temperance the past few weeks in Zoone. He had known how much she had been forced to deal with, how much she had to think about, and he had been happy to give her space. And, to be perfectly honest, he had been equally happy to avoid difficult subjects like going back to Eridea. But now he had made the decision to come home and . . . well, here they were.

"There are things we should discuss," Aunt Temperance said. "Maybe I'll make us some hot chocolate." She moved toward the kitchen.

Ozzie crossed his arms. "I'm not going to Dreerdum's."

"I'm not going to let you," Aunt Temperance said, stopping at the doorway to the kitchen.

Ozzie exhaled. "I'll talk to them. Mom and Dad. I'll tell them."

Aunt Temperance made her way to him, put her hand on his shoulder. "We'll talk to them together."

Ozzie nodded. "And . . . what about you? Now, after everything?"

"I had a lot of discussions with Zaria these past weeks," Aunt Temperance replied. "There are so many things I didn't fully understand before. About me. About my grandfather. Our family has a connection to Zoone, Ozzie. It always has, I suppose." She hesitated. "But that's not the reason I walked through that door down in The Depths."

Ozzie noticed that her gaze had wandered over to the mechanical cricket on the coffee table. Mercurio's cricket. She picked up the little creature, cupping it in her hands. "I spent so long hiding," she said softly. "Hiding from the past. Hiding from you. Hiding from myself." She carried the cricket to the nearby bookshelf and placed it next to her dog-eared collection of Shakespeare plays.

She's keeping it out, as a reminder, Ozzie perceived. *Maybe even a warning. Just like the statue that Lady Zoone keeps in her study.* He was suddenly struck with the vivid image of a little kid getting tripped and falling face-first on the cement. Except, to his own surprise, Ozzie wasn't the kid getting bullied—he was the one *doing* the tripping. Ozzie couldn't remember doing it, but it felt real, like it had actually happened. And it caused him to shiver.

"What is it?" Aunt Temperance asked.

"Something happened in the Machine," he explained. "I went through a different sort of doorway. I don't really remember it, but I know I saw a different side of . . . me. A me I didn't like."

"Captain Traxx called us the guardians of Zoone," Aunt Temperance said thoughtfully. "But Zoone is something more than just a place, Ozzie. I think it's me. It's you. That's what we have to guard and keep safe. Otherwise, it can get devoured. It can disappear. Then other things take over—insidious things."

She was speaking with such passion and vigor; in some ways, she reminded Ozzie of Lady Zoone, even though he wasn't even sure exactly what she was talking about.

"I now understand why my grandfather left me this apartment," Aunt Temperance continued. "Why he left me his key. There was a life he hoped I would embrace."

A life at Zoone, Ozzie thought. "You're going back?"

"I hope to. Many times."

"No, but I meant—you could live there," Ozzie suggested. "Permanently."

Aunt Temperance considered this a moment. "Yes, I could."

He sensed a "but" standing at the door, ready to knock. Just like old times.

"But I think there's something bigger out there for me," Aunt Temperance continued pensively. "Something more important for me to do than simply moving to Zoone."

What could that be? Ozzie wondered. *What's bigger than the nexus?* Then it occurred to him: *The entire multiverse.*

He stared at her, marveling at her again. She had

sacrificed so much, but now she looked truly alive. Truly happy.

Ozzie mustered his courage, stood up, and crossed over to her. "You don't need to worry about me. I'm going to be fine. You can go. You . . . you should go."

Aunt Temperance merely laughed. "Nice try. I'm staying with you, Ozzie."

Then what about the "but"? he wondered. *What about the multiverse?* "You already—you gave up a lot." He swallowed. "For me."

"Did I?" Aunt Temperance asked. "Sometimes I wonder. There's another way to look at it, you know. Maybe it's not about what we lose. Maybe it's about what we gain."

Ozzie thought of his parents, how they were always gone, always leaving him behind—but it lasted for only a fleeting moment because of the way Aunt Temperance had fixed her gaze on him. There was a glint in her eye.

A magical glint, Ozzie thought.

And he knew exactly what he had gained.

ACKNOWLEDGMENTS

As Captain Traxx tells Ozzie, "Everybody needs a crew"—and I certainly needed mine to help bring this book to life.

I'd like to thank my agent, Rachel Letofsky, who has had to go above and beyond this past year—your moral and emotional support kept me afloat. I'm really blessed to have one of the best editors in the multiverse, Stephanie Stein. Yes, I know all authors say that about their editors, but I'm still so thrilled that mine appeared on my favorite gameshow, *Jeopardy!* In addition to Stephanie, I'd also like to thank the entire team at HarperCollins, especially Maeve O'Regan in Toronto, who had to deal with my constant pestering as we launched *The Secret of Zoone.*

Thank you to my family for your much-needed and meaningful support this past year, especially my sister who said *The Secret of Zoone* was so good that it didn't even read like I was the one who wrote it! I also want to mention my Aunt Diana, whom I lived with my first year away from home at age seventeen. Her wonderfully eccentric spirit found its way into Aunt Temperance.

I also want to acknowledge the members of my chosen family who swooped in to save the day so many times these past couple of years—in particular: Sarah Bagshaw, Rob Stock, Jeremy Tankard, Heather Fitzgerald, and kc dyer. Also, a big thank-you to Jeff Porter for helping me with 3D printing Zoone keys!

Finally, I want to acknowledge all the different students I've worked with while I was building the worlds of Zoone. You often implore me to include you as characters in my books. So, I assure you, you are all in *Guardians*— you are various motos. Joanne, you're the moto decapitated by Fidget in Chapter 11; Jaden, Ian, and Tyson, you're the motos in the operating theater; Sion, you're the moto whose arm gets sliced off by the door; Elly, Emily, Julia, Sarah, and Sunny, you're the first motos to get blasted by Scoot's blender gun; Aiden and Arisol, you're the motos who take Ozzie and Fidget to the terrace. The rest of you can find yourselves among the army of those mechanical pests. These are important roles! Remember what I have always told you: It's the job of an author to cause problems for fictional characters. Yes, Arisol, I can hear your retort already: "Mr. Wiz, it's also your job to cause *me* problems."

You're not wrong, Arisol. You're not wrong.

973.072
M846t

Morton, Marian J   1937-
    The terrors of ideological politics; liberal historians in a conservative mood [by] Marian J. Morton.   Cleveland, Press of Case Western Reserve University, 1972.

    xi, 192 p.   21 cm. $5.95

    Bibliography: p. 147-185.

    1. United States—Historiography.   2. Historians, American.   I. Title.

35789

E175.M6   973'.07'2   78-183309
ISBN 0-8295-0229-7   MARC

Library of Congress   72